AF484195

Copyright © 2023 by Reena Lee

All rights reserved. No part of this book may be used or reproduced in any form whatsoever without written permission except in the case of brief quotations in critical articles or reviews.

This book is a work of fiction. Names, characters, businesses, organizations, places, events and incidents either are the product of the author's imagination or are used fictitiously. Any resemblance to actual persons, living or dead, events, or locales is entirely coincidental.

Printed in the United States of America.

For more information, or to book an event, contact:

E-mail: reenainspirations@gmail.com

Website: http://dualdestinybook.com

Facebook Dual Destiny fan group: https://www.facebook.com/groups/223485786930397/

Edited by Denver Murphy Editorial Services

Main cover design by De Monstapedia

Cover text and formatting by Aubrey Libitigan

Interior illustration by Khruri

ISBN – Hardcover : 979-8-9882524-3-6

ISBN – Paperback : 979-8-9882524-8-1

TO MY DEAR HUSBAND

Thank you, my love, for being my number one fan, the first person to believe in my writing, and the special individual who has been right next to me every step of the way. Your unwavering engagement has brought so many great memories, and the joy and strength to help me bring this book to life and become an even better writer.

Thank you for wiping away my tears during moments when I didn't think I'd cry but did. There were times I didn't believe in myself and thought I wasn't good enough, but you would always fuel me with the energy and drive to keep going. This book is truly in dedication to the beautiful love you've showered me and our children with— love that only comes once in a lifetime. I am genuinely honored to be a part of your forever, as you are to mine. You are truly the best thing that has ever happened to me.

Lastly, but never the least, the best part in writing Dual Destiny was seeing you act as each one of my characters to help stimulate my imagination. Not only did you support me while I chased my dreams, but you also chased it with me.

I love you.

TO MY WONDERFUL READERS

Thank you for your continuous support, love, and motivation. This journey has been an incredible experience and I couldn't have done it without all of you.

While writing this book, there was not a moment I did not think about you all. The thoughts of the emotions I'd put you through and what things you'd cry, laugh, and be angry with me about before you closed the book.

My mission is to share what chasing *dreams* is all about in a new age romance that will bring you on a heart-wrenching, emotional rollercoaster you'll never forget.

Join me and all the rest of the fans on my Facebook group at Dual Destiny Fan Group to stay connected with any updates, awesome arts, and live chats to meet me personally.

I can't wait to hear what you love about Dual Destiny and excitedly look forward to meeting you all!

In warmest regards,

Your author, Reena Lee

SPECIAL ACKNOWLEDGEMENTS

The team that made Dual Destiny possible

A life-long dream of mine to write a love story to touch the hearts of many had been made possible because of you all. Thank you for being with me at every stage of my book, from beginning to end.

Denver Murphy Editorial: editor—Denver, I can't express enough how much I appreciate your in-depth editing expertise across reviewing my manuscript the rounds you did. You truly live up to your reputation as many people have genuinely applauded you time and again. I am grateful to have carefully taken my time to recognize you during my search for the perfect editor and my experiences have been nothing but humbling to your mentoring. Thank you for believing in my work and the merit that comes with it.

De Monstapedia: main cover illustrator—Tee, thank you for being the first professional artist that saw my vision. You said, "Let's do this…" and made it all happen. Art is truly your life, as you once said; I can see it through the compassionate illustrations you've done for me. Your art has come a long way for me in my journey and I'm so happy to see it spread more to the world through my novel and many more authors.

Aubrey Labitigan: formatter, back cover text, and title designer—Aubrey, your diligence never ceased to amaze me. You are always punctual and worked earnestly with all my multiple rounds of tasks. I can't thank you enough for being there through the final stages of my book, all the way to publishing.

Khruri: interior illustrator—Kelly, thank you for the gorgeous final pieces of Dual Destiny. I am grateful to have met such a kindred soul who made genuine efforts creating my original characters. You always do it in a way that shows me my book is valued. May your beautiful artistic journey continue to move the hearts of many as it continues to do so with mine. I could not have asked for a more graceful artist such as yourself. You are one of a kind so keep shining and never stop believing that you can spark magic in many ways with your passion.

Lia Lo: Singer, song title: Tiam No Yog Wb Tiam—Lia, no words can describe how emotionally graceful your singing speaks to my heart and the many that will come to discover Dual Destiny. My readers are already overflowed with love when hearing this song, especially dedicated to YingShua and Su-Lia's life journey. I am forever grateful for your kindness which has allowed me to experience an exceptional collaboration. Thank you for making dreams come true when I once thought it was far from possible. I wish you nothing but success in your music journey and look forward to more of your wonderful works.

My families and close friends: You all know who you are. Thank you for the continuous emotional support and words of encouragement throughout my journey. You were all the first people I shared my ideas, work, and happiness with. I cannot express enough how thankful I am to have you with me in all phases of my life.

DUAL DESTINY CHARACTER LEGEND AND PRONUNCIATION

Main Characters Profile:

YingShua Pha (Ying-Shua) also addressed by TuPao as Tij Laug
(thee-lao/big brother)
Luang Prabang Province, Laos
Year: 1978
Age: 24–30

Su-Lia Chang(Su-Leah)
Asheville, NC, U.S.A.
Year: 2078
Age: 20–26

1978–1987 Supporting Characters:

Ia Vang (Ee-Yeah)
Captain Blong-Cheng
Thao Village Grandmother
Houa-Li (Hua-lai)
Meng Thao (Meng)
Nujai Ly (New-Jai)
Mainong Ly (Mai-Nong)
Yue Ly (Yew)
TuPao Moua (Tew-Pow)
Amelia—Meng's pet monkey
Dr. Henny
Supeng Pha
Sunshine Pha

2078–2084 Supporting Characters:

Mrs. Chang
Jinnee Kong
Kathy Meir
Mr. Benz
Director Leah
Dr. Hang

TABLE OF CONTENTS

DUAL DESTINY

A novel by Reena Lee

Prologue

"Shoot them! All of them!" a booming voice commanded.

The terrified screams of women and children rumbled through my ears, sharpening my senses. Men pleaded desperately for their lives but were still ruthlessly stabbed to death by the blades tearing through their innocent flesh.

The air was quickly polluted by the fire of burning bamboo homes. Breathing became harsh from all the smoke, as beads of hot sweat trickled down my neck. My legs couldn't stop running.

I glanced behind me and following was a woman who looked to be in her twenties, carrying her child on her back. Her eyes bulged in fear of death.

"Let me help you!" I stopped quickly, noticing her child was about to fall off. In an effort to grab the infant, I released the cloth strap. A loud gunshot fired at us.

It was like time had come to an immediate stop as I witnessed the mother's eyes roll back. Dark blood came pouring from her mouth and splattered all over me. The wailing voice from the infant instantly turned into cold silence.

My heart cried in pain, and tears came gushing from my eyes at the sight of the lifeless mother and infant in my arms; my hands a crimson red.

A soldier shouted and pointed at me, "Don't let *that one* get away!"

Panic ate through my veins as I tried to pull myself free from the body, knowing the soldiers would now be after me.

Sharp metal zinged past my ear, barely missing me, followed by a bullet that grazed the flesh of my left leg. I fell to the ground with a hard thud. Overwhelmed with exhaustion, there was no energy left in me—I couldn't move.

Was this the end of me, Su-Lia Chang? I asked myself in quietness, gritting my teeth.

Fear filled my heart at the thought of death. Scorching pain surfaced from my wound in waves of agony. The scene of heavy military boots marching in my direction faded when my consciousness became overwhelmed by darkness.

A Nightmare Escape

CHAPTER 1

"Wake up! Wake up!" a faint voice echoed through my ears.

As my eyes opened, goosebumps crawled all over my arms. My heart was beating faster than usual. Even the hairs on my skin rose.

It's cold, I thought.

"Are you okay?" a young woman's voice called out to me. "Come on, we have to keep moving or they will find us!" her voice urged in fright.

I refocused my attention, feeling pine needles poke into my back. My cotton, navy pajamas were soaked in muddy water and coated in leaves. The pearl half-moon glared down through the dark shadowy trees towering beneath the silken night.

"My head… It hurts," was the only thing I could mutter.

A skinny woman who looked in her fifties, with a blue and pink striped cloth wrapped around her head and squinty eyes, answered,

"Are you able to stand? Here, let us help you now—we can't just leave you behind. We've come this far."

The woman and another girl with short hair beside her grabbed me by my arms and carefully raised me up. "One of your legs has been injured, so you have to bear the pain until we get to our destination."

And then the horrific memories of noon suddenly came sinking in and my stomach churned. I vomited harshly as I remembered the smell of the villagers' burning flesh, and innocent lives being slaughtered by the communists.

The tears in my eyes continued to well. The trauma in my mind screamed even louder than the pain in my leg. I kept on walking and wondered how I had survived.

We set off without another thought. A group of five men, six children, and four women trailed behind us.

A few hours later we finally saw streaks of sunlight beaming through the tall thin layers of trees.

It was morning, finally. It had been a long night.

"Let's rest here. We should be safe for at least a day or two. We must do our best to make it to the Mekong River. That is where your freedom is, my Hmong brothers and sisters." The man had spoken from the front of the crowd as he tossed his head to the sky, hands resting at his hips.

Shortly afterwards, he turned around with a big smile and put a cigar to the tip of his lips. His curly brown and gray hair looked as if it hadn't been washed for days but, to my surprise, he had rosy cheeks like a chubby child who had just finished stuffing himself. His eyes were almond shaped and ominously black.

"That's Captain Blong-Cheng. He's in charge of this group and has helped many Hmong survivors of the war cross to Thailand," the old lady with the blue and pink hair wrap whispered and beamed.

My eyes switched from her back to Captain Blong-Cheng. As he walked through the crowd of travelers, his gaze caught mine. I looked away, not wanting to be noticed.

"How old are you?" was the first thing he asked. His heavy boots stopped with a thud. The greenery of his camouflaged attire came to view.

My guard was up, feeling wary. I muttered through an unwavering stare, "I'm twenty, sir."

He reached out with an open palm and his hand settled on top of my head. He stroked through the threads of my dark black hair that still had dried clumps of mud in them.

Given a split moment to observe this man, he seemed to be in rather a good mood considering an entire village had just been hunted and burned. There was no sympathy in his eyes.

I glared more as he patted my cheek. "Those hazel eyes are too harsh on me. You're still young and vulnerable," teased Captain Blong-Cheng. At the point I knew he was wanting to slide his filthy hands down my neck, I pulled away.

"Ah-hem, I'm tired… I want to rest," I said in a weak, breathless voice. Being hungry and dehydrated felt awful, made worse by fearing that this man was not to be trusted.

The afternoon came with a warm breeze as I sat surveying the mountains we were traveling through.

"Child, what is your name and which village are you from? We were passing by and found you unconscious in the woods. Luckily you were still breathing so we tended to your wound. That was when you finally woke up." The skinny lady who rescued me had decided to sit next to me on the log.

Hesitantly, I tried smiling. "My name is Su-Lia, and I am a Chang. I'm unsure where I am from, to be honest." It was the only answer I had, no matter how hard I tried to remember more.

"Well then, you can call me Aunt Chue. Our family name is Vang. We had a peaceful village…" She began to sob, and my heart sank. "I lost my husband… and now it's only my daughter and me. Her name is Ia, and she is the same age as you. You should stay with us, and we'll figure out where your family is when we get to Thailand."

Choked suddenly, tears streamed down my face. "Thank you for saving me." I wiped my tears away and then hers. "Don't cry, your husband must still be protecting you, for you to have survived this long."

I tucked my black hair behind my ears and realized a shadow hovering over me. It was Captain Blong-Cheng.

When I turned to look, he smiled with hands behind his back as if he had been eavesdropping on our conversation. "It's time to leave," he urged with empty eyes, and we both stood up quickly and gathered our belongings.

"We are only hours away from reaching our location. There," Captain Blong-Cheng said, pointing east to where we could see the free-flowing water of the Mekong River. "Our supporters and comrades will be waiting to get you on boats. We can get there this evening so let's keep moving."

He picked up a branch lying on the ground and began using it as a walking stick while whistling. The group was now heading downward through the mountain trail.

The crowd chanted with glee, and everyone seemed to have more energy to continue the journey. Happiness crossed my face at seeing the Hmong survivors looking forward to their safety.

"Finally, our freedom is only hours away!" One of the children, who looked six years of age, grabbed onto the skirt of his mother as she patted him on the head.

"Yes, my son. You have to keep that spirit, even when we make it to Thailand and start our new life."

The women and children talked about how they'd been walking up and down the mountain trails and in and out of the woods to escape capture by the communists in Vietnam.

The travelers also mentioned that there were some who lost their shoes and had walked on bare feet for days, and children who were exhausted and hungry after their food spoiled along the way. Worst of all, a group which had started with thirty or more people was now reduced to only fifteen because of loved ones being killed or captured. It definitely felt relieving to know the long horrific road was finally coming to an end for them.

I stopped for a moment to take a big breath as the fresh, airy scent of leaves, grass, and trees seeped through my nostrils. *Nature has never felt so real*, I thought.

The night came quickly. The moon rose to its place in the midnight skies. The wind lessened but that didn't stop the night being colder than any other. Everyone was dressed thinly and shivers from within soon surfaced.

"Where are the boats?" a scrawny man called out when he stopped to survey the destination.

The men walked in different directions to try to see if the boats were coming. The night was not only cold but a little too quiet.

The children began to whine and even the younger ones carried on their mothers' backs began to cry.

"Shhhh… you can't cry, or we will be heard," one of the mothers said, trying to calm her two-year-old toddler.

"The boats will get here soon, don't worry. We are still waiting on another group that is expected to arrive soon," said Captain Blong-Cheng.

A moment later, we heard cracking twigs and rustling leaves signaling footsteps.

From afar, I saw a much smaller group than ours emerging from the shadows. The first person I noticed was a boy, or rather a young man in his twenties, walking alongside a few other men.

He carried a black backpack of his belongings, and no women were in his group. It almost seemed they had traveled as a unit on their own instead of being participants in a large party.

As they made their way closer from the dark jungle, for some reason he looked familiar but I couldn't make out from where and when I might have met him.

Before long, the man was standing right next to me. He was quite tall, about five-eleven, with a muscular build and broad shoulders that towered over me.

The man didn't notice me to begin with and was paying attention to instructions for when the boats would arrive.

The other group members stood in the shadows, preventing me from making out what they looked like.

Observing and hoping to not be noticed, I couldn't help but gaze. Deep brown hair curtained down the sides of his smooth, beige complexion. It wasn't too long or too short but touched the nape of his strong neck. He wore a fitted black top with the sleeves cut off, presenting masculine biceps and firm arms. The shirt was tucked neatly inside his loose black satin trousers and deep red sash belt.

Minutes passed, and just as I was enjoying the perfect steal of his mesmerizing figure, he turned my direction. Dark chestnut eyes stared down at me.

Too late to look away now.

My heart fluttered for a moment, unsure if I was embarrassed for being caught staring or stunned at how strikingly handsome he was. His dark eyebrows narrowed as he observed me with intrigued eyes for countless seconds.

That face… where have I seen him before?

"Look! The boats are coming!" a different man shouted, pointing towards the river, breaking our gaze.

Quickly, I blinked away my previous thoughts and, while still being wary of the young man's presence behind me, I stepped ahead to observe the river. Staring at the ground before me, I saw his shadow overlapping mine composedly.

We watched as one of our group ran towards the boat. A split-second later the situation changed.

"It's the communists! Run! Save yourselves!" the man immediately shouted loudly at noticing the boats arriving contained soldiers aiming their machine guns.

The entire crowd of travelers screamed at once and scattered for their lives from the riverbank, back to the jungle.

Machine guns fire opened up, with those slowest to flee were the first to fall.

The armed soldiers jumped from their boats and charged towards anyone they saw.

"Spare my child's life, please!" the woman with the six-year-old child begged, cradling him protectively.

The soldiers' faces were devoid of emotion. They were clearly on a mission to eliminate anyone in their way. Especially the Hmong.

I turned around in an instant, covering my ears when I heard the woman and her child being shot ruthlessly. My heart screamed for the bodies that were falling like dominos—thinking any minute those bullets would kill me too.

Then I remembered and frantically searched for Captain Blong-Cheng. None of the bodies lying on the ground, soaked in crimson, were him. Then a glance up, he was standing behind the soldiers with his cigar.

A grim smile slowly formed. He had deceived us and betrayed his people! A traitor!

My rounded pupils shook in terror—no one can be trusted.

"I'm not going to die. I'm not going to die," I prayed while machine guns continued to roar around me. Overwhelmed in agonizing horror, I pressed hard against my ears. My temples throbbed, feeling like my mind was already gone.

Within a moment, a large hand grasped me by the shoulders and flung me to the ground. One side of my face hit the cold dirt, causing a burning sensation from the impact.

It was HIM! His firm chest laid against my back as he clung onto me, using his entire body to shield me from flying bullets.

"Shhh. Don't cry, not a breath can be heard or you'll die," he hissed sharply against my ear. As soon as the soldiers started heading in a different direction, presumably thinking they had killed everyone, he hurriedly helped me up and we took off as fast as we could back through the jungle.

It was a very dark night, making it a struggle to see any direction, but the man seemed to maneuver fluidly through the undergrowth like he knew the area.

I remained as calm as I could despite my face being drenched in tears; witnessing the bloodbath of so many people being shot down had stirred my intestines. I fought extremely hard to not throw up at the horror of it all.

After a while, the pain in my legs became unbearable. The bullet cut across my thigh, which had started to heal, began bleeding again.

"Wait, wait…" I said, my limp is so bad now I was forced to grab the nearest tree for support.

The man stopped to observe me.

He seemed to understand the problem right away, without me having to explain. He tossed my right arm over one of his shoulders and fastened a good grip around my waist. With his support, we kept on moving.

"Thank you…" I gasped in gratefulness. "Will they find us?" I added worriedly.

"You're safe. I know these trails well and I'll make sure to get you to the right location where the real boats are waiting," he assured.

I wanted to ask more questions but knew it wasn't the time to get chatty on such a dangerous night.

Before long, we came to a stop somewhere that seemed safe enough to allow me to sit down and rest.

Gathering dry twigs, branches and leaves, he was able to start a fire with matches he pulled from his backpack. He also brought out a bottle of water and a small first aid kit.

The man's calmness never ceased to amaze me and I wondered

how he could remain so composed in such a traumatic situation.

I watched as he walked over to me from the other side of the firepit. "Use this," he said, handing me the water. "Drink and clean yourself up."

Embarrassed, I touched my face and felt the rough gritty sand against my skin. Even my hair felt nappy.

The man tossed me a small brownish towel after I rinsed out the mud clumps in my hair and had refreshed myself.

He crouched down across from me, elbows propped on his knees, and raised one hand towards my face.

I flinched, startled by the sudden gesture but it didn't stop him from reaching. He gazed with remorseful eyes and brushed his thumb across my cheekbone.

"Does it hurt?" he asked in a worried tone like he didn't wish to cause me further harm.

"No..." was all that came out of my mouth. Those all-too-gentle eyes drowned me in silence.

It did hurt at first, but I had forgotten already. My gratitude and debt to him masked any remaining pain.

Afterwards, he proceeded to undress the cloth around my leg and inspected the condition of my wound.

"It's good—just a small opening from running. This cloth is dirty and could cause you an infection so I'm going to leave it uncovered. Letting it breathe will help it heal faster," he told me.

I squinted from the stinging pain as he applied alcohol to cleanse the raw-feeling flesh.

"May I please know your name?" I bravely summoned the

courage to ask.

He paused for a moment, like I was asking a silly question and brought his eyes to meet mine. "YingShua. Family name is Pha."

"YingShua… Pha," I whispered, staring off into nothing.

Where does my heart remember this name? a voice inside me asked.

"Thank you. My name is Su-Lia Chang," I offered, even though he hadn't asked.

YingShua looked up but didn't seem surprised. Maybe he just didn't care to know my name…

Then a curious thought came to mind. "So, if you knew where the boats were… how did you and your men end up with our crowd?"

"We are advocates for the peace of our people. It's our mission to ensure the Hmong can safely cross to Thailand. Also… because you were there. I got distracted."

"Distracted? Have we met before?" I questioned in a calm manner, feeling that sense of familiarity lurking inside me. I just couldn't figure it out or remember why.

"No. This may be the first and the last time." He stared down at the ground like he was disappointed.

Without more to say, I didn't probe any further in case it made him feel uncomfortable. I understood he was a man of minimal words.

After a few minutes the hunger in my body stirred. Starvation was a real threat; I hadn't eaten for almost two whole days. I pushed both my inner wrists into my belly. It was the way my mother taught me to prevent my stomach growling.

YingShua must have noticed because he stood up to go and dig in his backpack once more.

"Eat this. You don't look well." He handed me three strips of beef jerky and some crackers.

"Is there enough for you too?" I didn't forget to ask. I had no idea when I even started caring for this stranger.

"This is the last of it but I'm not hungry," he assured, looking away like he was shy.

I accepted the food and ate slowly after thanking him.

Then YingShua glowered like he heard something.

My gazed raised to follow when he stood to listen. "Stay here. I'll be right back."

YingShua walked away, his back towards me as I waited, hoping everything was alright.

After a while, my eyes began to feel fuzzy and tired. The orange glow from the firepit began to zone out. My vision became less vivid—even my consciousness was leaving my body. I was so happy to be alive despite the trauma and bitterness I had suffered. Somehow, I felt safe with *him*, YingShua Pha.

Unwillingness

CHAPTER 2

"Please… DON'T SHOOT THEM!" I cried out in the middle of my sleep, and my eyes burst open into the morning light.

While gasping for air, a sequence of throbbing pain weighed over my mind, imprisoning my will to break the illusion I was suffering in.

I clutched hard at my bedsheet. Strands of black hair stuck to the skin of my neck. Hot sweat rolled down my chest.

Another one of those nightmares…

The morning had come too quickly. Golden sunlight glowed against my eyelids. I was having an extremely hard time getting out of bed. My whole body was sore.

Does it hurt?

The gentle sound of YingShua's medium-low voice whispered in my thoughts, followed by the ambient sound of machine guns roaring through my ears. Voices of crying women and children played over and over in my head. I felt awful.

It does hurt now... my heart answered. Surprisingly, I had woken up in my own bed.

It was a recurring dream, one in which I kept going back to the same place and time. I was sometimes running away but, on most occasions, I'd be fighting for my life. It was rare for me to sleep peacefully.

This morning was different. Rather than wishing my dreams to be over because I hated remembering them, I felt an unwillingness to wake up.

The nightmare of running in fear ended with so many unanswered questions that my heart felt lost and left behind.

I got out of bed, reminding myself that it was just a bad dream.

While in the bathroom, showering, a loud knocking came banging at my dorm door.

"Su-Lia! Su-Lia, are you awake yet?!" That high pitched voice, who else would it be?

"Su-Lia, it's ten-to-nine. That just gives us ten minutes before Art History."

I could picture her ear and cheek being pushed against my door, trying to listen if I was still sleeping.

"Coming!" I shouted from the bathroom and quickly ran out to dress myself.

A soft pink blouse with light-blue fitted jeans felt simple enough. I tossed my hair in a high ponytail and fixed my bangs before grabbing my bookbag and slipping on my Star Light kickers.

I ran for the door and swung it open. Standing in front of me was my not-so-impressed best friend, Jinee Kong.

Jinee and I were childhood friends. We had grown up together in Asheville, North Carolina, and currently attend college in Hickory.

She had short black hair that stopped at her jawline and light bangs that laid weightlessly over her black eyes. No matter what mood she was in, I could never get enough of how gorgeously her eyes twinkled from behind her extra-long lashes and against her smooth pale skin.

"It's only been a week of Sophomore year and you're going to make us late," she said, rolling her eyes.

"I'm sorry, you really didn't have to come get me, Jinee." I grinned and added in a joking tone, "One of those nightmares again."

"Oh, what did you dream about last night?" she asked, suddenly interested.

"Not much," I lied. "Maybe it wasn't a nightmare after all. You wouldn't be able to imagine *him* anyways, even if I told you," I teased.

Quickly, I scooted Jinee out and shut the door behind us.

"What, that's not fair! You can't be having all the fun," Jinee whined and continued to tail behind me, laughing. She knew the jokes of my crazy dreams; after all, I was a big wanderer whether in reality or in spirit.

Life of always swimming in oceans of dreams was a challenge. At times, I even second-guessed myself if they were real or not.

While I was medically diagnosed to have a bad case of sleepwalking, shamans declared me as being gifted with a wandering soul, or in Hmong, *plig nyias*.

Wandering souls are understood to consistently travel through multi-dimensional places when their body is resting. When the soul returns to the body, it produces premonition dreams—a vision of potential events that may or may not interpret the reality of the future or past.

My gleeful expression slowly faded as my thoughts continued in a daze. Deep down, I was more disappointed than happy. It was hard to put up a good—what I called *normal*—front just so my friends would worry less about me.

Shortly afterwards, at the start of Art History, two hands dropped on my shoulders and spun me around. Big, green, feathery eyes expressing concern stared into mine.

"You've been very out of it today, Su-Lia. Is everything okay with you?" Kathy Meir asked. She was one of my close American classmates who loved the Hmong culture. Her red bouncy hair spiraled off her shoulders and contrasted with her yellow blouse.

I blinked and offered Kathy a beaming smile. "Yes, I'm fine. I just didn't get enough sleep last night."

"No sleep with a wonderful man in her bed," interrupted Jinee as she dropped her book on top of her desk, startling Kathy.

"A DREAM," I corrected with eyes rolling to the ceiling.

Kathy held her breath in amazement. "Oh? A man?"

I could see both girls exchanging weird expressions like they were both telepathically scheming how to get more out of me.

I grabbed both of Kathy's hands and gave her a smirk, pushing her hands off my shoulders. "There was no *real* man, I'll never get to meet him anyways."

Kathy moved away with a frown and tucked the back of her

hands beneath her chin. "Wish I could dream like you and see so many things. Maybe I'll be able to meet the man of my dreams."

"Trust me, it's not pretty," I told Kathy in a serious tone. "It's more like torture, if you ask me."

Before long, a loud knocking came from the classroom door. Mrs. Jones, our Art History professor, walked in gracefully.

All twenty-four students sat down quickly, and class went on for a good hour.

"Are you joining us for lunch later, Su-Lia?" Kathy asked after class ended and she flopped her backpack over one of her shoulders.

"No, I'll catch up with you girls later. I've got a few research papers to finish up."

My girlfriends looked at each other confused. They were used to me always suggesting lunch first; I love food but this just wasn't the day.

"Okay, since you don't look well, go do what you need to do and get some rest," Kathy insisted before we parted ways.

I watched as Jinee and Kathy disappeared into the distance.

Remembrance

CHAPTER 3

I came to Charlotte Academy of Arts and Design on a full scholarship. I knew the way to make it was to learn to be independent, utilize my wisdom, and be earnest in faith and in purpose.

Growing up, I never met my father, and my mother was only eighteen when I was born. She lived through being criticized by the community because she didn't have a husband, education, and a worthy title to her career. None of that mattered to me and nor was I ever embarrassed by it.

Regardless of the challenges, my mother always ensured I wasn't left alone in the dark or ever went hungry. She was the light in my life.

The words of my mother resounded:

"You are the best version of me, Su-Lia. Life is just like art. Opportunities are the sky, the creations of it are vast, and your imaginations will never run empty—you will always be seeking for answers for as long as your heart is full."

She was right and was never too quick to judge anyone. My mother was different. Whether I had real life goals or spiritual goals, she believed them all.

My phone rang and knocked me out of my deep trance. I picked it up to the sound of my mother's cheery voice.

"My daughter, I will be coming into town to see you this weekend. Will you be available?"

Mother traveled for a living, selling life insurance. She often stopped in Hickory since it was only an hour's drive away.

My eyes grew wet, I couldn't wait to see her. "Yes, Mom. I will be here."

We spoke for a few minutes and, just as I was about to slip my phone back into my pocket, a portrait at the far end of the hall to the right caught my eyes.

This was the first time I noticed the artwork hung along the walls. It seemed that the school had finished remodeling the area.

From a distance, the photograph had warm colors of yellow, orange, and red, contrasted with different shades of green.

I narrowed my eyes and calmly gazed as my feet began to walk towards it. The nearer I got, the more mesmerizing it became.

It was a portrait of a massive field of deep-red poppy flowers cascading beneath a beautiful bright-green mountain. The setting looked to be during the summer while the wheat was crisp and golden in color. Rays of sunlight shimmered through threads of poppy stems. If my eyes weren't playing tricks on me, it almost felt like the portrait had come to life. I could already fancy how graceful the flowers motioned in the whispers of the wind.

Whoever captured this moment in the portrait was an amazing

photographer. Every detail of the picture had a meaning:

The flowers as a symbol of remembrance; the sunrays as hopes for freedom; and the mountains as a promise of where home will always be.

Before stepping away, another part of the photo caught my eyes and I had to take a second look.

The heart of the entire portrait was found along the upper reaches of the mountain—a cozy home made from bamboo, thatched in golden brown. Flowers decked the front of the house, and a lengthy stair trailed up the mountain to it.

I could only imagine how breathtaking it would be to be able to wake up to such exhilarating scenery every morning.

A moment later, I heard YingShua's voice again, *"Because you were there."* I snapped out of my thoughts as my eyes searched around me.

Someone had walked past with a wisp of air, but it was no one I recognized.

Gathering myself, I managed to get one more glance before stepping away to carry on with my day.

The library was just around the corner. Entering, the old gentleman waved and greeted me with a gleeful smile.

"How do you do, Su-Lia?"

"I'm doing well, sir." I walked past, having exchanged greetings with Mr. Benz who was the general librarian of the college. He wore thick heavy glasses over ice-blue eyes but tended to still squint every time he spoke. His hair was thinned out platinum gray over wrinkly ivory skin. Mr. Benz wore a blue and black striped, collared shirt that tucked neatly in his navy pants, and light brown dress shoes.

The very back of the library was one of my most favorite spots to sit, study, or maybe even nap when I felt like being isolated from the normal afternoon crowd.

Next to me were four tall, wide windows that reached to the ceiling. Three stories down, I glanced at the cars trundling along in their daily traffic routines, accompanied by a handful of pearlescent painted aeromobiles flying at building level. A relatively recent invention, and still few in number given their expense, it was nevertheless attractive to see them in the air from time to time.

My research paperwork was finally finished after spending a few hours in the library. I threw my hands in the air and stretched, which made my shoulders feel good.

The digital clock on the library wall changed to 3:40PM and I heard my stomach growling. Having skipped out on lunch with the girls, my next stop was likely to be the school cafeteria.

"That will be $10.65," the system voice prompted. I tapped my phone against the checkout register to pay for my grilled chicken salad sandwich and bottle of water.

Thankfully, I had made it just in time before they closed and then decided to go out for some fresh air before the next class: Visual Arts.

I took a stroll outside the front of the campus, while finishing my food.

The air smelled so fresh now that all vehicles ran on electric motors rather than gas. Further out, I spotted the newest transportation line, The Skytrain, meandering across the sunset sky. Who would have thought that today's society would become so much more efficient and advanced compared to many decades ago, where walking had been the main source of transportation.

The world had changed a lot since then; the time and place I always dreamt about resided in the past, clearly without any kind of social media, mobile devices or entertainment platforms. It was incomparable.

How tough life was for those I often dreamt about; having to survive during war and poverty. Happiness wasn't even a choice during horrific times.

Stopping, not knowing how I ended up here, I stared up at a white building with tall pitch-black windows soaring over me:

Sports Virtual Simulation

Just what I needed. Nightmares are soul-draining. And they were starting to take a toll on my physical body. The exercise would pump me up and get my mind away from the reality of the world, especially bad dreams that messed with my head.

The system voice greeted me, "Su-Lia, a pleasure to serve you again. Please enter your weight and height."

The menu projected from the kiosk as I typed:

Weight: 110 pounds
Height: 5'4
Birthday: 04/17/2058

Archery was my most favorite hobby, and I played the virtual simulation game with my girlfriends often.

A step into a dark room, I turned on my sapphire-blue eye shield.

"Have a pleasant session, Miss Chang," the system voice rang and suddenly the room glowed red.

Dark silhouettes of rotating human figures with targets glowing from their chests all came at me from multiple directions.

Stage 1: Rotation

"Activate Light Mode," I commanded my Star Kickers and sequential air compression dispersed from beneath my sneakers. I drew my bow back, eyes darting from one target to the other, and shot multiple blazing arrows that streaked neon blue through the virtual scenery.

My sneakers made it easy to maneuver when the gameplay transitioned to higher elevations; allowing me to dash up flights of stairs, climb hills, and slide through tight areas while I hunted for targets. Pillars raised and descended as I raced through, keeping my eyes on every target that popped out.

Stage 2: Tunnel Trap

Skidding to a halt, orange neon spiral lights emerged from yards away. As the giant rings of light came closer, maneuvering targets transformed into virtual human figures of different sizes that looked like zombies.

I summoned more arrows to hand and leaped back as I shot six growling monsters, executing them as they withered away into the air followed by shrills.

"Session concluded." the system prompt as I took off my eye shield and jumped off a four-feet pillar, landing with grace. The doors split to my left and a burst of air conditioning cooled me down. I was feeling better already.

Target executions: 24/25

I smirked at seeing my score flash from the wall in red. My flexibility and skills were still great despite the years I had not put them to use.

Visual arts was not until evening so I decided to head back to my dorm to shower and work on the rest of my paintings.

The academy was quite generous; every student had a private space that came with an equipped kitchen, small living room, and bathroom. My study area had a gray linen couch that converted into a nice, fluffy rose-pink bed.

Sheer, lavender curtains billowed out to my balcony where I was sitting to apply finishing touches to my landscape piece. A little later, I stretched while walking back inside, feeling exhausted from staying busy all day. Hot chocolate tasted good on a chilly evening and a nap was calling for me before class.

The impact of hitting ice-cold water burned through my skin. I struggled to push myself up, but the current was so strong my efforts only served to pull me deeper. At which point, I could feel liquid welling up in my lungs and my throat tightening.

Seconds later, I heard a loud splash as though someone had jumped in after me.

Underwater was dim. I couldn't see anything except a faint figure which looked like a man coming toward me, perhaps with the intention of rescuing me.

He had a very familiar presence, but I wasn't able to make out his face just yet.

Before I could think any further on this, he grabbed me and pulled me over to him. One of his arms ringed around my ribcage and the other forcefully swam us up to the surface. I couldn't seize anywhere else, so I clung around his neck for support.

We fell together onto the lakeshore ground. His back hit the wet, mushy sand as I landed on top of him, and we both panted for air. My fingers clutched at his bare chest while his hands gripped around my shoulders to hold me in place.

The taste of muddy water was horrible. My insides rumbled, and I tossed my head aside to gag out the remaining dregs, before wiping my mouth with the back of my hand.

I turned around, hair a drippy mess while my shadow hovered over an extremely familiar pair of chestnut eyes.

"YingShua?" I asked in a quiet gasp, still catching my breath.

He stared intently with worried eyes, like he was searching for an answer. "Su-Lia, where did you go and why did you do that?" he questioned sternly, gaining control of his breathing.

"Do what? I… took a nap?" Confusion hit me as my eyes scanned the area. The question didn't quite register. I had just closed my eyes and here I was, lost again with a pounding headache.

I saw his chest raise as he held his breath before making a statement, "You were trying to drown yourself."

"Drown myself? Why would I do that?" Although I remembered struggling in the water, I didn't know how I ended up in that nasty lake.

Right, I must be dreaming again.

I shook my head. "No, *that* was not me trying to drown myself. I must have fallen from up there." I pointed upwards but at nothing in particular, feeling a bit silly telling the truth or at least I imagined that was what happened.

One of his eyebrows raised like he didn't believe me. He propped both his elbows into the gritty sand beneath him, "You climbed this tree and fell?"

I looked up and there was actually a tree overhanging the spot in the lake where he had pulled me out.

Obviously, I wasn't doing a good job convincing him, so I tried again, "Look, I didn't want to be here in the first place, but I don't know how to explain to you how I ended up here again. This place, what happened to us—even YOU—are all just things in my dreams. Before long, you will disappear," I told him, raising my chin.

"You mean, *you* will disappear like yesterday?" YingShua replied, eyes fixed on me like he was awaiting for confirmation.

"Yesterday?" Then I thought hard. "Oh right! You never came back."

"I did after finding out a soldier was lurking around the area. I had to put him to sleep," he explained.

"You killed him?"

"He attacked with his knife first, but I caught it and knocked him out before he pulled his rifle. I came back to check on you, but you disappeared."

My eyes enlarged and I hurriedly asked, searchingly, "Are you hurt anywhere?"

He shook his head.

Momentarily, YingShua's eyes dropped down to my body. He cast his eyes quickly to the side, like he had seen the wrong thing.

Then it clicked. I was soaking which made my pink blouse transparent, revealing my bra and cleavage beneath.

To add to my embarrassment, I was sitting casually on top of the man, and had been talking to him the entire time while he was enclosed between my legs.

YingShua swallowed hard while staring away with a flushed face. He seemed to be holding his breath.

I jumped off immediately and turned around to cover myself. "I didn't mean to do that."

"You shouldn't dress so thinly," he commented before getting up from the ground.

YingShua brushed off the sand from his back and pants like nothing had happened. He then approached with bare feet until he aligned his shoulder with mine.

"If you think this is a dream, then continue to stay inside *this* reality if you know what's good for you. It's a dangerous time to be wandering off," he cautioned.

The words caught in my chest. I was speechless. He sounded adamant. Although he spoke in rough tones, I could sense he was only worried.

YingShua walked over to collect his bag from the shore while I stole glances at him.

He looked decent even in just a pair of black trousers, secured by a red sash belt. The fabric stuck to his long legs. Water drops from locks of his wet hair coursed down his neck, towards the valleys between his back muscles. YingShua slipped on his black top and returned to me.

Keeping his eyes to the ground, he withdrew an outfit from the backpack. This man seemed to have everything in that bag, as though his life depended on it.

"This isn't much but it's my mother's. She has a petite frame like you." He held a small bundle of clothes in front of me. I could see they were sewn nicely in black, red, and green.

"Are you sure I can wear this?"

"Yes…" YingShua slowly turned his back and waited patiently while I changed out of my damp clothes.

I slipped on the simple Hmong vintage top and pleated skirt first. Then I tied the dress apron on, before looping the dull-red sash belt twice around my middle and fastened it at the back. At least that was how I remembered to dress myself in traditional Hmong attire. The fabric smelled and felt just as fresh and crisp too. The details and pattern of the gorgeous handmade embroidery trailed along the plum and red skirt of fine stitches shaped like stars, roses and vines. My sneakers were still wet, but I put them back on anyway.

YingShua turned to face me, and I could see his face lit with astonishment.

"It's quite… short," YingShua said after examining the fitting and blushing when seeing the top didn't cover my slender belly.

"I like it, actually." Spreading the dress on both sides, I twirled once and came to a stop as the skirt swayed to the side and returned, touching my thighs.

I held my breath, hoping YingShua would say something to me, but he only remained gazing with soft eyes.

"You said this was your mother's outfit?" I asked him to break the silence.

"My mother passed away before I could give it to her as a gift. She was usually poorly dressed so I worked hard to afford new clothes for her," he replied in a sad, hesitant tone.

My heart hurt when I noticed the quiver in his eyes. Even he had a long story he couldn't tell anyone.

"I'm sorry. I didn't mean to ask about something so personal." Without thinking twice, my hands reached gently upwards and I brought him down, wrapping my arms around his wide shoulders.

Shocked at my physical response, YingShua froze stiffly like he wasn't sure if he was permitted to return the same gesture. While his heart thumped faster, his hands twitched at his side, curling into loose fists.

The wind whispered by crackling trees while the glittering lake motioned serenely and birds chirped in the sky. The timeless moment felt like infinity wasn't long enough.

I felt YingShua's arms slowly rise and, before long, they wrapped tightly around my back and to my waist. He pressed my lean body against his as he dug his face into my hair like he longed for a moment to hold onto someone. Seemingly, he had a story he wanted to tell but, for such a long time, there was no one to listen to him.

The Longing

CHAPTER 4

"This is goodbye. The next boat arrives in two days… I'll make sure—"

"Wait, how long have I been gone?" I interrupted, not wanting to miss anything.

"A day," YingShua replied, observing me carefully.

I pushed back, breaking his embrace, feeling out of place. I really thought I had been gone a long time but had it really only been one day?

Previous events entered my consciousness and I remembered the last time I was here. I was lost and had chosen to follow a group. We were ambushed by Pathet Lao soldiers and Captain Blong-Cheng fled the scene.

"Captain Blong-Cheng… is he a good man?" was the first thing I needed to ask.

YingShua zipped up his backpack and swung it over his

shoulder. He turned towards the horizon, where mountains guarded the greenish lake. "He is a part of the corruption that's taken place since the war. For years, trail paths and village locations were leaked to the communists, leading to many innocent Hmong villagers and refugees dying in vain. This is why I vowed to stay and help my people escape the corruption, in order to prevent losing more lives."

YingShua picked up a rock and swung it fiercely across the lake, where it skipped four times before dropping beneath the surface.

"I couldn't bring my shattered spirit to Thailand alone while the remains of my parents is under the soil of Laos and many others are being hunted down like animals. This is another reason why you need to make it to the next boat. And remember to trust no one."

I walked up to his side.

Captain Blong-Cheng's dark eyes came to mind and the thought of him ignited me with anger that seeped through every inch of my bones. I won't forget those black, eerie, unsympathetic eyes and the bloodshed he caused his own people. His desire for survival was nothing but a cold scheme and betrayal.

I tightened my lips and told YingShua, "I'm not getting on any boat. I want to share a common ground on your vows. The people you want to save are mine too."

He turned to catch my gaze, his expression troubled. "You must get on that boat. I can't guarantee your safety if you stay here."

"I'm not worried." I looked up into the sky as soft gray clouds started to form. "I don't understand any of this and feel confused about coming back here again, but now I want to have a purpose. Making me leave won't do me any good."

YingShua held his breath and stared at me, with a look of concern across his face like I was making a crazy decision.

I grasped the bottom of his shirt, clutching a fist against his abdomen as he continued to regard me with disapproving eyes.

The stubbornness in my tone had been clear and I could see in his face it registered with him that I wasn't changing my mind. Whether in dreams or reality, I was still the same person.

"So where do we go now?" I said, looking away, beginning to walk. YingShua didn't bother to argue. He understood I had my mind set.

Moments later, he caught up with me. "We'll walk south to catch up with the other group of people, where a few of my Unit members will be waiting. I only stopped again…"

Waiting for him to finish, I kept on with my pace until I realized he had finished talking altogether.

"So, you came back to find me?" My heart filled with hope.

He was reluctant to answer, which was typical of him, but I could see the flush in his face. He wasn't used to showing the nature of his thoughts to just anyone.

"Why haven't you asked where I went, then?" I purposely asked.

"Where you go is not important to me as long as you don't get yourself killed," YingShua muttered, but his cold words were undermined by the worried expression he retained. Rather, he looked agitated about losing me for a day.

Slightly smiling, I answered, "Good. I wouldn't know where to start anyway…"

We walked for a long while under the warm sun, maneuvering in and out of the jungle, and along different trails.

Sometime later, the jungle grounds turned into moist green

vegetated soil. We came upon what felt like a magical view of deep red poppy flowers, trailing along the downside of the mountain. The beauty of the moment was an extraordinary bliss of escape.

Faster and faster, my steps quickly transitioned to a run, and before I could think about what I was doing, I was already thrashing through the field.

Air weaved through the flower petals while straws of green wheat swished against one another, brushing my bare legs. As I twirled, hands thrown to my side, flowers touched my fingers. My vision streaked in shades of yellow, orange, and red; the colors bled into the evening sky like soft flames of fire.

YingShua trailed behind me. In each of my twirls, I captured expressions across his face that I'd never seen before; seemingly, a side he only showed when he assumed no one was looking. Although he didn't quite allow his lips to form a smile, his eyes gleamed in ways that suggested he had a thousand words he wished he knew how to express.

I turned around and noticed YingShua lunging over with a sudden change of mood. He grabbed my wrist with an immediate jerk. "Get down! I heard footsteps of people heading in this direction," he warned firmly.

The wishful bliss I had been experiencing disappeared in an instant. Panic hit my face at the realization we'd been followed and were now under surveying eyes.

In short breaths, YingShua squeezed my shoulders as we heard foreign languages speaking from a closing distance.

"Did you see them come in this direction?" we heard one of the soldiers ask.

"Yes, keep on searching," a familiar voice answered. It was Captain Blong-Cheng. My eyes narrowed. It was no surprise he had brought the enemy.

YingShua nodded while staring at me carefully. Beads of sweat glided down his jaw and dripped along his Adam's apple. He swallowed hard and proceeded to pull his Hmong knife out of its wooden sheath. My heart sped at the sight of the extremely sharp looking blade, but I knew it was a necessary defense weapon.

We listened carefully. The crisp sound of military boots breaking through the wheatfield, with flowers being crushed under their steps, was getting closer and closer.

I stayed as quiet as I could and, just as I saw YingShua was ready to strike, rain started drizzling. Within seconds the weather turned into a downpour. He abruptly stopped and continued to wait. We both listened with keen ears.

"Let's head back!" shouted Captain Blong-Cheng to his men. "We'll look again tomorrow. These people are not far from here."

YingShua dropped his body back onto the now-wet ground with big breaths like he was relieved he didn't have to kill anyone. The quick shift of the weather saved us from being discovered.

"YingShua?" I called out, while shivering at the coldness seeping through my skin. "Are you okay?"

He blinked and looked up at me, only to realize I had been talking to him. He sat up and quickly helped me to my knees. We crawled through the wet field and to the foot of a mountain where we could see an abandoned farmer's hut further up.

"Let's take shelter there." YingShua pointed before taking my hands in his. We used all our strength to hike up the elevated trail until we finally reached the bamboo hut. The dwelling was tiny and very thinly made but sufficient to fit the both of us as we sat and waited for the rain to stop.

He pulled out a small white candle and lit it. By now it was much darker and the only thing we could see was the bright orange-red glow of our faces.

I folded my knees up against my chest and wrapped my arms around them, propping my chin over my knees. My lips shivered and I could taste small cracks of blood from where they had become dehydrated.

YingShua gave me a long look as he shrugged off his backpack and quietly sat across from me. He set down the candle between us. "Give me your hands," he said, pulling them slightly above the flame. To my surprise, his hands weren't cold at all, and mine slowly began to warm as my fingers sat between his.

"Where is your village?" I'd wanted to ask him this for a while.

YingShua lifted his eyes to meet mine. I gazed intently with an eagerness to know more about him.

Staring down, with the flames dancing across his wavering dark eyes, he began: "I don't know of a place to call my home. My parents raised me in a small village in the southern mountains of Laos only until I was ten. Both of them suffered from diseases and passed away when our town was burnt by the communists. Since then, I have been on my own and have learned to hunt for food and to survive however I can."

My mind drifted off while he told his story:

YingShua lived through life on his own accord with no one to lean on, fending for himself all these years and, while throughout his journey he experienced grief, sadness, and loneliness, he always kept a straight face, pretending he was tough. In moments when he should've cried, he didn't and, in times when he was hurt, he never showed it on his face. He was forced to grow up by himself and witness the corruption of even some of his own people colluding with the enemy. Although draining at times, he kept on going, day-in and day-out, to help his people survive because of his drive to fulfill the freedom and peace he wanted for them. He was selfless.

YingShua let out a small cough and sniffed a little.

"Are you not feeling well?" I asked in concern as he let go of my hands and leaned his head against the wall.

"I'm… okay. We have a long way to go tomorrow. You should get some rest." He folded his arms across each other and closed his eyes.

Then I noticed a small ray of moonlight that caught my attention from the seams of the hut—to my right. I was reminded of the first night we met. Even though it was hard to see each other's expressions, I could always sense when his eyes were closed, his ears were still sensitive to my every movement.

"The moon is full and bright tonight," I commented but received no response. Shortly, I heard his hands fall to his side with a thud.

"YingShua?" I looked over to him and saw his whole body shaking in the dimness.

With haste, I crawled to him, reaching for his forehead beneath his wet hair. He was growing a fever and his face was turning pale.

"You're burning up," I told YingShua and quickly grabbed a small tan towel from his backpack. The coldest water I could get was from the rain, so I soaked the towel, squeezed it, and came back inside to lay it across his forehead.

I held the towel in place for a few minutes and YingShua's head fell against my shoulder. The towel dropped to the floor and into the darkness. I couldn't find it.

"Su-Lia…" YingShua called out faintly.

I listened closer but he didn't finish his sentence until seconds later.

"Will you… stay?" YingShua asked calmly before shivers took over his body again.

Immediately, I embraced him. "I'm not going anywhere. Why would you worry about that during a time like this?"

"What if… we might not meet again?"

"We will." I tightened my lips and patted his back. He was the complete opposite when it came to sleeping. It was nice to hear his thoughts for once.

YingShua lifted his head, likely realizing my knees were wobbling as I tried to balance his weight. He attempted to sit up but I pulled him forward and offered my lap for him to comfortably sleep on instead.

"Here, keep this on your forehead." I finally found the towel and placed it over his head again to help him get back to sleep.

All night I slept with my head against the wall with a stiff back. I listened to the crickets and tree bugs cry from the cold nature around us. I began to miss home and would have loved to open my eyes, like any other time, in my nice fluffy bed. But if I were to continue to stay in *this reality*, I wouldn't think twice because I wanted to be there for YingShua, who had no one.

The Stone

CHAPTER 5

The birds sang from outside as the morning light glared into the hut. I sat up frantically, having realized I hadn't woken up in my bed like I thought I would.

I was alone, with a black jacket draped over me, even though I remembered YingShua had been sleeping on my lap the whole night.

Quickly, I opened the door and jumped from the hut that was set about three feet off the ground.

"YingShua?" I called out, making sure I wasn't too loud. I tried his name a few more times as I walked faster and faster down the hill, before coming to a stop.

YingShua was sitting by a stream. He must have woken up early to go and catch some fish. Next to him, he had put up two sticks and a string to dry his clothes. I noticed my pink blouse and jeans next to it.

I stepped onto the cool sand. "So, you are here…" The air blew through my bangs.

YingShua looked up and handed me a cooked fish on a stick. "Eat, so you won't starve. I heard your stomach growl all night and I couldn't sleep."

Embarrassed, I replied, "Well, I'm glad you got enough sleep then to be up so early." He obviously was unwilling to admit he had been completely out of it while I slept sitting up all night. "I'll gladly take the payback with food, thank you."

I assessed him for a bit in search of signs of his wellness since I remembered how much he had shivered the night before.

"Don't worry, I'm better thanks to you," he said, acknowledging my concern.

"You're welcome." I sat down to eat and, shortly after, I changed out of the vintage Hmong clothes and offered them back to YingShua. "Here, this was a lovely outfit."

YingShua stood up without taking them and walked away. "It's yours. Keep it."

"Huh?" Baffled, I watched him toss a bowl of water to douse the fire.

"There is a family who will be meeting us along the way. They will set out with us. We should reach my other Unit by evening if we don't encounter any issues," YingShua said with caution.

I nodded, finished eating, and we set off just as quickly as the morning sun rose from the horizon.

Four hours into walking under the scorching sun, we noticed a foul smell. It became stronger as we got closer.

We peered further down and kept on hearing a voice calling after their mother and father: "Kuv niam aws…Kuv txiv…"

Our hearts sped as we ran to the scene in alarm. We were met by the haunting sight of a body lying at the side of the road for what had seemed like days underneath the heat of the sun. The young man's head was twisted to one side like he'd been struggling for hours.

"What happened to you?" YingShua touched his head and asked.

"I'm in so much pain…" the young man said between faint breaths. His eyes were bulging out, begging for his life to be saved. His tongue was white from dehydration.

"Tell us, who did this to you?" A choking sensation caught in my throat at the sight of blood from his stomach, where it looked like he had been stabbed multiple times.

"Not. Our people…" the young man said with his last breath, before passing away with eyes darting up to the sky.

YingShua grimaced painfully and slowly closed the boy's eyes shut. He stood up, reaching out to help me when he noticed my legs were weak.

As we left the poor boy and walked along the narrow road to find the village, we encountered other bodies like his.

It was such a hard experience to go through and we wondered how many people from the village had been killed in this way. If Captain Blong-Cheng wasn't responsible, then it must have been thieves.

Upon reaching the village, it was like a ghost town. No one was in sight except stray dogs crossing our way and wisps of dirt blowing by. I heard a crying voice suddenly and I grabbed YingShua by the wrist, pulling him towards the sound.

"Be careful…" he said, moving in front to take the lead.

"Kuv pog… Kuv pog." The girl kept on wailing for her grandma. "Please, don't leave me too."

A house at the far end of the village had the door opened. We stepped inside to have a look.

Startled, the little girl in a blue dirty dress hugged her grandmother who was lying in bed. "Please don't take my grandma!"

"No, we are not here to do you any harm," I responded calmly.

The grandmother turned her head a little. Her eyes were milky with cataracts but she could still see enough to know people were around her.

"Who's there? Houa-Li, stay behind the bed," the old lady said in a raspy voice. She looked like she'd been bedridden for days and had only just started to come back to her senses.

YingShua noticed one side of her face was heavily bruised, like someone had beat her. Dried blood stained a corner of her forehead.

"Here, drink this…" Gently, YingShua crouched down to the side of the old lady, elevating her head with one arm so he could pour water slowly into her mouth.

"Young man, we were in shocking terror the morning before…" She began telling her story in traumatic tears. "The moment I heard my granddaughter come running and crying that both her parents had been killed, I immediately hid this child to save her life. I dropped to my knees and grieved, praying to the heavens to protect us. They can steal all our food and take all our water but give my son and daughter-in-law back to me…" She wailed for a long while in YingShua's arms as I held Houa-Li in front of me by the shoulders.

Tears wouldn't stop dripping from my eyes. The anger in my heart at hearing her story was indescribable. Sadness weighed heavily in our chests and we knew we couldn't just leave them in such a poor state. With that, YingShua and I made the decision to stay a few days.

While YingShua was out feeding the chickens, pigs, and cows, and made two-hour trips to carry heavy buckets of water back to the village, I stayed with the old grandmother and Houa-Li to help them around the home.

"It's healing better today," I said, applying green and yellow medicinal herbs YingShua had brought back from the woods to her forehead, while redressing her head bandage.

"You remind me of my daughter-in-law," she said with trembling lips and eyes full of grief.

"I'm sorry…" was all that I could reply to her. She had lost her entire family except her granddaughter, Houa-Li, who was only eight years of age. There were no words I could say to heal her heart, other than to help her regain her strength and nourish her mentality.

During that time, we learned that there had been about ten families. Half of them had left the village for Thailand a month prior and the rest had decided to risk staying for the sake of their livestock. Four families, including her son and daughter-in-law, were all killed and the family who was stabbed along the way back to the village was the one we were supposed to meet and take with us.

"Here, have some water," YingShua said, handing me a tin-cup.

I brushed the sweat off the side of my neck, looking up at him as he held a hand out to block the hot sun from my face.

The days had been very humid. It was nice to be outside to help wash the old grandmother and her granddaughter's clothes and blankets. I learned to make them a few meals in between, burning my hands a few times in the process. YingShua was definitely better at the house chores and especially the cooking part. The short days with them was like living as a family—something I hoped to have myself in the future.

As I was taking gulps of water, I noticed YingShua staring at me with soft eyes, like he was lost in a deep daze. I tilted my head and teased, "You look like you want to help me wash these clothes."

YingShua blinked and glanced down to see a bucketful of water, soap, and clothes mixed with blankets. He grabbed a small wooden chair from inside the home and sat down next to me in front of the entrance.

"Don't your fingers still hurt from the burns?" he asked, dipping his hands into the cold bubbly water and stopping mine in the process of working.

"I'm okay. They don't hurt any more. As you can see, I'm not a proper Hmong girl; obviously not a cook and I've only learned how to hand wash clothes recently, but all these experiences are things I've come to appreciate the most. Back home, I only knew to go to school and study."

"The place where you are from: what is it like?" YingShua asked.

To my surprise, the man who rarely asked about my whereabouts was interested to know. I continued to squeeze and twist clothes inside the deep wooden bucket.

"Where I am from... is very different from here. There are many tall, shiny glass buildings in the city that reach the sky. We have vehicles and multiple lines of transportation that are programmed to take us to places without the need to drive them. We have machines that wash our clothes for us and clean our homes. Manual labor is less needed, you could say. The technology where I live is far from here; we have mobile devices that are multifunctional where it provides direction to take us to places, allows us to explore what they call the internet for many things. The device can teach us how to cook with recipes and we may contact our families and friends with just a voice command…" I stopped for a moment to remember my mother's cheery face. *I do miss home.*

YingShua stared off, deep in thought. It was quiet suddenly.

Did I say too much and overwhelmed him? I wondered.

"I'm sorry that you have to suffer here with me until you can return to your home. It must not be pleasant to be here," he commented in a sad, remorseful tone.

"This dream certainly feels real. I'm unsure when this journey will come to an end, if it ever does, but one thing's for sure—you make me feel at home," I assured him so he knew I was not disappointed.

YingShua's eyes widened like he was ready to say something, but he held back. Surely, he was happy to hear my response.

Shortly after, I noticed a shiny piece of stone dangling from a deep red leather necklace YingShua wore around his neck. Closer inspection revealed it was not only blue but also had gold, fire-like twists that feathered across its asymmetrical profile.

"I've never seen anything like this before…" I said, reaching to touch it.

YingShua removed it from his neck and held it in his fingers. "This stone was the last gift I received from my father before my parents passed away. They told me it was a protection stone." He dropped it into his palm and squeezed. "It's been unusually warm against my skin lately, like an energy runs through it."

"That's because that stone is special, child," the old grandmother commented from her bed. We quickly rinsed our hands and went to check on her.

"Are you awake and feeling better?" I asked, grabbing a hold of her hands as she got herself up.

"I am feeling good, my dear," she said, grinning, and causing crows' feet wrinkles to appear around her eyes. "You said the stone was given from your father, young man?"

"Yes, father gave it to me after he returned from war, saying it was a stone that fell from the sky," YingShua explained.

"This stone is special, child. As an old shaman, I've seen these while walking through the spiritual world. It's a sacred stone from the stars; a gift of protection against misfortune. The energy manifested in the mineral gravitates to spiritual and physical awakening. It is also a blessed piece that can bring forth love and reconciliation in a timeless manner. Must be why you both have met," she said, beaming from me to YingShua. "But I must say it has a lifespan. Unlike stones that live for hundreds and thousands of years, this one is the rarest due to its fragile profile and hollow inner depth. You see those fine lines?"

YingShua handed it to her as she looked at it with squinty eyes. "This is a measure of time," she explained. "This is all I know. The rest is up to fate."

The old grandmother took my hands into hers and continued, "Su-Lia, I usually can sense how strong a person's spirit is. Your heart feels, your eyes see, your body moves and yet your spirit is barely clinging to your body. If you make a decision, make it wisely, child," she told me.

"What does that mean?" I asked quickly, keeping my eyes on YingShua.

"Don't worry. When the time comes, you'll know what to do." She smiled and patted my hands.

"Grandmother says you are both leaving tomorrow..." Houa-Li said, coming through the door with sad eyes and changing the atmosphere.

"Yes, we are." I brushed my hands over her soft head. "Let's make you dinner so you don't sleep hungry."

Later on that evening, YingShua and I finished drying the clothes and blankets and made dinner. There wasn't much to make but some rice porridge with chicken was quite delicious.

"You're both really setting off tomorrow, child?" the old grandmother asked while I fed her.

I saw YingShua come to check on us. "Are you sure you don't want to come with us?" he asked.

"This is my home. I will remain here until the coming of my day. Houa-Li said she won't leave me, even when I've urged her to go with you," she replied.

It was sad to hear her words, but she spoke with a happiness in her voice that made us feel better about leaving.

"Your granddaughter is a blessing," I told her.

Her hand touched my shoulder. "And so are you to him."

YingShua looked up at me, flustered and visibly shy.

"My vision is not the best but that only strengthened my other senses. She's a rare find too. Don't lose her again, young man," she said, turning to YingShua to remind him.

"I am more in debt to him than anyone knows. I am the one always being lost and found by him," I joked while feeling silently surprised that the old grandmother seemed to have known more about us than we did ourselves.

YingShua only smiled and stood up to face the old grandmother and told her, "Please take care of yourself and thank you for your hospitality."

The old grandmother nodded. "You both have been more than

helpful to me and Houa-Li. We will most certainly miss you and are grateful for all that you have done for us. The innocent souls of Thao Village have been given proper burials and will bless you for your kindness."

Roosters crowed the next morning and we were ready to leave. YingShua had his usual black backpack, and I made a cloth bag for myself to pack clothes, some dried fruits, and food. Houa-Li purposely woke up early and came running to give us hugs.

"Take good care of your grandmother. She will depend on you a lot going forward. I know you are so strong and mature for your age. When we come back in this direction, we'll make sure to pay a visit." I patted Houa-Li on the head and her face lit with happiness.

We parted ways, and I couldn't help but take one last look at Thao village as we left. I wanted to breathe the new air one last time. Thankfully the breeze flowing along the road, trailing leaves in its wake, kept away the reek of death.

"Since we are going deeper into the jungle, you'll need this more than I will," YingShua said, opening his hands to reveal the blue and gold stone.

I stared up at him with questioning eyes and blinked as he bent down and whispered to my ears alone:

"Be good. Don't wander off again..." With that, he secured the pendant around my neck in silence and walked off ahead of me.

"Wait, but this is yours!" I called after him, but he only waved for me to hurry along.

To Believe or Not

CHAPTER 6

Your spirit is barely clinging to your body. The old grandmother's words kept on replaying in my mind.

"Su-Lia. Su-Lia…" YingShua's voice echoed. "You've been quiet for a while. What's wrong?" He stood in front of me, appearing worried.

"I've been thinking about what the village grandmother said to me. She was trying to tell me something but didn't go into further details."

"I'm a believer in the elderly who give spiritual insights," YingShua said, beaming with reassurance.

"Is that why you put this necklace on me?" I grasped the stone to have another look. The energetic beauty enlightened my thoughts; all-around the surface felt jagged to the touch but fragile in a way. The colors spread in pearly dark-blue with feather-like swirls of melted gold.

"You wander off or get lost from time to time. You'll need the extra protection."

"Are you saying it's a gift?" A smile flashed across my face.

"I'm only lending it to you." The obvious flush on his face told the contrary.

We continued trekking deeper into the jungle. With his long knife, he slashed taller plants and wood vines out of our way.

A half day into our journey, YingShua stopped and closed his eyes abruptly. He had good ears and was always wary of his surroundings.

I stopped and scowled, not quite comprehending the gesture. "What's wrong?"

"Let's walk faster." YingShua stood up and grabbed my wrist. Without a word, he firmly pulled me along.

"Is someone following us?" I asked, and before I could get an answer from YingShua, we came to a halt.

"Stay very calm. We don't want to give this animal the opportunity to chase us," he said beneath his breath with a very serious expression like our lives were at stake.

I dared to raise my gaze to meet the creature's glaring amber eyes:

Its fangs were gnawing through its freshly killed prey. The animal beneath him was already torn to pieces, making it hard to determine the species. I'd never seen a tiger in person before, other than those caged up in a zoo; its stripes of black, white, and orangish-brown looked so vibrant in the deeper yellow-green jungle, making the scene even scarier. An adolescent, these animals were known to be extremely fast and the strength of it looked unimaginably terrifying.

YingShua gestured for us to slowly back away. We watched with keen eyes from twenty feet, hoping the tiger would continue to go about its business. The quieter we could escape the better. But luck was not on our side.

The animal noticed us and it popped its head up with alerted ears.

"Go! Run as fast as you can and don't look back!" YingShua commanded.

I ran at the drop of his words but when I looked back, he stared at me for a quick moment before running in a different direction. My eyes followed him as the tiger bolted after him. YingShua must have known that escape for both of us was not an option.

"YingShua!" I shouted frantically before running parallel to his silhouette. I was unwilling to let him face this creature alone—even at the cost of my life.

My heart felt like it was going to pop out of my chest; I'd never run so fast and efficiently through the jungle before. My eyes paced from YingShua to the animal. I managed to skip over elevated vines, evade broken branches, squeeze through stands of bamboo, and shove banana leaves out of my face.

By the time I reached YingShua in a thrashing stop, all my belongings were missing from my cloth bag. I loaded two fist-size rocks, readying my throw to distract the tiger from YingShua.

My hands were trembling but, with all my might, I took my best shot and flung the bundle of rocks.

I missed; the animal noticed me right away.

YingShua jerked his head in my direction with stunned, panicked eyes. He breathed heavily as he switched his focus between me and the tiger, quickly calculating his movement should the animal strike out in my direction.

A dread of fear threatened to overwhelm me as the animal stared at me with merciless eyes and began moving slowly in my direction. The thought of being mauled by the beast shook me to my core but my main concern was what I could do to distract it from YingShua.

I immediately took off.

"Su-Lia! No!" YingShua shouted after me as he whipped out a thick rope, tightly wrapping it around his knuckles.

The tiger managed to gain enough momentum for the distance between us to close rapidly. It was then I realized a dead-end cliff was up ahead.

Just as I turned around, the animal lunged forward, pinning me underneath him. The horror on my face grew when I witnessed the tiger's dark massive jaws expand to reveal long, piercing canines.

I had forgotten how to breathe. *Help me…* My mind drifted and I shut my eyes in defeat.

A split-second later, I heard YingShua grunting from atop the animal, swinging a thick rope around its neck.

"Be careful!" I shouted as YingShua forcefully yanked the animal to the side and off me.

Panting for air, I rolled onto my stomach and pushed up onto my hands and knees. My hair was thrown into complete mess while I gathered my strength in horrid panic, thinking of how we might possibly make it out alive.

YingShua continued to choke the animal with all his strength and proceeded to unsheathe his knife, but the tiger roared and fiercely swung at him with its sharp claws.

"YingShua!" I called out to him as he staggered away. Thin streams of red blood streaked out of his injured arm.

The tiger rose on all fours and charged my direction once again. YingShua sprinted over and took a flying stab into its back. Even that didn't taint its speed.

The commotion happened so fast before my very eyes: terror struck my face at seeing the mass of the tiger's muscles flex while bounding in my direction. It leaped into the air to strike and, as I threw my arms over my face, I twisted and lost balance. The world slowed down. Shoved off the cliff, the animal's fierce momentum hauled me into the air with it. My world tumbled in a circular motion as I saw orange and black streaks of fur flash before me. The fatal strike may have missed but it had nevertheless cast my life towards impending death.

"Su-Lia!" YingShua reacted with immense speed. He dove off the cliff, thrust his knife into the ground for grip, and caught my arm with his injured hand.

Hung in the air, my mind went into a fog. The plea in my eyes spoke of my desperation to stay alive. Bulging veins appeared on YingShua's forehead as sweat came dripping down from the strands of his dark hair. He bared his teeth and clenched them hard as he pulled again and again, even though his bleeding worsened. More streams of blood coursed down his trembling arm.

"Su-Lia. Keep holding on. I won't let you fall." The pink in his eyes intensified as fearful tears began to well up.

He cared for me.

As frightened as I felt, seeing YingShua cry for the first time gave me strength.

Gritting my teeth, I gathered all my might and reached once more. He winced in pain when I clutched onto his forearm but that didn't lessen his grip. Being unable to defy gravity at this point, my fingers kept on sliding down.

"I can't... lose you again." His sincere sobs broke my heart. We both knew the mixture of blood and sweat was causing constant slippage. I felt the black leather band of YingShua's mechanical watch. It was the only form of grip keeping us connected but that wouldn't save my life.

The leather band snapped in my grasp and sent my pupils darting in shock. *It is over*, my mind screamed. All my hopes shattered into pieces.

The wind roared through my ears until I could no longer hear YingShua's voice calling in anguish. The intense pressure tore through my face while my black hair billowed around me.

As many times as I'd admired the vast blue sky, the fading image of YingShua made it that much more beautiful as I fell further down... and down...

I snapped from my long dream.

A loud scream vibrated from my throat before my eyes popped open. Tears gushed from my eyes and a rumbling pain flared from my gut twisted inside my stomach. I turned to vomit in the toilet, feeling like I had just died.

"Excuse me, are you okay in there?" a girl's voice asked before she knocked at the door of my stall.

Gasping, I looked around in confusion and quickly gathered myself, wiping all the moisture from my face and mouth.

I didn't die. And I'm back! It was just another nightmare.

Finally able to breathe, I exited the stall, using my hands for support. Two girls stared with curious expressions, like I had just emerged from a train wreck. They made way slowly for me to get through.

Exhausted, I turned on the sink faucet to wash my hands and stared off in a blur until noticing the water turning pink made me resharpen my attention. It was a sink full of washed blood.

What is this? I wasn't bleeding from anywhere. I brought my hands to eye level to get a better look—nothing. Nowhere was I hurt.

"Do we need to take you to the nurse's office?" one of the girls asked worriedly. They too had noticed the pink water. Their eyes grew shaky when they saw my face.

"I'm sorry. Don't be afraid. I just have a sleeping disorder," a small voice answered their horrified expression. The two girls backed away and exited quickly.

Indifferent to it, I went about my business, cleaning my hands. People thinking me as weird was nothing new.

Momentarily, I heard a clack against the sink counter. Two brown eyes stared at me. "Excuse me, this fell onto my side of the stall," an Asian girl with black hair and dark eye makeup told me. "Looks broken."

The emo girl walked off leaving me in deep confusion. A minute later, I glanced at the white countertop again, bemused while observing the familiar object. As I picked up the watch, I noticed one of the old, flaky leather straps was torn off the main face of the device. Not long after, it finally registered and the image of YingShua's watch, semi-coated in his blood, snapping from his wrist streaked across my vision.

A sense of incredulity came over me, followed by shocking

waves of anxiety. I felt suffocated to the core. Everything hit me at once: disbelief, panic, distress—all in one turmoil of emotions I didn't have answers to.

Did I really not have a sleeping disorder? More importantly, had I really not been dreaming? Trembling fingers crawled to my sweaty neck, up to the noise in my ears, and combed through my hair while my blood pressure continued to rise. I clenched my fists as my eyes raised to view my reflection in the mirror:

Lines of dark gritty dirt were tucked between my fingernails. Dry sweat was stuck to my face like a shiny layer of glue. My eyes were poofy from traveling through the air at such intense speed. And somehow, I had ended up back in my own time, as if I had been retracted by gravitational forces.

All those occasions I'd gone back to the same places and returned a mess, was it really that I had been physically there? But how was that even possible? Were they really dreams or not?

Then I touched the dip beneath my neck. With shocked eyes I stared intently at my own reflection. I wasn't hallucinating; the necklace was REAL.

His Voices

CHAPTER 7

Unfastening the pendant, I held it in front of me so I could confirm its existence. I was really *not* sleepwalking or having a nightmare.

The life I had known felt like it had vanished. My body started to shake while my legs went numb and weak. I was on the verge of collapsing. "If this wasn't a dream then YingShua is… real."

My vision kept going in and out as I tried to gather enough strength to use the wall to guide my way out of the women's restroom.

A while later, I had made it into the open air and stared up at the building to make sure it really was my college campus. I hadn't ended up in my bed this time, but in the library bathroom of all places.

Walking past classmates in the hallway, I ignored all the strange stares people gave me. I knew what I looked like, and it didn't matter to me.

What mattered more was understanding what was going on. It occurred to me that I must have been delusional, but every time I convinced myself of this, YingShua's watch and the stone necklace was evidence to the contrary. There was absolutely no doubt that every event that happened to me had been real.

My mother must have used the key I'd given her to let herself into my dorm room because she was there when I got back. She looked worried as I closed the door behind me.

"Mom?" I called out in a soft voice like I was glad to see her.

"Su-Lia? Where have you been? We've been searching for you all week." My mother ran to me and pulled me into a hug.

"What day is it?" I queried as I closed my eyes, resting my chin on her shoulder.

My mother stopped and pulled back from hugging me like I had lost my mind. "Well, it's Sunday. I've been here since last Friday when your friends told me they couldn't find you. I'll call them to let them know so they can stop searching."

"Let's sit down, please," I insisted, feeling extremely exhausted. I really just wanted to fall down and dive into my thoughts, hoping it would miraculously present me with the answers I needed.

"Is everything okay, Su-Lia? You look like you came back from the jungle," my mom said semi-seriously.

I stopped and turned around. "I did, actually."

My mother must have noticed the seriousness of my tone or the fact that my face remained stony. "What?" she asked hesitantly. "What do you mean?"

I debated if my mom would think I was crazy if I told her what was happening to me. I bit my tongue—no one would believe me. It would not be seen as possible. Everyone would just tell me I have a bad case of sleepwalking.

"I need a shower…" I told my mom instead, and she didn't ask more.

"Well, okay. I'll clean up your area and make you dinner."

"Thank you," I told her and closed the bathroom door.

"Be good… Don't wander off again."

All I could hear was YingShua's voice and my last glimpse of him before I had returned to the present.

"I can't… lose you again." I paused from washing the shampoo out of my hair and stood in a daze. The warm water flowed down my body as I brought my chin up so the spray could refreshen me.

The shower was calming. The answers were slowly coming to me the more I collected my thoughts.

I reached to scrub my back and felt the rough skin on my left shoulder blade—it was my childhood burn mark; an ugly oval-like texture that looked like wrinkled deep-pink flesh almost the same size as my own hand.

~Reminiscing:

When I was six years old, I had been naughty and kept running through crowds of people while playing with all my younger cousins during an event. It was our yearly spirit-calling gathering at our home, known as *Hu Plig Peb Caug.*

Once a year the Hmong would practice this tradition as a way to call back each family member's spirit; both living and those belonging to their ancestors. During the intervening twelve months, the spirit may wander off, get lost, or be frightened away, requiring this practice to call it to return.

The tradition is believed to keep the spirit and body in good health. In addition, it is a time of bringing all the ancestors to the household feast as the home is swept to remove all bad fortune and to welcome the new year.

My mother yelled for me to stop running and, just as she finished her lecturing and lifted a super-hot pot of water, ready to blanch her freshly killed chicken, I tripped, and my mother lost balance.

The pot tilted, pouring a portion of steaming hot water over me. I fell and hit the floor, screaming in agony.

All at once, my mother flung her pot away and several of my aunts dashed over to take off my shirt. They quickly observed the burn and rushed me to hospital, where the doctor at the time determined it to be a second-degree burn.

The incident ruined our gathering that day. I cried a lot from the pain, and when we returned home later that evening, I slept soundlessly.

Mother felt horrible so she promised for my birthday, due a week after the incident, to take me camping.

A very blurry image of a boy who looked a few years older than me came to mind.

"Su-Lia, will you... stay?" I'd heard that soft plea before—when I was a child.

My eyes popped open, and I remained holding the breath in my chest, making sure my thoughts were going in the right direction.

Didn't YingShua say the same thing when we both spent the night in the old bamboo hut? I wondered if the boy and YingShua were the same person.

My heart sped. He had always been familiar… I just didn't remember where I knew him from. The memory from when I was six years of age was so old it made it hard to clearly remember all the finer details.

"Su-Lia honey, dinner is ready," my mother's voice came through the bathroom door.

"Be out in a sec," I replied loudly so she could hear me.

"Have you been under a lot of stress lately, my daughter?" my mother asked. Her eyes firmly watched me with a glint of concern. Of course, mothers knew their own daughters best.

"I'm not ready to talk about it. But I promise that once I've cleared my mind, I will tell you everything," I assured her.

She set down her fork and spoon and put her hands in her lap. "Whatever it is, I know you'll figure it out. You've always been a smart girl. As long as it's not life-threatening, then I trust you."

It has been life threatening, I confirmed silently with an even expression. Being chased by a tiger was the scariest thing I'd ever experienced. Falling off the cliff, guns firing, and homes burning was all life threatening. Witnessing death was tormenting, and being stained in blood and sweat was haunting. As distracted as my mind was, I remained extremely composed. To worry my mother, who was also alone in her life, and meaning we only had one another, would not be fair. I could wait.

Later on that evening we heard a knock at my dorm door.

"Su-Lia, your friends are here to see you." Mother opened the door and smiled as Kathy and Jinee both came running with worried expressions and jumped up to hug me.

"Gosh, where have you been? You scared us for a whole week," Jinee said, squeezing me, before withdrawing slightly to inspect me.

"You definitely don't look well. I've never seen bags underneath your eyes before. Girl, where have you been?!"

Kathy stepped back to examine me too and made a *tsk-tsk* sound. "You sure that dream guy of yours is taking good care of you?"

My eyebrows rose when I saw my mother behind them suddenly scowl. She quickly walked to my side with hands on her hips. "Dream guy? Is there something I'm missing here, Su-Lia?"

I caught a glimpse of Kathy and Jinee quickly exchanging glances, as if they both had said the wrong thing.

"Ah-hem, I've just been having weird dreams, Mom. It's been messing with me. That's it." I tittered and glared at the girls.

"Do I need to get another shaman to look at you? You do seem like you've lost weight. You came back looking like a hot mess. Should we start with seeing your doctor for your sleepwalking then?" By now, my mother appeared seriously worried.

"No, Mom, I'm fine. My friends were just making jokes, so don't worry."

Mother blinked a couple of times and glanced back at Kathy and Jinee.

"Yes, Su-Lia's mom. Don't worry. We were only joking," Jinee said, nudging Kathy.

"You better be joking, girls. I don't want a man sneaking into your dorm or I'll have to stay a few more days."

"No, no, no," we all answered in unison.

"You don't have to, Mom. No men are allowed here anyways, since it's an all-girls' school."

Mother stopped for a moment. "That is true," she said, quickly cheering up and then telling the girls, "Well we still have food on the table if you haven't eaten."

Kathy and Jinee nodded. "Thanks Mrs. Chang. We love chicken curry noodles!"

"Well, help yourselves then," Mother replied with her cheery face and smiling eyes. She then turned to me. "In the meantime, I'm going to the grocery store to stock up your fridge, since you barely have anything in it–probably why you've lost weight. You need to eat better meals."

With that, my mother left. The girls quickly sat me down on my linen gray couch by the window.

"Now tell us… where have you been? Has your sleepwalking become worse? We heard girls whispering in the hallway earlier about someone who washed blood in the sink, was that you?"

I glanced down to my hands and stared at them before answering, "It was… his blood stain."

"His? Who? The man you've been seeing in your nightmares?" Jinee quickly asked.

As I listened to the question a dread came over me. My heart was torn on how I was going to explain these inexplicable events to my two best friends. How was I going to even start?

Kathy and Jinee's pupils decreased in size as they waited for my answer. Their lips hung under mixed emotions like they didn't know if they should be excited or scared.

"Everything… that's been happening to me recently has NOT been a dream."

They both turned to look at one another.

"I was *not* sleepwalking," I finished firmly and paused to observe their reactions.

Jinee pulled back. "Are you saying your disappearance this entire week was because you've been with him?"

"YES." I held my breath, hoping I'd convinced them. "He is a real person who doesn't exactly exist here—or now—in our time."

The girls froze in place with blank expressions. Jinee gulped and inquired more, "So… this guy came to life from nowhere?"

I quickly shook my head. "No, he didn't come to life. He is living about 100 years in the past."

"That explains the blood—he's a vampire!" Jinee snapped as if she was enjoying this guessing game.

Kathy smacked Jinee on the knee. "Vampires don't exist, dude. Okay, explain the blood in the sink?"

Jinee's guess did have some merit but I turned to Kathy to answer her instead. I closed my eyes before starting as all the memories of our final moments sank in, "We were ferociously chased by a tiger. It clawed him while he was trying to protect me, and then it charged at me and tripped me off the cliff along with it. His arm was badly wounded when he caught mine, but I lost grip and we separated. Then I ended up back here."

I opened my eyes and my two girlfriends had tears streaming down their faces and tissues up their noses. "That's such a sad dream… you both still got separated in the end." They obviously thought I was telling them one of my nightmares again.

"You both don't believe me, do you?" I asked in slight disappointment.

They quickly wiped their cheeks. "No, no—we believe you, Su-

Lia." They both wrapped their arms around me when I continued frowning.

I pulled out the necklace and quickly grabbed the watch from my bag. "Look, this is his. Even this necklace… he gave it to me."

"Are you serious? You brought this back from his time?" Jinee said, grasping the necklace for closer inspection.

"That's what I've been trying to tell you both."

Kathy and Jinee stood up and looked at each other again.

"That's not possible," Kathy said, shaking her head and switching her eyes from me to Jinee. "So how does he take you to his world—era, whatever you call it?"

I shook my head quickly. "No, he stays in his time… I keep going back and I don't know how and why."

Jinee covered her mouth but her eyes remained wide. "That is insane! And everyone thought you were a crazy spooked Asian girl who sleepwalks at night on campus. But firstly, are you okay?"

The question caught me off guard which led me to observe my right arm. "The scars… are healed." I looked up at the girls at complete loss.

Kathy stood up and took my wrist, examining one arm to the other, her thoughts forming words. "Wounds heal on our bodies… with time," she said bewildered, and switched gazes from me to Jinee.

Jinee drew forward to also witness my arm. She looked up to both Kathy and me. "Time only moves forward… which explains why you thought you were dreaming."

The girls let my arms down and we all sat together again to steady our breathing.

"I need to understand how I can go back at will. Something is triggering it and I have to find the answers," I said, breaking the silence.

"But it's dangerous," Kathy cautioned.

"YingShua has no one…" I muttered.

"We'll help you." Jinee quickly agreed and nodded towards Kathy. Although it worried the girls, they knew they couldn't change my mind.

I looked at them with grateful, relieved eyes. They believed me even though it was mind-bending to them as well.

The Answers

CHAPTER 8

A week had gone by, during which I attended class as usual and got caught up with my schoolwork. It was very hard to stay focused with everything that had been going on. I'd slept a few nights in peace, thankfully, but even that bothered me because I needed to know if YingShua was safe. My heart felt very unsettled.

"Better thank me. I told our professors you were out sick. I wrote lecture notes for you too." Jinee raised her chin and grinned proudly.

"And I made sure your mom wasn't stressed. You were missing for a week, so we took her out to get her nails done and went shopping," Kathy added with a beaming smile.

"Thank you. You girls are the best. I'm strange but only you girls understand my kind of crazy." We all giggled.

Over lunch, I had the opportunity to recount a few of my experiences with YingShua and events that happened to us. The girls were amazed and the more I shared the more they wanted to know.

Jinee took the broken watch into her hands and positioned her glasses for a better look. "I can't believe you brought this back from the past."

Kathy crossed her arms and sat back in her seat. "I agree, how do you explain something like this to your mom? You'll make her worry for sure."

"Our lips are sealed. Your mom almost had a heart-attack last time she was over. By the way, you never told us his name, Su-Lia," Jinee inquired with big blinking eyes. "You know, the man you slept with all night in the bamboo hut."

Kathy rolled her eyes. "Stop it with your dirty thoughts, Jinee."

"I can't help it that she had so many opportunities with him and she didn't." Jinee said, laughing. "You're so gullible. He wants you and you don't even know it. Take my advice: snatch him up next time you see him." She winked.

Jinee definitely seemed to have some silly advice but that was typical of my childhood friend. She enjoyed the exciting life and night adventures—but not my kind of adventures.

I blushed before answering, "Hey now, we just met by chance. He doesn't feel that way about me. You could say we kind of just help each other out, since we are both alone in our worlds."

Jinee curled one side of her lips, like she knew I wasn't honest with my feelings, and popped a cherry tomato from her salad into her mouth.

"Anywho, his family name is Pha? We rarely hear those last names except back in the day," Jinee commented.

"There used to actually be a large clan of the Phas, but we heard many of them died during the war in Vietnam," Kathy commented. She was American but her heart was just as Asian, particularly when it came to the Hmong culture. "You know, changing the topic, there is a watch shop down the street if you want to take it in to get it examined. I'm sure they can probably estimate when this vintage piece was made. I'm just not exactly sure if they can fix it since it's so old."

My eyes lit suddenly. "Good idea. It's broken but I'll see if they can get it working. Maybe getting it to work can be the first step to going back." The thoughts were rather wishful but felt like a start.

After lunch with the girls, I was eager to locate the watch shop. I only had to walk three streets down, thankfully.

"Welcome to Her's Watch Repair shop," a very old gentleman said, standing slowly from his seat behind the glass counter.

"Hello," I replied, noticing the watch shop owner was Hmong. His nametag read *Chen Her*. He looked to be in his mid-seventies, had a bald shiny head, and a dark brown mustache with some streaks of gray in it.

"I'd like to repair this watch, sir."

The old gentleman spread out his hands and accepted the timepiece. He adjusted his thick, heavy glasses, and before long, his eyes had a glint of surprise in them. "Where did you get this from, child?"

How do I explain it to him? That I got it from a dream that wasn't really a dream?

I cleared my throat before gathering the most appropriate answer, "Someone lost it and I'm looking to return it to the owner…"

"Is that so?" the old gentleman asked. "Whoever lost it will be happy you found it. Unfortunately, after taking a look, I won't be able to repair the device since it's such an antique. We no longer have the proper instruments to fix it due to the mechanism inside being so old. However, I can replace the band with a similar one. Did you forget that everything you see now are solar-powered, digital, and holographic smart devices? It's already 2078, child."

"Right…" I cursed myself thinking I really was losing it to forget which world I lived in. It felt like I'd been gone so long. Indeed, he was right. How could I expect a watch *that* old would be fixed 100 years into the future?

He handed it back to me. "Let me know if you'd like the strap replaced. The least I can do is help you make it wearable before you return it to its respective owner."

"Please do, thank you, sir." I laid the watch on top of the glass counter and paid the fee for him to quickly replace the torn leather band with a brand new one.

I walked out of the shop and waved back towards the old man as he sent me off with glee.

The next stop was the library; I wanted to keep on looking for answers.

"Su-Lia, is that you again?" Mr. Benz whispered loudly from the far-left side of the book aisle. He had just finished organizing the returned books that were checked back in from the metal book cart in front of him.

"Yes. I have a question." I walked quickly over to him. "Do you… have any books that can tell me more about dreams? Can dreams take you back in time? I mean if they really, physically can take you back to an era that once existed?"

The librarian had a wide-spread smile across his face as if the topic sparked interest in him. "Which era are we talking about, Su-Lia?"

I bit my lips and answered, "During the Vietnam War—maybe after? I dream about that time quite frequently but…"

The man started walking deeper into the book aisle. I trailed behind him with curiosity.

"By mentioning going back physically, it sounds like what you are looking for is not dreams but time traveling."

Time travel had hit the nail on the head. "Yes!" I snapped. "That's it."

He quickly searched through aisle D–H and pulled out a book called *Dual Destiny*, written by T.P. Moua, and handed it to me.

"Physically, time traveling has always been a myth no matter how many people claim it to be possible. However, based on spiritual culture, each person has one destiny that exists in their lifetime. After reading this book, it gave me a different perspective on one's spiritual capacity. The world is filled with energy forces that the human eye will never be able to see, but this gifted soul was born with a dual destiny."

"Dual destiny? What does that mean?" I had to ask.

"It's where a person's soul and physical being can exist between separate times. The connection involves manifestation in whichever timeline the spirit resonates most with. It's a supernatural phenomenon discovered in only one single case back in the 1970s. Ever since then no such occurrences have been found—which is why this book made it to the shelf."

"Thank you, sir. Let me check that book out for a few days."

"It's all yours but let me request one favor…" The librarian man scooted closer and patted me on the shoulders. "Take good care of yourself, would ya?"

He was right, I had to make sure to bring back an explanation to YingShua of all my disappearances. I recalled the few remarks he made:

"You like to wander."

"Don't let me lose you again."

"Will you... stay?"

All the words he spoke were as if he'd always been waiting or looking for me. Did I go missing that many times and worried him? Evidently, our connection went much further back than I imagined.

~The Modern Wanderer:

In modern times, they are known as 'wandering souls'. Hmong elders called these spirits 'plig nyias'.

Wandering souls are precognitive dreamers who are gifted with an extended vision to the past and/or the future.

~Spiritual Growth:

When the physical body manifests in a different place or time, minor amnesia is a common side effect. This may cause the person to forget past events for a short period of time. With age, the individual may regain their memories when their spirit energy matures.

For example: like normal dreamers, the individual can wake up from their sleep and forget what they dreamt about.

However, wandering souls—born with a dual destiny—can physically exist between separate times depending on which time their soul most resonates with.

The deeper I dived into the book, the more I began to understand what dual destiny was: a wandering soul that shares a spiritual connection to the past/future through dreaming and, in very rare cases, manifestation of the physical body.

But what caused these events to keep on happening and when do they ever stop?

~Destinite: The Fallen Star

Destinite is a sapphire and gold, mirror-looking space stone that has a smooth asymmetrical profile. A rare space stone that at one point in time hit the earth's surface and dispersed into pebbles.

YingShua did wear a stone necklace but what were the chances…? I continued reading:

Wanderers share a strong spiritual connection with Destinite. This metaphysical mineral has soul-capturing magnetic properties.

The stone's lifespan is limited due to earth's environmental nature being incompatible with space minerals.

An impact to the fallen stone can disturb the bonding properties between the rock, body, and spirit. As a result, it causes energy-wave shocks that disperse an opposite summoning to the past/future.

Thus, through time, the mineral may lose its attributes as the stone deteriorates due to its delicate profile.

The late shaman's words crawled through my skull like ants marching through each root of my rising hair.

At one point in my childhood, Mother told me I suffered a strange fever for several weeks. She said my spirit may have been lost in the woods after going missing for days during a camping trip:

"You are a gifted child. A very lucky wanderer but I must warn you to be careful. It's dangerous because if you go too far, you may lose yourself forever. I've temporarily sealed this gift of dreams so you will become healthy again."

Avoiding *the gift* was extremely hard. To think the late shaman took three hours to bring my lost soul back to my body, and I'd be living well without nightmares. But as I matured my spiritual presence became stronger. The seal to stop my soul from resonating with the past had evidently broken.

At times, there was no way of deciphering what was real and what were dreams. That only led to the ultimate medical reasoning: a bad case of sleepwalking.

After an hour into reading *Dual Destiny*, I began to hear rain droplets clacking and gliding down the window. It occurred to me that if the lights went out, I'd have a hard time getting out of the large library, so I gathered my belongings into my bookbag.

Just as I stood up and started walking through the book aisle, violent thunder boomed, and everything went pitch black. I stopped calmly and searched for my phone so I could use the flashlight.

Shortly, I heard the librarian gentleman ask, "Is everyone alright? I just got off the phone with our staff and they advised me the electricians are working hard to fix the outage."

Students in the library started chatting from a distance and I could see their silhouettes gathering as phones were being turned on for light.

"Stop that person! Someone just stole my bag!" a girl's voice shouted.

The commotion set off the whole crowd and everyone scattered into different parts of the library.

At this point, no one knew if the thief had any weapons or how threatening the situation was because the darkness did the person a good favor.

The noise from the crowd suddenly got louder.

"He's heading in that direction!" I heard someone else shout but without knowing the direction they were referring to.

"Stop him, don't let him get away!" Another female student yelled.

Finally, I found my phone and, just as I was about to turn it on, what looked like the thief came thrashing through and shoved me off my feet. My whole body was flung backwards and my phone went flying out of grasp, landing somewhere I couldn't see.

Stars came flashing through my eyes when the back of my head struck the bookshelf. Books came tumbling down on me from the impact.

I scowled, feeling a bit perplexed as my head started spinning; it was as if my hearing had become ten times more tuned in and yet the weight in my body was declining.

The throbbing intensified as the minutes passed. I couldn't find any reason for it except I was somehow claustrophobic. But I had never experienced this issue before.

What was happening to me?

A moment later, the atmosphere shifted into complete silence. I couldn't hear or feel students anymore, which seemed insane. My senses were all over the place and messing with my head.

Am I going crazy here? I waited in the dark, shuddering in goosebumps while my breathing became short.

Now panting, a sharp high-pitched sound whistled past my ears, as if I was the only person meant to hear it.

Then a force of gravity sucked the breath out of me. The darkness in my vision burst into an enormous energy, filled with blue skies and white clouds.

Reset

CHAPTER 9

M OOOO! MOOO!

It all happened at extreme speed. I only remembered the transition as streaks of flying colors, and suddenly, I found myself staring at six giant dark brown animal eyes.

Startled, I pushed myself away from the three cows; giants hovering over my bed of thorny hay, beneath which was moistened mud. Not *another* animal, I silently pouted and hoped they weren't about to eat me too.

"Ack!" One cow stuck its tongue out in an attempt to lick my face but I pushed at it and squirmed away.

"Shoo–shoo! Out of the way," a small voice called from a distance but I couldn't see who it belonged to until the animals obeyed the command.

"Who's there?" the girl called out, with a hand shielding her eyes for a clearer lookout.

The foggy image of a girl with short black hair, a white top, and a multi-color designed wrap skirt came to focus.

"Su-Lia?" She immediately came to grab my arms and shoulders. "How did you end up here? I thought you went to Thailand already?"

It took me a moment to remember her: the girl and her mother had helped me during the Mekong ambush.

"Ia? No, I never made it across. I'm actually… *back here?*" I said while my eyes scanned around, confirming I really was back in Laos. My intense headache from the library was gone… I've really returned!

"Su-Lia? Su-Lia?" Ia waved in my face. I snapped from the distraction as she helped me stand up from the dry stack of golden hay beneath me.

"Yes, it's me," I said, nodding quickly. "I'm glad it's you too."

She stepped back abruptly and covered her nose, her expression one of distaste. I was perplexed for a moment until the awful smell of cow dung reached me, making me feel like puking in my mouth. *Great*, and I thought it had been soft mud.

"There goes my favorite Star Kickers," I said, squeezing my eyes shut before opening them again. Even when disgusted, I couldn't help but burst out in laughter with Ia.

I scooted over to the drier, grassier area of the field and we walked up the elevated land, deeper into the more jungled area. I stopped when Ia gestured for me to wait so she could quickly run into the house to grab me a change of clothes.

"Hold on!" I grabbed Ia lightly by the arm, halting her. "Can you… tell me where this place is? And what year?"

Ia gave a slight grin. "Well, it's 1978 of course. We are in the province of Luang Prabang. This specific area is deeply secluded. Breathtaking, isn't it?" She swung her hands around in a slight twirl as she sprinted up to the home ahead.

Stunned and speechless, my expression grew ecstatic as the overwhelming confirmation poured over my body, soul, and mind.

I circled around to discover the enormous lush green jungle, where the foliage of thick lavish plants rustled as the fragrance of crisp, freshly-broken wood bark seeped into my nostrils.

Sunlight pierced through the canopy of trees as if water was glistening from the sky. Exotic birds of bright colors flew from one area to another, singing melodic songs like they were entertaining the guardian spirits of the land.

Joy filled my heart.

My prior passages were so full of immorality and bloodshed that haunted me every time I returned. However, this time I was awestruck by the opulent scenery of this captivating *past*, and the rare destiny that beckoned me. *This* reality was waiting for me to live it once more.

While observing the area, I understood why Ia mentioned the location was secluded. Anyone who would have reached the place wouldn't have realized a house existed. It was deeply camouflaged in the giant jungle; wrapped with large green vines that hugged the textured bamboo surface of the home.

A short while later, Ia stopped before me with a small stack of clothes and towels. "Let's take you to the small, steady stream down the trail of this farmer's home. You reek of cow dung."

"The farmer's home, you said? So, this isn't your home?" I asked.

"No, it's not my home. I am only staying here temporarily until Nujai returns from his duty. The farmer and his wife are Nujai's older brother and his wife, Yue and Mainong."

"May I ask who Nujai is and their last names?"

Ia's face flushed so I knew it must be someone she admired. "Their family name is Ly. Nujai is the man I met during the Mekong ambush. It was too dangerous, so he brought me here to hide out until the paths are safer. The men go out to scout them daily and make sure travelers are safe to cross to Thailand. They are a secret unit of four who have pledged their life to the Hmong."

Happiness crossed my face. "I'm grateful to hear that what they are doing is making a difference."

It was good news to my ears. Nujai seemed to be connected to YingShua. He was possibly a member of the unit with YingShua during our encounter at the Mekong River. They were able to save quite a few escapees like Ia. Meeting Ia was a great thing. Our fates were connected again and hopefully that was a sign of seeing YingShua.

"Yes. Believe it or not, they've helped and saved thousands of Hmong travelers and even American soldiers who were hurt during the war. They've been doing this since they were very young, like ten- and fifteen-year-olds! Very smart and clever guys, I tell you.

It's dangerous because of bad people like Captain Blong-Cheng colluding with the enemy. There are many like him but the Unit thankfully proactively paves the way for the travelers to get to safety. The Unit coordinates with the good Laos people, who assist in bringing the boats to a safer shore and the Hmong can get to Thailand."

Surprised, I had to ask, "You know about Captain Blong-Cheng too?"

"I didn't..." Ia said in a soft tone. "I learned of him from Nujai— he is a blood sucking traitor, and I can't believe we swallowed his lies and almost died traveling two days and one night with him."

"What about your mother? Is she here too?"

Ia frowned deeply and it registered with me that she must no longer be alive. "I'm… sorry," I said, reaching to take her hand. I stopped to look her in the eyes as she raised her teary face to me.

"She passed away after the incident. I saw her life taken right in front of me, and Nujai managed to help me escape. The hardest part was not being able to cry… so I wouldn't be heard." I could hear the sob in Ia's voice. It reminded me of the time I was with YingShua, wounded and barely able to run; holding on as long as I could.

The walk took us about twenty minutes from home, where we reached a stream that flowed serenely over sparkling white pebbles. To our left was a small waterfall which spilled over the limestone ledge like fine threads of white cotton.

"We are here. Take your time bathing and don't be afraid. This area is very private, so no one can see you," Ia stated, handing me a tan cotton shirt and an old orange wrap skirt with pink zig-zag designs. The colors were strange looking but it's what I had to work with.

"You should bathe with me so I don't feel awkward," I invited her.

Ia's face lit with excitement and she agreed to join me. I unbuttoned my white blouse and, just as I dropped it down my shoulders, Ia noticed my childhood burn mark.

"That looks painful," she commented with a grimace.

I let out a small chuckle. "It's the ugly, naughty part of me that will never disappear. Instead of blanching the chicken, I made my mother blanch me instead."

"You're fine. I have an ugly mark on my body too," Ia said, lifting up her T-shirt and pointing to just below her ribs. It was a bullet wound that had healed into a dark scab.

"You were shot before?" The look of the wound soured my stomach.

Ia nodded. "Yes, I lost so much blood and almost died while running from the communists. Nujai saved me. He carried me for several miles until we got to this place. The landowner and his wife took care of me. Since this territory is more secluded, this is like home for the Unit."

The sensation in my throat tightened. "You went through such a hard time." I pulled her in for a friendly hug. "I'm grateful to have met you, Ia. You have a good heart so you can't die that easily."

Ia responded to my affection with a beam across her face like she was my very own sister. She dragged my hands suddenly and we went running into the water with splashes.

In the middle of wrapping up our bath session, Ia looked up and excitedly grabbed me by the arm.

I frowned. "What is it?"

"Look, Nujai and the men are back."

"Men? You said this place was private and no one would see us?" I asked in a frantic tone.

"Apparently, they came back early, I guess." She was more excited to get out of the water than she was embarrassed that we were both still in the middle of bathing. Who knew that the path we had taken was the same backtrail the men used to return from scouting.

In haste, I sat down low in the water to cover myself. A bathing wrap skirt pulled over my chest would still be considered as me being exposed. I started to swim up to the shore to grab my clothes but froze; the rustling footsteps from a distance turned into thrashing splashes. Someone was coming.

The throbbing in my chest became intense. I squeezed my eyes shut and, without another thought, the breath in me was wiped out by two strong hands pulling me. My back splat against the man's torso and my eyes popped open. His arms locked tightly across my collarbone and around my ribs. A tingling sensation ran up and down my throat; although constrained, I was calm because I knew who it was holding me.

"Su-Lia," YingShua said between short breaths. The rhythm of his heart raced quicker than he could finish his sentence. "I didn't let go… I never did." Disappointment weighed in his tone—as if he was upset with himself. He buried his face into the coil strands of my wet hair, his lips touching my shoulder; a behavior I'd never seen from him before. It was like he felt responsible for what had happened to us.

There were so many emotions going on inside of me. I had zero strength to climb out of his arms while being overfilled with joy to see he was in one piece. "I know…" My body fell against his chest in relief. Then I remembered the tiger claw wound and looked down to grab his arm. It had healed already but the scars were still fresh.

I turned around to finally face him and gently pushed up his dark-wet hair so I could see his entire face, especially his frowning eyes that held emotions he would never speak of. "Are you sure you're okay?"

"I am now…" He tightened his grip around my lower back. The softness of my breasts pressing against his upper abdomen caused him to fluster.

Embarrassed, he pushed himself away to gather his composure. He proceeded to take off his black jacket and threw it around me to make sure I was covered up.

"I'm sorry that you're still bathing, Su-Lia. I was not in my right mind," YingShua said, shame evident in his tone.

In my right state of mind, he should have been slapped across the face for invading my privacy, but I couldn't bring myself to do that. I was too happy to see him to be upset with him.

"What's with you two?" a man's voice called from the top of the hill. "Get dressed already, if you're done."

"Can you grab me my clothes?" I hurriedly asked YingShua when I heard the rest of his unit members talking from up the hill. Ia stood with them, and God knows how she had already managed to get dressed so quickly.

YingShua handed my clothes backwards to me without looking while I climbed out of the water. I changed into the old orange wrap skirt and fastened a silver belt to hold it in place. An outfit I'd only seen in old Hmong movies that females wore, which felt very uncomfortable with no walking room but quite simple at the same time.

YingShua turned around and opened his hands to receive mine, noticing I had trouble flexing my legs. "Stay still…" he said, crouching down and taking out his sharp dagger from one pocket of his gray cargo pants. Applying the blade to the fabric of my skirt, he cut a straight line down one of my legs, making a nice slit from mid-thigh length to my calves.

"That's much better." My toes wiggled as I extended a leg out with relief, and we walked up the hill to meet the rest of his Unit members.

"This is Nujai," Ia said, introducing her crush first. Nujai was just as tall as YingShua, but he had a very slender body and long legs. His hair was short cut like someone who was in training camp.

All three men wore similar outfits: a black fitted shirt with gray cargo pants. They had old tan gadget vests and stored their knives and tools in matching black backpacks they carried on their shoulder just like YingShua.

"So, you are Su-Lia?" Another member came into focus who had longer, straight hair to his neck and a blue bandana across his forehead.

Ia continued, "This is Meng Thao. He's the animals' favorite."

Meng's mouth dropped. "She's a beauty. How do you keep your skin so clean and soft? You don't look like someone from here, I presume?"

Meng reached towards me in an attempt to grab my small wrist, but YingShua raised arm to stop him.

"Meng, keep your hands to yourself," YingShua told him with a hint of disapproval in his eyes.

"Oh right, I shouldn't touch you or he'll have my head." He winked from me to YingShua with a joking face, smiling with a mouth full of teeth. "It's just rare to see this kind of beauty. She looks like she's never held a farming shovel in her life. I can smell the scent of orchid flowers in her hair from here. Most women smell like dirt these days."

Ia gave Meng a scowl. "That's insulting!" But she took the humor well and laughed it off with the rest of the members.

"Her eyes are not black but hazel with green in them. That's interesting. Is she a mix of a different kind, other than Hmong?" Nujai said, looking closer at my face.

Silence filled the air and I saw Ia blinking with a smile, like it was something she had never realized too.

Flushed, I couldn't manage a single word.

My eyes bounced from one person to the other, feeling a bit embarrassed—though it was true that I really didn't have farming duties back at home. And I couldn't help that my parents gave me hazel-green eyes instead of dark brown. Skin care was a daily routine for me, but how could I explain all that? Everyone already saw me as a lazy joke who was without any kind of useful responsibilities. That was far from the truth and didn't mean I couldn't learn to live the proper life and be useful during this time.

YingShua pulled me back slightly by the arm. "She's not familiar with this area. Please make her feel comfortable, would you all?"

"Yes, sir. Whatever you say," Nujai and Meng answered, and we paced back up the trail. Just as we were approaching the vine-covered bamboo home, a couple emerged to greet the men.

"You all came back rather quickly," the gentleman said.

"We met the Hang travelers halfway so it wouldn't take too long to send them off yesterday evening," YingShua answered.

The homeowner then noticed me and whispered to his wife who raised an eyebrow like I was foreign to them.

I cleared my throat before answering their expressions, "My name is Su-Lia Chang. I am delighted to meet you."

They both acknowledged and grinned. "Oh yes, that intriguing name we keep on hearing," Mainong acknowledged and glanced at YingShua beside me.

Mainong was a cheerful mid-thirties pregnant woman who glowed in her blue and black Hmong attire. Underneath was a stretchy white shirt, covering a belly that looked at the brink of giving birth. Fine black hair ribboned down her back, while beneath her blinking dark lashes were warm coffee-brown eyes.

Yue, her husband beside her, had a slight mustache and frizzy-looking hair. He was wearing an almost matching blue and black Hmong crop top with his loose Hmong trousers. They both seemed a pair at peace, about to complete their family with a child on the way.

"Well, let's all get inside and have a meal since you all are back, and especially because we have a pretty guest tonight," Yue declared, throwing his arm in the air invitingly.

"Thank you," I tittered and looked up at YingShua as he grinned down at me.

Mainong had already prepped some food as if she knew the men were returning that late afternoon. Fresh green cabbage in pork broth, slushed cucumber, and stir-fried squirrel was served. The menu was not suited to my tastes but I couldn't complain.

"Thank you, Ia and Su-Lia, for helping with the meal," Mainong said to us after we had eaten and we were sitting to wash the dishes in the backyard.

"You're very pregnant so the least I can do is help you cook," Ia replied.

I stared at them and smiled hesitantly, "Sorry, I'm not the best but I'll learn to do better."

The girls giggled. "Your hands are too delicate. We're used to these duties." They both lifted up their palms to show me; the skin was very dry-looking and rough on the surface. I could tell they had worked hard all their lives, which put me in a rather incompetent position compared to them. I didn't care about having soft hands or dewy facial skin. It was more of a luxury at home. I found a lot more interest in the lifestyle and struggles they, and the ones they loved, went through—how they survived and found peace even during uncertain times.

After finishing the dishes, YingShua waited for me in front of the entrance without me knowing. I brought the dirty water to toss outside, and he caught me by the arm and brought a finger to his lips.

"What are you doing?" I asked in a small voice. Stillness filled the air when I noticed those same gleaming eyes in the moonlight as when we first met. The way he looked at me always made the fluttering in my chest uncomfortable and raised heat to my face.

"Come with me, I want to show you something…" Then he pulled me away from the home and went running into the woods.

The moon became brighter as we headed higher, towards the top of a small hill overlooking the home from the opposite side. The sky was deep blue; just as I remembered from being back in this time before. I still couldn't bring myself to believe how real everything had turned out to be and it felt like it was only the beginning, another reset of my journey to the past.

Resilience

CHAPTER 10

"Keep going..." Usually, YingShua would lead the way but this time he wanted to be behind me to make sure I wouldn't fall while we hiked up the rocky trail. I could sense his unwavering eyes watching me as he walked with his hands in his pockets.

Finally, we made it to the top and I turned back to catch his staring face. He blinked away quickly and simply said, "We are here." YingShua took a seat on the soft, grassy ground and curled his knees in between his arms.

I took up position next to him and started hesitantly, "So… this is what you wanted me to see?"

"There's supposed to be a shooting star tonight," YingShua answered while keeping his eyes to the sky ahead of us.

I looked for a moment before turning to him. "How do you know which direction the shooting star will fly?"

"It always goes the opposite of sundown. It's rare but whenever a full moon appears three nights in a row, it usually is followed by a shooting star. Today is the third full moon so I hope we'll catch one tonight… and that you'll remember me."

"But I do remember you—I've never forgotten you," I answered in confusion.

"Not the first time you came back…" YingShua said in a soft, disappointed voice.

I was silenced for a moment, unsure how I was going to respond. "Well, can't you just tell me?"

Just as I waited for an answer, at the corner of my eyes I noticed a scintillating light that streaked across the broad sky. It was really a shooting star, tailing a purplish ray of light behind it. I stood up in awe as my eyes followed the spectacle.

A few more stars flew through the sky during the following minutes, triggering surprising memories that brought forth terrifying images—blinding me like flares of fire. Scenes from fourteen years ago played across my vision; I saw them as fresh as the day I was there:

A village was under attack by ruthless soldiers. The smell of burning bamboo homes had woken me up and many feet were running past me as the ground shook in terror.

"Someone please help me…" I heard my soft six-year-old voice calling out to any villager that came by, but no one could hear me. I was buried under a dead body, so heavy I could feel my ribs at the verge of breaking. Then, finally, a boy noticed me and said, '*Come with me and don't wait here to give up your life.*'

I stood like a dark silhouette that had frozen in time at the painful remembrance buried long ago.

"Su-Lia?" YingShua walked up behind me with discerning eyes.

A moment later, I mustered enough courage to ask, "YingShua… it was you, wasn't it? The boy from my childhood?"

He remained silent, like he was waiting for me to continue.

"I would have died had you not dug me out from the horror and pulled me onto your back and ran. How am I to forgive myself for forgetting the most important part of our relationship? The beginning…

"Since then, I believed I was only having nightmares and it never occurred to me that these were actually real events—memories that I had forced myself to forget because I hated having them."

YingShua squeezed my shoulder and crouched down to see the regret in my eyes. "I didn't mean to make you feel that way. The last time we saw the shooting stars together was during the toughest time of my life. Tonight, I wanted us to watch it as a reunion."

I closed my eyes to allow the memories to sink in. "We ran so far up into the mountains and when we turned back, the village was still engulfed in flames. We could smell the ashes from the deeper jungle and, just as you were crying your heart out, above us we witnessed flying stars streaking across the partly smokey skies. You dropped down to your knees and cried out to your parents."

YingShua walked ahead, admiring the gleaming stars. "My parents taught me that when stars travel the sky it means someone is protecting you and a new beginning is to start. I always believed the stars sent you to me. You saved me from taking my own life. I didn't want to keep on running and surviving if I had nothing to look forward to. But when I met you, it gave me every reason to survive. I became a peace fighter after the war and that was where I found the rest of my unit."

"I've heard from Ia all the great things you and the men have done for our people. You've really fought earnestly," I answered with a proud smile.

"It wasn't until I realized a handful of our own people were betraying their families and joining hands with Captain Blong-Cheng; I wanted to pave a way to help those in need. The lives of our people mattered because everyone fought so hard in the war.

"The day I heard a nearby village was raided, Meng reported three women and an infant had been killed. When I arrived, we only found two women and the infant. I saw scattered footsteps imprinted on the ground, so I knew a group had come by the scene." YingShua reached into his pocket, turned around, and pulled out a deep pink hair accessory. He handed it to me. "You've always liked your hair tied in a ponytail, so I had to find out if it was really you."

I was surprised he had my scrunchy—it must have come off my hair during the incident. "The night at the Mekong River, did you know it was me?" It was a question I'd waited to ask.

"I didn't. It was by chance…" YingShua stepped closer to me and brought his fingers to touch the back of my left shoulder. "I was the one who treated this water burn. The original bandage had fallen off and the flesh became infected. I was only ten at the time but knew the aloe vera plant was a natural medicine to cure burns. Fourteen years later, when I shielded you from flying bullets, your shoulder was coincidently exposed—that was how I knew it was you."

Childhood amnesia was no joke. I was more in debt to YingShua than I had ever known.

"So, you knew all along…" I replied in a weak voice.

YingShua only gazed. The longing in his eyes lingered upon me as his fingers slid down my arms and curled his fingers around mine. "I knew. *Each* and *every* time—I would never mistake you for anyone."

A breeze played through strands of his soft, dark hair and brushed over my parted bangs. His touch was tender and his watchful eyes were captivating, like he intended to ignite the fire in me. But I knew the longer I allowed it, the harder it would be for me to leave him and the world I had come to know.

Was it too late for him to know the truth? Is it wrong of me to make him hope and waste time on someone who shouldn't exist in his life but did somehow?

All kinds of guilty thoughts stabbed me like flying knives.

"YingShua, there's something you need to know…" I began.

"What is it that I don't already know?" he answered in a whisper as disappointment consumed his face.

"I can't make you any promises. I'm not sure if we can be together. Today. Tomorrow. Or ever in this lifetime." Tears welled up in my eyes as I knew I was telling him things he didn't want to hear.

YingShua frowned for a long while before he dropped his hands to his side and answered, "You're not from here, I know."

"You already knew that too?" I said, gasping. *Then why hadn't he said so?*

"Ghost, spirit, or angel—I've accepted you for whatever you are. During our childhood, war weighed heavily on our land. Life running from the communists was much scarier than being with a timid soul to keep me company. I would rather chase your crying voice in the dark of the night, scared I'll be left alone. You disappeared for days, months, years even, without an explanation but I couldn't bring myself to ask you why. I figured, if I didn't ask, that you would come back. And you did."

Despite his sincerity, I found myself slightly amused. "What if I told you I was neither ghost, spirit, nor angel?"

"Then what are you?" YingShua asked, looking confused.

"I'm from the future," I told him and made sure he heard I was more serious than ever.

"The future?" he replied with intrigued eyes.

Nervously, I paced back and forth before stopping in front of him to continue: "To make this short, you are living in 1978. Me—I am from 2078. I live in the future, and you live in my history books, the past. In reality, we can't really exist in each other's time but somehow here we are," I explained, hoping to make sense to him.

I began unfastening YingShua's watch from my left wrist and wrapped it around his. "Your original band was torn but this is a replacement from the future—where I am from."

YingShua gazed at his watch, not as shocked as I expected. The bright moon reflected against the clear glass surface. "Thank you for repairing the band. This watch was my father's. It once ticked with life but later on it stopped ticking. My future has stopped ever since. The future, to me, has always sounded glorious. Perhaps knowing that you came from the future—I have hopes for my own."

His response was the complete opposite of what I had imagined but I was happy to know he was genuinely accepting of the strange fate we had, and that my existence allowed him to look forward to his future too.

"I know this all sounds crazy but don't be afraid of me, okay? I'm just as human as you are, except I breathe in a different time and live in a different world far from here."

"Su-Lia, I've never been afraid of you, nor was I bothered enough to ask. I believe what I've seen is sufficient to know you are special, but one thing I don't understand is… how did this happen to you and why have you come to this time of uncertainty? You've experienced more than enough near-death situations—you could get yourself killed and never return to your time."

YingShua pulled his worried expression closer to mine, cupping both my shoulders.

Overwhelmed and lost for words, my eyes lingered on his for a moment. "As far back as I remember, it just keeps happening to me. I can't control it, except that it happens in my sleep, through dreams. While searching for answers, I came across a book called *Dual Destiny*.

"As there are many dreamers in this world, there are rare dreamers like me who are gifted with an extended vision to the past and/or future.

"The elders call these individuals Plig Nyias, while the book terms them wandering spirits born with a Dual Destiny. A rare supernatural phenomenon where certain souls can physically exist between separate times.

"This is the only reason I can make sense of why I keep on returning. But why *here*? I don't know the answer myself."

I peered into YingShua's eyes to search for something he might help me learn. "What is this connection that you and I have? Of all places, time, and people... that it's always you?

YingShua's jaws clenched before he began, "I know that your disappearances are out of your physical control. I've witnessed it with my own eyes...

"During the cliff incident, I was more than confident I could pull you back up. Then there was a glare from that stone. It cracked as particles shimmered into thin air. My chest immediately throbbed as I witnessed you slipping right through my hands.

"For days, I begged my unit to help me look for you. We traveled beneath the cliff, miles around the area, yet there was no trace of you. I knew what I saw must have been real and that you were still alive somewhere."

YingShua caressed the necklace. He looked down and my eyes followed as he told me, "Your physical appearance must have something to do with this stone. I believe this is where our connections began long ago. This rock, as the village grandmother once said, is a special stone of this time and place."

My pupils dilated, connecting the dots, remembering 'The Fallen Stone - Destinite' section of the book:

Wanderers share a strong spiritual connection with Destinite. This metaphysical mineral has soul-bonding magnetic properties.

"Destinite." The name escaped my lips as I stared intently at the pendant before me.

"Is that what it's called?"

"Yes," I told YingShua.

"Before my father passed away, he fought in the war. He said he found this mineral after he and his comrades saw a big glare in the night, thinking it was a bomb. But it turned out to be a fallen meteor that had landed. He always said it was like a star that fell from the sky. A blessed piece."

YingShua's side of the story was coinciding with everything that had happened:

The hideout after the Mekong ambush…

The tiger incident…

The library theft knockout…

Every time it occurred under some kind of circumstance that disturbed the stone.

I took a better look at the piece, where roughly a quarter of the profile had been smashed off. Staring, my mouth started speaking: "My spirit resonates with this stone and every time it fractures, it sends me in the opposite direction. The village grandmother and even the book states that this stone holds a deteriorating lifespan. So, does this mean that once it is gone…?" I stared at YingShua intently.

"You will return to your time," YingShua said in a soft tone, swallowing hard. He pulled back slightly to look me in the eye. "Because I don't know what fate this stone will bring us… don't let me lose sight of you. If anything…" He paused, tightening his lips before continuing in an even more serious tone, "If not with me, I want you to be home—in your future. At least that assures me you are safe and not here risking your life."

It was the hardest thing he had to tell me, but I would be selfish to not understand. YingShua was selfless; he was willing to part with me if it meant I would be safe. This was how he knew to protect my life; although it stung my heart it was reality. Our timelines were so far apart. Promises were invalid.

I nodded slowly, feeling a little shattered but I had to stay positive and not forget to make my time with him worthwhile. Regardless, hopeful thoughts spoke through my lips, "Maybe if we take care of this stone, we can last a little longer and I wouldn't have to go home so soon."

Our attention was drawn back into the horizon. The stone was glazed by the early morning transition of night to dawn, setting off the smooth surfaces' hue of sapphire mixed with gold, making it look transparent. The night had gone by faster than we had realized.

Su-Lia, do you remember when you thought you slept with a stiff back all night in the bamboo hut?"

I nodded, continuing to listen.

"You actually didn't. You slept in my arms soundlessly. The fever

I had wasn't enough to keep me down, especially when you were with me—I couldn't sleep. Not knowing when you'd leave again, I was the one who stood up all night, listening to your stomach growl."

I led out a small laugh. All this time, I never realized the sentiments of YingShua's care, genuine beliefs, and hopes for a lost girl like me. His confession was mind blowing and I came to understand that he had accepted me, our fates, and everything that had happened to us even before I discovered it myself.

"Why did you sometimes act like I was a stranger to you?" I asked amusingly even though I strongly suspected his uncaring front was a way to protect the shame of my minor amnesia.

"Because… your secrets belong only to me," he said, beaming.

While understanding our destinies could never be foreseen, making our confessions was teaching us that resilience was the essence to embracing our fates.

Growing Instincts

CHAPTER 11

Yawning, Meng walked out of the home and raised his hands into the morning air to get his stretches in.

We both crouched down to avoid being seen, chuckling to ourselves. We had not slept and looked like zombies.

"Here." YingShua secured the necklace around my neck again. "I've bound it with plant fiber. It should help protect the delicacy of the stone."

I beamed up at him and tucked the pendant inside my cotton shirt. "Together…"

"YingShua, it's four in the morning, what are you doing so early?" Meng asked when he saw YingShua returning. He had deliberately used the back trail to hide his whereabouts.

"I did my morning walk and took a bath by the stream," YingShua lied while watching me tip-toe quickly into the house behind Meng.

"Your morning walk and bath? You still have the same clothes on from last night." Meng curled a corner of his lip but YingShua ignored him and proceeded to the back of the house to rehang the towel he had borrowed.

Just as I closed the door, I ran into Ia which startled me. She gave me a weird look and said, "Where did you come from? I thought you were still sleeping."

"I…" I looked behind Ia and also saw Mainong. "I went looking for my clothes but couldn't find them. Where did you hang them?"

Ia blinked and smiled. "Oh, yes, they're in the backyard. They should be dry by now."

"Good, I'll go change then." I held my breath and hurriedly squeezed my way between Ia and Mainong.

"Come and eat after you're done," said Mainong.

"So, what's on today's agenda?" Yue asked while everyone sat around the table for breakfast.

"There is a Moua family of four—a father, mother, and their two sons—that are stuck three days' walk southwest from here in Tha Ngon. Due to heavily guarded territories by Trail 13, the family was delayed and missed their boats yesterday. We should check to see if they are still there and maybe take the Monkey Trail as an alternative route and rearrange a different boat for them. In the meantime, let's prepare extra food and blankets—the family will need it," YingShua instructed.

Ia leaned over in an attempt to whisper but YingShua interrupted, "Su-Lia, get ready after breakfast. You're coming with us." He turned to Ia. "I'm sorry to burden you but if you can please lend Su-Lia a few extra changes of clothes."

The whole table stared at YingShua as he turned his eyes to meet mine. He ignored everyone's surprised expression and, although he would have known we would be facing a dangerous day, he didn't show the slightest concern—as if he was confident he could protect me at all costs.

I stared at him hesitantly and understood he had been serious when saying to not let him lose sight of me.

Ia scooted back to her position and pouted. "I was hoping to have a partner to help feed the cows and do chores."

YingShua only smiled over the table and replied, "There's a lot I'd like to teach her first."

Nujai placed his palm on Ia's shoulder. "You stay here to help Mainong since she is about due. We should be back in a few days."

Ia nodded and went back to chewing her food while Mainong couldn't contain her smile and commented, "I'll make sure extra food is packed." She looked over to me. "You'll worry him if you stay."

I acknowledged this and did just as YingShua asked. We set off by noon and the Unit estimated our arrival at the Monkey Trail would be the next day.

"Here, this is a knife I sharpened for you. Keep it on you in case you need to use it," YingShua said, slipping the four-inch pocketknife into my cloth bag containing some clothes and food Ia and Mainong had packed for me.

"I don't even know how to use this." I looked up at him with worried eyes. I was afraid of sharp things.

YingShua patted my arm and curved his lips. "I'll teach you when we stop to rest later."

Nujai and Meng both waved as we set off, with each of us carrying rolled blankets and a backpack full of gadgets, food, and water.

"Just out of curiosity, how do you earn a living doing this— where do you get so many supplies and so much food from?" I had to ask at the start of our trip.

"We don't do our duties for money but many generous travelers who we've helped donate belongings they no longer require, and we store it to help other survivors in need. We hunt along the way back to bring food home. The extra we preserve to feed the hungry," Nujai answered.

These men were quite impressive, I thought, feeling amazed.

"Where do you get your information about these people?" Something I'd yet to learn.

"The Laotian boatmen," Nujai continued. "They usually are given head counts on who is arriving, especially the ones we work with. They tell us the few that end up not arriving, establishing an approximate location based on information from groups they parted from that made it across. Nine times out of ten, we end up finding those who get separated and they then help us discover where their lost family members are."

"You all do such generous work," I commended. I had read in history books about the thousands of Hmong who survived, and knowing that over 100 years ago compassionate men like these were a part of the freedom movement was something worth treasuring.

"Also, be ready to wrestle the monkeys along the Monkey Trail tomorrow," Meng said.

"The female monkeys are somehow very attracted to Meng," YingShua replied, answering my confused expression.

Meng combed his fingers through his hair. "I am indeed attractive. Even animals love me."

Nujai snorted. "We'll see about that tomorrow. It's more like the monkeys like giving you attention and you scaring off women."

"Hey, don't make fun of my looks. Women these days just don't know what's good for them," Meng said, raising his eyebrows. He pushed up a sleeve, revealing one of his muscular arms. "See these? I can carry two of Su-Lia since she's so thin."

"You wouldn't," YingShua answered in a serious tone followed by a slight grin and a roll of his eyes.

I smiled, quite amused by their conversation while admiring their brother-like friendship.

Meng's face dropped to a frown, and he looked at the ground. "Yes, sir, I wouldn't touch her. If looks could kill, I'd be dead."

We all laughed and looked ahead to our long day of trekking through the dark jungle. It was estimated that by nightfall we should be close to the Monkey Trail.

The sterling moon rose into the inky-blue night. Animals' howls echoed, giving the impression our footsteps were being follow closely, setting off my nerves in all sorts of directions. I looked back but all that was behind us was the dark, still jungle.

"Let's stop and rest here tonight," YingShua told the guys.

We made good progress, our destination was only two days away so the men selected a resting point where they thought it was safe to get some sleep. Thankfully, the night came with warm breezes to balance the cooler evening while the men started the campfire.

Nujai and Meng went to pick large spreads of banana leaves so they could make a sleeping space for themselves before settling in for the night.

YingShua laid four extra-large banana leaves across from Meng and Nujai. He created more sleeping spaces around the fire. "We'll rest here."

"Here?" I asked with wide eyes, feeling extremely shy.

YingShua nodded nonchalantly. "It'll only get colder later." He helped me set my cloth bag on the ground and withdrew the knife from it.

"I'll teach you how to use this now," he said, placing it in my hands and cocking his head to the side for emphasis.

We both walked away from our sleeping space so we wouldn't disturb Meng and Nujai.

"You start by making sure the blade is pointing towards your wrist, but with the sharp side away from you." YingShua positioned himself in front of me and rotated the knife away from him. He settled his fingers over mine and closed them into a tighter grip.

Then YingShua stepped back a few feet away and said, "Pretend I'm someone you hate." He parted his strong legs and bent forward a little, into a fighting stance. "Show me what you've got first. Take your best swing."

I took a hesitant step and then another. My weapon had a cover but I'd never wielded this kind of knife before—especially with the intent to kill or protect. It felt scarier than shooting targets while practicing archery. My eyes glanced from the blade back up to YingShua, thinking of the many scenarios in which I might have to use it.

Given the time I'd taken, he should've laughed at me, but didn't. He remained calm and waited patiently with eyes firmly on me.

Holding my breath, and without any further thought, I charged at him aimlessly like my life depended on the blade alone. Just as I was inches away, I cowardly squeezed my eyes shut and swung right past him. With haste, YingShua extended his arms to catch me before I ran into the tree a short distance behind him.

I opened my eyes and looked up at him through my messy bangs.

YingShua stared down at me, clearly baffled. He swallowed slowly and blinked once, and then again like he hadn't expected such a move or had ever seen one before.

Awkwardness filled the air. Then I pushed against his chest to make room but choked and started coughing heavily. I felt a deep pain in my stomach, and when we both parted, I realized I was holding the dagger with both hands, hilt jabbed into my abdomen.

I dropped it and gasped, not believing how this had even happened.

"Not only did you attack me with your eyes closed, you would've stabbed yourself and ruined your face." He tried not to grin and gave me more room to breathe.

Utterly embarrassed, I tried to defend myself despite still coughing, "I've never. Held. A weapon before." I cleared my throat and continued, "I've only ever used a knife to cut vegetables and meat. I've never had enemies."

"You'll have many here." He replied like he was still joking but I knew he was serious. He too wanted me to learn to protect myself.

YingShua bent down to grab the weapon and secured it back in my hands. He stepped back. "Let's try again," he said, but this time he pulled out one of his own daggers and sliced it through the air a few times to give me examples of how I should draw and wield my dagger.

"The best way to hold a blade is either the forward grip, which means pointing it at your enemy. It's better for slashing," he said before effortlessly spinning the dagger in one hand so the tip of the blade pointed directly at me. The sharpest edge of the weapon glared a reflection of red-orange flames from the fire glow.

"The other is the reverse grip: holding the handle with the blade pointing towards the ground. This enables more stabbing power." His weapon was now firmly in his grasp as he slowly curled his arm around until his wrist aligned with his sharp looking eyes. "This move will give you a stronger aim at your attacking enemy." He then refocused his attention on me and stepped back into his earlier stance.

I nodded, feeling more excited than nervous now it was finally registering. I blew my bangs out of my eyes and positioned myself again, dagger pointed towards YingShua.

After preparing myself, then settling my weight on one leg, I charged once more. This time with a focused gaze, calculating in which direction I should swing.

With a leaping strike, he evaded quicker than I had anticipated. YingShua lunged backwards and dodged my two consecutive horizontal slashes.

I advanced into taking another swipe but was caught off guard when YingShua ducked beneath my attack like something had alerted him. He swooped me up off the ground and flung me around to the side. I could tell he was intending to return me to my feet but I lost balance. YingShua turned back to catch my arms but wasn't fast enough to prevent me toppling backwards, and I fell, dragging him down as he circled his injured arm around to cushion me.

We crashed and YingShua grunted in mild pain as his elbow impacted the ground, dropping his face centimeters away from me.

"Your wound," I gasped worriedly from beneath him. In attempt to push myself up, I noticed something out of the corner of my eye:

An extremely long, red, brown, and black segmented creature surfaced from powdered dirt and hurried away. Shutting my eyes, I managed to ask, "Is it gone yet?" The thought of its million yellow creepy legs crawling over my feet made my stomach turn sour.

YingShua watched it disappear with keen eyes. "Centipedes are venomous. I was bitten by one when I was ten and had days of fever."

I opened my eyes to the sight of YingShua staring down at me. He smiled warmly, with a hint of amusement.

Waves of heat rushed to my face. "Where… were you bitten?" I spoke slowly, trying hard to stay engaged, but my mind kept on being distracted by the details of his features. I'd paid attention to his looks before but had never been as close to him as I was now, breathing beneath him.

"On my calf…" YingShua answered quietly, his curious concentration melted over me like gliding lava. The high structure of his nose was perfect. I could tell he had become familiar with the scent of me from how he breathed. And those plump parted lips that hesitated time and again about the right things to do and say.

Then he blinked. "But I survived and so will you after this." A charming curl of his lips spread across his face like he adored me secretly. His gentle fingers wiggled beneath my head as he said, "You're getting much better."

The dagger remained tight against my chest while he stared at me, cradled in his arms.

Although he was teaching me, I felt I was more of a burden; but it was not time to give up yet.

YingShua helped me up and decided on changing the training

direction. "How about if Captain Blong-Cheng came at you like this," he said, dashing at me and grabbing one of my arms. He wrapped his well-built arms around my neck, tugging me against his torso. "Which area on my body would you stab first so I would release you?"

My arms stiffened around his masculine biceps. He held firmly but in a gentle way. I swallowed hard before answering. My heart sped. I quickly calculated my escape route, wondering if I stabbed him in his arm, he might still be able to grab me with his other hand. But if I stabbed him in his stomach, he could swing his body away.

Without a moment of thought, I attempted to attack the side of his legs but he caught my swinging wrist. To my surprise, my legs collapsed like I had lost all strength in them. My knees hit the ground with a thud.

"Su-Lia, we can stop here," he said before reaching out for me.

I threw my arms out to prevent him—I wasn't going to be a disappointment again. "No, we can continue."

My free hand dug in the dirt for a moment, and it finally clicked. I released the knife from the hand YingShua was gripping by the wrist. The weapon fell but before it made contact with the ground, I snatched it with my other hand and slashed it across YingShua's abdomen.

YingShua leaped back in surprise, freeing me. Before he could take his feet off the banana leaves, I tore them from under him with an amused face. While he was distracted with trying to stabilize himself, I took the opportunity to attack him to the ground, pinning him across his neck with one arm, my dagger pointing centimeters from his face.

"I got you to release me," I said, smirking.

YingShua looked at me with pride and teased, "And I once

thought you were a timid soul."

I hopped off him and extended my hands to help him back up.

We brushed away the dirt from our clothes and YingShua faced me to begin the next lesson.

"The first thing to know when handling a weapon is how to wield it with enough momentum and strength so your aim is absolute."

He walked behind me, taking the back of my hand into his as he taught me in detail.

"Your grip around any of your weapons should be just as firm as the strength that comes from your body's force. When you swing, swing not from your wrist alone but make sure that the strength comes from your thighs, which enables your abdomen to contribute even more momentum—ending your final swing in a sharp, penetrating blow."

YingShua swung the knife in my grip in different strikes. I followed his lead and, eventually, he wanted to call it a night.

"It's okay. You can go to sleep while I'll finish up." Just as I turned around, YingShua grabbed from behind, scooping me into his arms.

"I can walk…" I told him with hands around his neck, but he didn't answer. I noticed my shoelaces were loose as I watched my feet dangle off his forearm.

He laid me down gently onto the sheet of banana leaves, back flat on the ground.

Dark trees soared over us, but past them the sky had filled with diamonds again and it lightened my mood. I was still scared to close my eyes to the unknown—ever since childhood I had only closed my eyes when I was tired enough.

"Sleep. You've not slept all day," YingShua reminded me, turning towards the firepit.

"Neither have you," I remarked, hoping he'd reply but he didn't. His large back was turned against me.

I bit the bottom of my lips, not really wanting to close my eyes just yet. I tried talking again, "I've learned a lot tonight. You've taught me so much and—"

YingShua rolled over to face me. Startled, I froze and clamped my mouth shut.

For a moment, I thought I'd be scolded for being chatty, but he slowly reached to cover both my eyes with one of his palms. "Su-Lia, if you're afraid to sleep. Don't be."

While I couldn't see, I knew how he looked when he was ten. He laid on his side, ears and cheek resting against his arm, with eyes that refused to close until the moment I drifted to sleep.

The pitch black in my vision made my eyes heavy. He remembered my habits when I was a child. Those nights I couldn't sleep because I was afraid of the howling wind and the trees looking like creatures staring down at me with long branch hands. It was like reliving our childhood moments.

In no time, a warm, fuzzy feeling danced over me, and before I knew it, I was already lost in a trance, forgetting I'd already fallen asleep.

The next morning, I was up before the men were. The tree bugs buzzed past my ears in multiple directions. Beautiful orange and blue dragonflies the size of my fingers flew through the air; their wings flapping at what looked like a thousand miles per hour. The scent of greenery freshened my senses but it only lasted for a moment before

I heard rustling from where YingShua was sleeping. I scowled while raising my posture slowly to see what was causing the disturbance.

The sight before me sent me into instant panic: the shiny black segmented tail, tipped with a sharp pointy stinger belonged to a scorpion the size of my fist!

My chest pounded and ordinarily I'd be screaming but, to my surprise, I just calmly and cautiously unsheathed my knife. It was a weird feeling to want to kill something that threatened our safety, but this was an opportunity to use what I had learned.

YingShua slowly opened his eyes when he noticed I was kneeling over him, but I ignored his perplexed expression. "Su-Lia?" he questioned in a soft tone that was undermined by the alarm in his eyes.

I watched the scary crab-like creature behind him with keen eyes as it crawled closer and closer to YingShua's ear, raising its tail. He must have understood I wasn't being crazy and was about to save his life from something venomous because he remained still.

Anxiety ate through me; thinking if I missed, YingShua was either going to lose an ear or the scorpion would immediately sting him. I wasn't confident but I breathed to gather my composure. I had only one chance to kill it and I wasn't about to do it with my eyes closed.

YingShua watched me with an approving expression. "I trust you… on three… one… two… three!"

As I took a stab with fully aimed force YingShua simultaneously managed to move fast enough to escape the blade. A big breath broke out from me as soon as I witnessed my achievement. My aim had proven absolute.

I pushed myself back in triumphant breaths—I couldn't believe my eyes that I managed to aim so perfectly, just as YingShua taught me the night before. Relief fell upon me as I watched the scorpion's tail twitch and legs squirm as it slowly died.

YingShua grabbed me by the arm and pulled me away so I was next to him. "You did it. Are you okay?"

Meng and Nujai woke up from their sleep. "What's this noise all about," Meng said, kicking the banana leaf off him and propping his arms on his knees.

Nujai rubbed his eyes and quickly walked over to where we were. "A scorpion? That's huge."

"Who killed it?" Meng asked, and YingShua glanced towards me proudly.

"She almost cut off my ear trying to save me."

We all chuckled and started off our morning by finishing Mainong's prepped dried cow meat, and rice wrapped in banana leaves.

Back in the future, I rarely needed a knife to survive other than to help me cook. In the past—my current present—I felt an urge to train and grow my survival instincts. I enjoyed being pushed to make decisions I'd never made before.

Monkey Senses Monkey Do

CHAPTER 12

The Monkey Trail was an interesting path along the suburbs of Kasi territory–away from Trail 13. Miles before we got there, we heard sounds of anticipation, as if its inhabitants knew there were visitors. The squealing, howling, and grunting became louder as we walked closer.

"Are these monkeys used to travelers?" I turned to ask Meng, since he looked excited to see the animals.

"They aren't used to travelers, but they know it's us," Meng answered, pulling out an old camouflage military hat and waving it over his head to attract attention.

"Meng has a special monkey friend," YingShua said, looking ahead as though knowing exactly what this reunion was.

The air was suddenly quiet and the squealing stopped for a few seconds before a loud high-pitched hoot came like it was from right above us.

Out of the corner of my eye, I noticed a long shadow on the

ground of a head popping up and down, and before we knew it Meng said in excitement, "There you are, Amelia!"

"Amelia?" I asked YingShua when I saw the energetic monkey jump from the tree and land in Meng's arms.

"Amelia is the monkey's name. Five years ago, an American soldier crashed in the middle of the jungle and died, leaving his pet monkey. Meng was first to notice the scene as Nujai, Yue, and I were passing by.

"We all helped each other and managed to pull the pilot from the burning plane. We gave him food and water, even tended his burn wounds, but he was unlucky and didn't survive. The gentleman's injuries were too severe. His body just never recovered.

"Meng lost his parents also at a very young age. They were captured by Viet Cong soldiers and tortured to death. Meng had an uncle whom he traveled with, but he abandoned him and his two younger brothers. They died along the way from starvation. Meng was the only one who survived.

"From there, Meng went through the jungle, helping injured soldiers and travelers during the war. He carried the same purpose, wanting peace for his country, and that was how we first met.

"After we helped Meng bury the American soldier, Amelia crawled into Meng's arms and pointed to its silver neck brace which said, *Amelia, USA*. The monkey kept the soldier's hat and handed it to Meng to show its appreciation. Out of all of us, she picked Meng as her new owner, but Meng couldn't take her with us because he felt it was too dangerous. He believed Amelia belonged with her newfound family, which was here—why we named this part the Monkey Trail." YingShua told the story briefly as we stared at Meng playing tricks with his pet animal.

Even Meng had endured a long, tough journey, but my mood lightened when he swung the monkey over at us playfully.

"Amelia, meet our new friend, Su-Lia Chang," Meng said, bringing Amelia in front of me. The monkey squirmed back into Meng's arms and shook its head like it didn't like me.

"Don't worry Amelia, Su-Lia is mine," YingShua said, smiling.

The men nodded to confirm YingShua's claim. Embarrassed, I remained calm—pretending to not have heard.

YingShua immediately corrected himself, "I mean, Su-Lia is my long-lost childhood friend, just like how you are to Meng."

Meng relaxed his shoulders and threw an arm around YingShua. "My friend, you don't have to put a tag on her, we already know."

YingShua unlocked Meng's grip and changed the subject: "Have you made up your mind to take Amelia with us? You did promise her that the next time you see her you'd bring her."

Meng stared at Amelia. "Yes, for sure this time you're coming with us." The monkey's eyes grew round like it understood they would never part again and kissed Meng on the cheek while hanging its long furry arms around his neck.

Nujai's happy expression disappeared when he heard an army truck in the distance. He put a finger to his lips to quieten everyone. "Let's move away from this area. Someone is coming."

I jerked my head up at YingShua, worried. He nodded and we hastily climbed into the woods to position ourselves away from where we might be seen.

"Shhhh…" Meng whispered to Amelia, and before long we heard the loud truck slowly wheel through and came to a sudden halt. We weren't able to make out exactly who was in it but suddenly heard a gun firing, followed by screaming voices of younger girls and middle-aged women.

"My husband!" a woman cried out, throwing herself over her husband's dead body and begging the soldiers who were speaking in foreign languages.

"That's a stolen American truck. A Dodge M37," YingShua informed the group. "These are not real American soldiers but cons that are a part of Blong-Cheng's corruption pretending to give travelers a lift."

My eyes grew wide at the information and I winced when one of the fake soldiers roared to the women, "Throw all your belongings, money, and anything valuable in this bag. Anyone who refuses, I will shoot."

Three other men who wore dark black uniforms and black army hats had all their guns pointed at the women. Dead on the ground were four men—likely their husbands, sons, or relatives. The soldiers kicked the bodies to the side of the road. Deep red blood streamed from their heads and no women dared to cry too loud or their lives would not be spared.

We watched as each woman got off the truck bed and removed their necklaces, old silver jewelry, and got out their money.

"That too," one of the soldiers said, pointing to their bag of food and extra clothes. He snatched it from them as they cried silently.

The sight produced dark chills that crawled under my skin. I bit my lip so hard I didn't even realize the blood in my mouth until YingShua noticed and cupped my ears between his palms.

He whispered, "Don't look if you can't bear it..." and wiped away the blood from my trembling lips with his thumb. He held his breath as if trying to hear me breathe more steadily.

I nodded and squeezed his hands but didn't close my eyes. Just as I thought I was getting stronger, every gunshot brought back haunting nightmares of the past.

"No!" Nujai gasped and Meng moved swiftly to stop him so he wouldn't accidently get us noticed.

YingShua and I both jerked our heads and saw to our horror that the last girl at gunpoint was Ia.

"How did she end up there?" I queried. Our eyes darted to the helpless girl and saw another, larger, reddish-brown army truck pulled up right in front of the M37.

YingShua's information was indeed accurate. We all watched to see who the driver was and, sure enough, Captain Blong-Cheng got out with a large cigar in his mouth. The fake soldiers were all a part of his disgusting plans.

They were helping him steal from these travelers, killing all the men. No doubt he was paying these fake soldiers a bundle of money to traffic the women and girls.

"Get up there!" one of the black suited men ordered, touching his gun to Ia's back. There were a total of eight women who got on the truck bed, Ia being the last. As she reluctantly climbed up, one of the soldiers lifted her skirt inappropriately, but she clearly dared not speak back.

Captain Blong-Cheng pushed his men to the side and told them, "Don't touch her—she's mine tonight."

Nujai was angered beyond comprehension at this point. The wetness in his eyes told how much he cared for her. Saving Ia was a priority but it needed to be done without putting anyone else in danger.

"We have to save her," I told YingShua in a desperate voice.

He nodded but didn't speak.

Witnessing this was worse than I could have imagined. Burning villages and leading travelers to their deaths was bad enough but human trafficking was the absolute worst.

"Nujai, calm down. We'll find a way to save her—you have my word," Meng said, grabbing Nujai by his shoulders and gripping firmly.

Meng gestured at Amelia, assigning her a task. "You see the reddish truck? Follow it and bring us to their location once they've stopped at their destination."

The monkey stood in front of Meng and saluted like its original owner had taught her. She was rather an impressive animal who almost seemed to understand human instructions.

Amelia waited until Captain Blong-Cheng and his men got back into their vehicles and started up their truck. Meng nodded and Amelia ran down the short hill, finding the right opportunity to jump onto the truck. It clung tightly to the rear bumper.

"Will she be okay, Meng?" I asked.

"She's definitely a smart monkey. She'll be back in no time."

Four hours later Meng sat by the edge of the trail, waiting for Amelia, but he didn't see any sight of her.

"She'll be back… soon," Meng said beneath his breath as he looked up worriedly at me and YingShua.

"We can keep walking forward. I'm sure Amelia knows your scent and will have no problem finding us," YingShua suggested.

Meng shook his head. "You guys go on ahead. I'm going to wait here for Amelia. It's probably just because their hideout is farther than we'd expected."

"No, we'll wait here with you, Meng. We shouldn't separate," I added and YingShua agreed.

We glanced over to the other side of the trail and saw Nujai sitting by himself, staring off in hopeless despair.

YingShua settled his hands on top of Nujai, who looked up. "You have my word… we'll track down where they are and save Ia."

Nujai got up slowly but showing a little more confidence. "It's going to be dangerous, YingShua. I can't let you and Meng risk your lives for me."

"Where has it never been dangerous around here?" YingShua remarked. "If anything, we have to locate their hideout as quickly as we can. It's eight young girls and women. Those men have dirty intentions, and I don't have a good feeling about this."

Meng appeared next to YingShua and added, "Cheer up. We'll save Ia as soon as Amelia returns." He appeared to be putting up a strong front to reassure Nujai.

"All these years we've been together, I've only thought about devoting my life to helping our people escape safely and reunite families along the way. We've encountered near-death situations where I never regretted the experience with you and Meng. I've never thought I'd need you to help me save Ia too. I'm sorry for asking for more than I should," Nujai said, squeezing Meng and YingShua's arms as he looked down to the moist ground beneath. Tears of gratitude started dripping from his eyes.

I couldn't help but puff up my chest with bravery and also put my hand on Nujai's shoulder. "Nujai, Ia is not only precious to you but to me as well. She saved my life once before, during the Mekong ambush, so even I owe her this. We all will help save Ia. I'm willing to face whatever cost it takes."

Nujai looked up and both YingShua and Meng grabbed him in

for a tight hug.

The moment was definitely one we were never likely to forget. They were all close friends who came from different backgrounds and experiences in life but, they were also like three brothers who would risk their lives for one another.

A whole day passed with no sight of Amelia. The evening came and we continued to wait until it was fully dark.

"You're a good monkey. You'll be back," Meng said and snapped a twig that was in his grip.

I stood there in my own thoughts until I saw faintly a small figure approaching from the far end of the dark jungle trail. I peered a little harder and excitement hit my face. "Amelia is back!"

Meng jerked his head to see—it really was his monkey.

"Amelia!" Meng called, thrashing down the hill, almost falling to his knees a few times before he caught Amelia in his arms.

"I just knew you would come back!" Beaming, he held the monkey in front of him with two hands and kept on snuggling it.

We all quickly grabbed our belongings and ran towards Meng.

Then, after a moment, Amelia tapped three times on Meng's shoulders before hooting and squealing some noises. It then pointed back where it had come from. He nodded and turned to us, saying, "Amelia knows where they took Ia."

Amelia wasted no time. It jumped from Meng's arms and started leading the way. We all followed hastily.

Saving Ia

CHAPTER 13

Captain Blong-Cheng's hideout was farther than we thought and ended up being in the middle of nowhere. We traveled all night till morning to get there.

"This is Phahom territory. I'm not surprised he chose this location. With so many mountains surrounding the camp, no one ever knew where they stayed," YingShua observed.

Amelia finally came to a stop and jumped on Meng's shoulders. It softly hooted to let us know we'd arrived at the location.

"Good job," Meng said, running his fingers down Amelia's back. He had Amelia go into his backpack for the time being.

The entrance was heavily guarded by dark suited men, and thick layers of barbed wires fenced the location. It was clear that if a person were to get in, it would be difficult for them to escape. A hint of discouragement weighed on my chest but I shook it off and found my confidence again—it was time to use my brains rather than be frightened by what my eyes saw.

We hid on higher ground so we could monitor activity until nighttime. A big fire was lit between two large brown tents. A few of the men were out feasting on small piglets they had roasted on long sticks.

The time came and YingShua and his two friends sat to discuss their game plan. It was scary and dangerous, but necessary in order to save Ia.

"First, we have to get into the campground before we can proceed. Here, get into these clothes Yue packed. They're a close enough match for us to look like one of them. These hats as well."

YingShua pulled out a stack of dark gray and black camouflage clothes.

"Where did you get those?" I asked.

Nujai answered, "Yue used to be our unit's leader. He instructed to always be prepared to blend in when in danger. We learned to speak Laotian and even a bit of English. That has helped us escape many times."

Mainong's voice came to mind. *I've packed you some men's clothes. Just in case.*

I was confused at first but searched through my bag to find clothes sewn to appear like the soldiers' in the camp. The men were still chatting amongst themselves, so I kept my discovery to myself.

"You stay here," YingShua said, taking a few steps towards me. It was dark but the campground lights offered me his silhouette.

I agreed out loud but not exactly inside. I didn't want to feel useless during such a dangerous mission.

"We have watched for a long time now. Every hour, a line of Blong-Cheng's men will march past. We'll use this opportunity to blend in. I can hear them coming from the west side of the camp, so they should be arriving soon."

Everyone agreed and, as they put on their clothes, YingShua added his instructions: "Meng, once we get through the camp entrance, I want you to first locate their supply tent; arm yourself there. From what I can make out, it should be the one nearest where their trucks are parked—easier for them to load and unload."

YingShua reached into his pocket and gave Meng a box of matches. "They usually have gasoline for their vehicles, so find it and we'll connect the tents so they all burn together."

Then YingShua turned to Nujai, "Ia will be glad to see you first. So, Meng and I will work on distracting the camp and freeing the girls. We'll catch up with you once the soldiers are trying to put out the fires. The west gate is the least wired and it takes a longer time for the lights to beam over it."

"Is it my turn yet?" one of the enemy soldiers asked, bringing our attention back to the camp.

"No, the Captain is not done yet," replied another.

We were unsure of what was going on until we heard a deathly squeal come from one of the tents.

"She's sickly!" Captain Blong-Cheng declared, dragging one of the younger girls by her long hair and tossing her out of the tent. She fell on her palms against the muddy ground, shaking uncontrollably while her eyes rolled up into the sky.

"Kill her or she'll cause us all to be sick."

"Yes, sir!" Both men got up with their rifles and shot the girl on the spot. White foam came bubbling from her mouth.

Captain Blong-Cheng proceeded with his demands, "Check

every single one of them, if they look sick, kill them all. I didn't pay for sick whores to serve me."

"She's a girl who experiences abnormal seizures," YingShua commented while observing. "He drugged her, and she had a reaction to the drugs."

"Why would he drug such a young girl?"

Meng took a breath before answering, "What any dirty bastard would do. Drug them, assault them, torture them, and kill them."

What depravity, I thought, feeling like my intestines were going to come out of my throat. Blong-Cheng was worse than I'd ever imagined.

Nujai surveyed the camp with worried eyes—no doubt hoping to spot Ia but she was nowhere in sight.

"Looks like this captain has gained a whole group of followers throughout the years," YingShua said when he saw ten other men bringing the girls to stand in a straight line so they could check each one.

The captain walked by each frightened female, staring at them intently for any signs of abnormality. "I paid a heavy price for you. Anyone who disappoints me won't be spared."

The third female was an older woman, likely in her fifties. The captain grunted. "Why do you idiots not look for the young flesh? This old hag can't serve me. Lead her out."

The old woman's face lit with hope to survive. Two men pointed their weapons at her and escorted her out the main gate.

"Thank you! Thank you!" The old lady started running off and, just as she seemed far enough to be free, the guards unleashed their large black dogs. The woman made it to the woods but it wasn't long until we heard tormented screams, like her flesh was being torn off her bones.

"She can be the dogs' new toy for the night," Captain Blong-Cheng said, puffing on his cigar before bringing it up to another girl's face. She shut her eyes tight. "You look like a virgin."

"You're disgusting," a voice called from the end of the line. The captain moved away from the virgin girl and noticed Ia.

Nujai's eyes grew wide upon realization that it was Ia who had spoken out. She shouldn't have bothered for the sake of her life—presumably not knowing how threatening the situation was.

"I need to go now," Nujai growled, grabbing his M16 rifle.

Meng stopped him. "We agreed to stick to our plan, so don't be impulsive. Ia isn't an easy girl to deal with and you should already know that."

Nujai returned his gaze back to Ia to see what would happen next. He was getting impatient.

"What did you say, young lady?" I heard the captain ask, as he walked over to the end of the line where Ia stepped out from behind the girls. She stared at him with hatred in her eyes.

"I said, you're disgusting," Ia repeated without any sign of fear.

"Disgusting?" The captain let out a laugh and instantly grabbed Ia by the neck, wringing it. "I'll show you what disgusting is." She gripped his wrists and clawed her nails into his skin, forcing him to release her with a wince of pain.

Four soldiers at once pointed their guns at Ia but the captain shouted, "Stop! No one touches her." Blong-Cheng snatched Ia by the shirt and tore part of her blouse off. He grabbed her again and she bit him, provoking him to slap her with the back of his hand, knocking her to the ground.

"Fool. You should've stayed quiet," Nujai said, baring his teeth. But the hatred Ia showed Captain Blong-Cheng was no surprise given she had lost her family. "Let's go—now!" he ordered.

After the men were suited, YingShua made one last glance towards me. He looked confident but with a hint of worry. "If we don't make it out in an hour, I want you to take Amelia with you. The monkey knows the way back home."

Amelia's head popped out of Meng's backpack. She saluted.

"Wait…" I caught YingShua by the hand and squeezed it. "You'll come back. *I'll* make sure of that."

YingShua narrowed his eyes for a split-second. "Stay here…" he said before turning away.

The men quickly crawled down the hill as they waited for a group of Captain Blong-Cheng's men to march by. As soon as the soldiers passed, they tailed along to blend in.

I sat hidden, keeping my eyes on the men and watched them successfully make it into the camp. My heart throbbed for their safety, and I hoped everything would work out as planned.

Ia… I know you're doing this to save those around you. Be strong just a little longer, I prayed silently.

Then my eyes popped open to the sudden shout of Blong-Cheng's men.

"Sir, our tents caught fire!"

Knowing YingShua and the guys were responsible made me feel a little more at ease. I let out a long sigh.

"What? Who would set my tent on fire? You all go put it out!"

the captain shouted before grabbing Ia from the ground by her hair. "I'm going to handle this whore first."

Many of Blong-Cheng's men went to put out the flames as the initial fire had spread to the smaller tents around it.

The whole camp was in an uproar of panic, providing the perfect moment for me to do my part.

I slid down the hill and stopped to observe the entrance. By now, the six men tasked with guarding it had gone to put out the flames.

I carefully snuck under the barrier and bypassed soldiers without suspicion since I was disguised in a dark suit and a black cap.

My entering the camp was not part of the plan, but I couldn't let YingShua and the others down.

With Ia so obviously wanting to save the girls, I made them my first priority. As the commotion continued, I found they had been left to sit against one another on the ground. I stopped quickly before the guards came back or anyone else noticed.

"Look now, I'm here to save you. See that entrance," I said, pointing. "As soon as I cut these ropes, I want you all to run as fast as you can past those gates."

All the girls nodded quickly and took off at once, as instructed. I watched them while remaining wary of the danger around me. Just as I turned around, a pair of hands grabbed me by the waist and flung me into one of the tents.

I fought hard, kicking and biting until I heard the person call out in pain. It was too dark to see his face but I knew the voice.

"YingShua?" I grabbed him by the arm, regretting that I had bitten him so hard.

"Yes, it's me." He snatched one of my wrists. "Are you crazy coming in here?"

"I wanted to speed up your plans," I hissed back innocently.

YingShua sucked in some air. He wasn't exactly upset with me, but the vibe felt like I was adding to his worries.

"I saw you the moment you snuck through the entrance," YingShua said, exhaling and rolling his eyes good-naturedly.

"What about Meng and Nujai?" I asked quickly.

"They both went to find Ia. I was supposed to have gone with them but when I saw you I had to grab you before anyone noticed the missing girls."

"Let's go catch up with—" YingShua instantly pulled me back against the tent walls and covered my mouth before I could finish.

He dropped his hands to grasp my hips, leaning closer to me than he would normally. He was keenly watching a dark shadow. The silhouette tread slowly like he knew we were inside—about to make his strike.

YingShua was very calm despite his deep, short breaths I could hear faintly in the pitch-black space.

Instantly, a machete the size of an arm pierced through the thin leather wall; the enemy attempted to strike us a few times but missed. YingShua jerked me to the side and immediately seized the man's wrist with a twist and threw a hard kick against his stomach, pressing against the wall. The entire tent flipped over the enemy and, right away, we noticed guns and weapons in clearer view. YingShua snatched a rifle as I grabbed a bow and arrows, and we took off at once to escape.

Nujai and Meng had made it to Ia before YingShua and I did.

"Stupid girl!" Captain Blong-Cheng shouted, kicking Ia in the stomach when she couldn't get up.

Nujai ran straight to the scene with his rifle cocked and loaded, "You bastard! Get off of her!" The first gunshot was fired at the captain's legs, and he fell over with a painful cry.

Meng jump-kicked the captain's wound, adding to his pain. "Sick bastard old man…" He pointed his rifle at Blong-Cheng's face, making sure he didn't have any dirty tricks up his sleeves.

"So, you scumbags came to burn my camp." The captain spat at Meng's feet; his eyes full of hate.

"Shut your trap!" Meng stamped at his shoulders, collapsing Blong-Cheng onto his back.

Nujai dashed through the dirt and onto his knees. He grabbed Ia by the arm, checking her as quickly as he could to make sure she was okay.

"Nujai?!" she called weakly, still in the process of recovering from the hard blow to her stomach. She was finding difficulty breathing but seemed to be fighting back the pain. "I thought… I would never get to see you again," she continued softly through bloody lips. She raised a shaky hand to Nujai's face as tears welled up in her eyes.

"It's me. We're going to get you out of here, right now," Nujai told her. His eyes darted to Ia's torn blouse, now hanging off her arm. He quickly took off his jacket and wrapped it tightly around her before helping her up to tentatively stand.

"Take Ia and go—right now!" Meng commanded in a firm shout, just as two of Blong-Cheng's men were closing the distance to him.

Nujai clenched his teeth, as though reluctant to leave Meng in a bad position; one where he was going to be outnumbered. However, noticing YingShua and me from a distance must have reassured him because, with a nod of acknowledgement, he took off with Ia.

Two men surrounded Meng and shouted, "Put your gun down or we will shoot."

Dropping his rifle, Meng put his hands behind his head in surrender. One of the soldiers came behind Meng and struck his legs. Meng's knees hit the ground with a thud. The other, taller and more heavily built soldier, with a bandana on his head, walked in front of Meng and curled a corner of his lips in mockery. Without a word, he snarled and spat at Meng, raising his rifle to Meng's head.

YingShua was visibly fuming and instantly aimed his own gun at the soldier.

Captain Blong-Cheng limped over to Meng. "You're not so tough now, are you?" he said, smashing his fist into Meng's jaw, sending blood and spit spraying from his mouth.

Meng's head was swaying back and forth in a daze, trying to grasp his senses. His eyes remained glassy for a few seconds until coming into focus. He wiped the blood from his lips with the back of his hand and managed to say, "You're just a damn, bloodsucking leech of your own people."

"Kill this motherless bastard!" the captain shouted, but just when the stocky soldier was about to pull the trigger, YingShua shot him through his temple, sending the man to his instant death.

Alarmed, the other soldier jerked his head in our direction and drew his weapon near his face to aim.

YingShua pointed the barrel at him and, suddenly, I heard a loud click like the stolen rifle had malfunctioned. Panicking now, YingShua pulled the trigger again, and again, but to no avail.

"Su-Lia!" Just as he was about to grab me to take cover, an arrow whistled right past him at lightning speed. YingShua's head snapped towards the now-executed gunman. His body fell with a loud thump and both YingShua and Meng turned to regard me with stunned eyes. Their shock was quickly followed by astonished relief.

Without a word, I took YingShua by the arm and we both sprinted to Meng.

"We need to leave, now," YingShua warned Meng, a moment before the captain unsheathed a sharp, shiny bowie knife.

YingShua shoved Meng to the side and caught the captain's arm before it could make contact with Meng.

Having been forced to drop the blade, Captain Blong-Cheng threw an unidentifiable white substance into YingShua's eyes.

"YingShua!" I cried, lunging over to slash the bow across the captain's face.

He spun around and came at me, catching me by the shoulders. "Come here!"

"Get your filthy hands off me!" I kicked him once before stabbing him with my dagger.

The captain grunted in pain and, as soon as his grip on me loosened, I turned around and aimed the razor-sharp blade directly at his eyes. He moved fast enough to avoid me blinding him but the blade still managed to slice his cheek open. A scar for life.

"My face!" the captain wailed, raising his hands to the vicious wound, blood streaming down the gaps between his fingers. He fell against one of the tents and rolled onto his back.

YingShua grabbed me by the arm and tugged me aside when another soldier rounded the tent and took a shot at us. YingShua swiftly tossed his small metal knife and it pierced the soldier right in the forehead.

After securing my dagger away, I grabbed YingShua to observe his eyes, worriedly. "What is this?" Feeling the ends of his eyes, I told him, "Hang in there. Just follow my lead." My heart hurt seeing him struggle. I've always been used to him leading me and everyone else.

I tossed YingShua's arm across my neck and shoulders while we maneuvered through the campground.

A short while later, we finally reached an area where lights surveyed the western part of the camp every four minutes.

"Nujai left us this thick cloth sheet on the ground so we could climb over the fence without getting snagged," Meng said, having initially stepped on it by accident.

YingShua nodded, blinking hard to sense his surroundings. The lights had only just finished their sweep of the area. "We'd better go now."

Meng carefully tossed the sturdy cloth over the steel thorned fence and was the first to climb.

YingShua grabbed me beneath my arms, helping me up while continuing to try and clear his vision. Then he took a big leap and climbed quickly over the seven-feet fence safely before the captain's black Thai dogs caught up to us.

The Crossbow

CHAPTER 14

"They made it!" Nujai said in slight excitement to Ia as we approached. Ia's face broke out in a broad smile. They had waited about two miles west of the camp. While it was still dark, morning was approaching.

Cold chills awakened my goosebumps. The sudden wisps of wind were causing me to shiver but I kept on moving with YingShua's arms still around my shoulders.

"Su-Lia!" Ia limped over and I reached out to steady her.

"Ia, how did this happen to you?" I looked at her condition with an expression of concern. "Are Yue and Mainong alright?"

"I'm worried about them and can't say. Mainong was having contractions before I left the house. Yue asked me to grab herbs for chicken and, on my way back from the nearest village, someone hit me on the nape of my neck and I passed out. I woke up in the back of a strange truck. How did you know they had taken me? It was the day after you left that I was kidnapped." Ia coughed and Nujai gave her a small jug of water.

"Don't talk anymore. You can tell us when we get home," he said with a gentle look, brushing the particles of dirt off her eyelashes.

With the sound of dogs barking some way behind them, YingShua grabbed his two good friends by the shoulders. "We need to split up. Let's meet again by the Monkey Trail. If you don't see us by the end of day tomorrow, keep going till you are safely back home. We've burnt all of their goods in the largest tent so, by now, Blong-Cheng will be coming after us for sure. They have smart Thai Ridgebacks and, if we stay here, it won't be long till they catch up to us."

Nujai nodded and turned his backpack to the front, pulling out his dagger and a handful of lemons. "I found a small lemon tree nearby and made sure to pick some, here…" He quickly cut the fruit into pieces and handed them to us. "Wet your clothes with the juice and rub the peel on your clothes and skin. This will help prevent the dogs from detecting your scent."

We all quickly took off our black and gray camouflage outer clothes, keeping on our layers beneath; I had on black high-waisted denim shorts and a white button blouse. I left on the black cap since it kept my hair together.

Meng squeezed YingShua by the arm. "What about your eyes? You shouldn't have done that. I really owe you my life."

"I'm okay. It's not going to do anything to me," YingShua said, signaling an end to the discussion and allowing us to hastily part ways.

A mile after splitting up from the unit members, my mind was uneasy and worried.

YingShua could pretend he was fine as much as he liked but he didn't fool me. His eyes were deep pink and the skin around it was growing rashes.

"You're not okay," I said, stopping him in his tracks. He looked away to hide his face, but I locked his jaw between my palms. My thumbs traced the outline of his eyes. "We need to find the closest pure water source and get it washed out of your eyes. My mother has always used natural treatments on me when I was younger—like honey."

"*Honey?*" YingShua questioned in a soft tone, blinking hard.

A warm blush surfaced on my cheeks upon hearing the word. Of course, the world has changed so much in 100 years. *Honey* would be a sweet word to call the ones you love in my time. He wouldn't understand.

"Are you not feeling well, Su-Lia?"

Fearing he'd noticed, I bit my inner lip.

"Everything will be better when you leave this place. I'm sorry for troubling you."

He'd misunderstood but in some ways I was glad he hadn't seen my embarrassment.

The past was not my home. But it had become like a home to me. I had made wonderful new friends and got to be with YingShua. The man who I dreamt about in the future had become the man now in front of me. He gazed with eyes that told me the contrary of his words. He wasn't ready to let go, and he didn't want to know when our parting might be.

Thinking I could never be with him was tearing me to pieces. Home was so far away… yet it was also right here in front of me.

A frown weighed heavily on my pale face, and I dropped my eyes to the ground.

YingShua continued observing me and remained in silence for a moment longer. "Is it because you miss your mother?"

I do. *But I'd miss him too.*

Shrugging off the complex feelings, I managed a smile. "Yes. I miss my mother. I have wondered how she's doing and if she's worried about me by now."

"She is worried. I know. My mother was always worried for me when she was alive. But don't *you* worry. I will find a way for you to return. You have my word," YingShua vowed. However, I knew the look in his eyes—it was the same shattering pain that hurt every time there was hope.

"Anyways," I said, quickly resuming the topic at hand, "honey is good for inflammation. If only my device bangle worked in this time, I would be able to utilize it for many purposes—like locating resources and accessing immediate information about things I want to know. No network exists during this time that is compatible with my holographic watch." I looked up and all around us was just jungle.

YingShua grinned and pulled his face away. "There's no use for that bracelet, watch—whatever you call it—here. The burning will wear off. I can see enough for now," he assured me and started walking ahead.

"But…"

"Honey is a rare find but there's a river two hours walk from here. We'll stop." He turned back and smiled gracefully. "If you're concerned that much, you can personally treat me."

That made me happier but it was soon replaced by a sense of guilt. Our strange fate felt like a load of bad luck but with YingShua I had no regrets.

It was now a total of three days since I'd returned to 1978.

The Vietnam War was behind us but that didn't mean there was no betrayal or corruption within the Pathet Lao and North Vietnam followers. It meant the Hmong were still chased to their deaths and captured. If our history books could be told of the great things YingShua and his unit had done for the Hmong, how wonderfully they would be remembered in 2078. Where hope had been lost, the peace fighters made a new life possible for thousands.

"Su-Lia?" YingShua picked a ripe mango from a spotted mango tree and used his pocket knife to cut it open. The juice poured out of it like shiny sweet tea. "Eat this…"

In such deep thoughts, I hadn't noticed my belly growling. "Thank you."

A while later, YingShua picked up a long piece of bark from the ground, as though suddenly hit by inspiration.

Looking around, he found a large grayish rock with a flat surface, sat down, and pulled out his medium knife. He chopped the bark to size—which turned out to look like a semi-flat airplane with a pointy beak.

"What do you plan to do with that?" I bent down, wrapping my arms around my knees to observe.

"Making a crossbow," he answered and chopped a long piece of bamboo almost the same size as the wooden piece, flattened it, and then started a small fire.

YingShua sat as he dangled the thin fiber over the flames. "This is to soften the limb. It helps with flexibility," he said, in response to the look of intrigue on my face.

"You're quite good at archery. What do you hunt for in your future?"

Perplexed, I replied, "I don't practice archery for hunting."

YingShua stopped and looked up at me like he was interested.

"Archery has always been my childhood hobby. It's what I do to relieve stress."

"You should do more with your skills," he suggested. "I'll teach you how to hunt with this crossbow." He took the parts away from the fire and held them up to his eyes, making sure his measurements were correct.

"Hunt?" My eyes widened. "So, you're building me a crossbow?" I almost thought he was joking.

YingShua answered with a grin, "If you're hungry, you should also learn how to hunt and/or defend yourself."

I crossed my arms, tempted to refuse. In my mind, these were jobs for men, but I suddenly had a change of mood. "Fine. I'll try it."

It didn't take him long to finish making the crossbow, since he already seemed to be proficient at assembling them from wood, bamboo, and inner tree bark fibers; it was quite interesting to see YingShua weave and twist the crossbow string and secure it to each end of the bamboo limb.

He grabbed a few other shorter parts of bamboo and created thin, sharp, bolts for the weapon.

I was impressed by the finished crossbow, and walked around with my arms crossed admiring it. "I remember my grandparents talking about these, but I've never seen one in person. Especially one being made."

YingShua turned around to test-shoot it, aiming at a squirrel dashing up a tree. No sooner had the bolt been shot then the animal fell down, hitting the ground with a thud.

I ran to it to check where the bolt had pierced the squirrel's flesh.

YingShua slid the crossbow in front of me. "Now you try…"

After a quick study, I guessed it worked just like a bow, except on a smaller scale and with me having to pull the trigger to release the bolt. It seemed easy enough.

YingShua stepped aside and watched. The first three bolts, I failed miserably, and the next few shots were just as horrible. My aim wasn't reaching far enough.

"This is harder than normal archery," I said, letting out a sigh.

YingShua walked up to my side. "It's quite different. A usual size bow and arrow, you don't have to worry about setting the trigger prior to positioning the bolt, because you can aim and control the amount of force when drawing. The crossbow is a bit heavier, with multiple functions to understand."

"So, what defines the speed?" I wondered aloud.

"The similarity is still having a clear vision of your target before you aim, but the difference is the *distance* to ensure your bolt will penetrate with its full potential."

He could have just told me I was standing too far from the target, but I still enjoyed seeing his side profile from the corner of my eyes:

He looked sharp and observative to a fault, where he was always first to notice details no one else did. His thick dark eyebrows gave him a serious, intimidating look but provided a deep charm that fascinated me about his features.

YingShua had me walk a few steps in front of him. Before I could register, he gently aligned his long arms over mine and held the crossbow beneath my fingers.

"The distance…" I turned slightly to speak and noticed our cheeks were against each other's. Our lips were almost touching.

YingShua shifted his eyes and noticed too but he remained focused and spoke calmly, "This will feel forceful but stay close," he warned. An instant later, he shot the bolt.

My heart dropped upon realizing YingShua had just injured a man behind a tall bush. With a stern face, he grabbed me by the arm and tugged me back behind him.

We saw three more men in black army-like suits and guns approaching from a distance.

"They caught up faster than I thought," YingShua growled, and we took off at once, knowing them to be the captain's men.

Running through the thicker jungle was scary. The vines grew bigger and more intertwined, slowing us down. YingShua had to use his knife to chop the heavier vegetation so we could get through.

Snakes slithered up and across the nearby trees, blending themselves with the foliage. The reptiles continued to give me cold chills each time one was spotted.

I squeezed my eyes shut, turned towards YingShua, and gripped his backpack tightly. He turned to glance at me just as we were approaching a crossing over a rushing stream.

He stopped to inspect the vine bridge by shaking it and pushing it in different directions, making sure it was safe before he turned to me.

"You walk ahead of me…" he said with approving eyes.

Trusting him with my life, I gave him my hand as he pulled me carefully in front of him.

The bridge was only two-feet wide. Thick brown and green vines had been weaved like bird nests along each side. I held on tightly and made nervous steps, hoping the long bridge to the other side would hold until we made it.

YingShua paid close attention to my every movement while he glanced multiple times at the water below.

Surprisingly, I did well until taking my first step on the ground at the very end; my sneakers were full of mud, and I slipped, tripping over a protruding tree root.

"Careful!" YingShua warned, catching me by the elbow and pulling me back against him. He glanced down and saw the state of my footwear.

"Those *future* shoes won't stand this moist soil for another mile until we get to dryer land." He turned his backpack round, handed me the crossbow, and crouched down in front of me.

I stared at my sneakers and then at his broad back waiting for me. "I can't, you're already carrying too much. I'll walk." As I attempted to get past him, his firm hand caught my calves.

"Get on…" he demanded, waiting patiently.

A moment later, I hesitantly climbed on his back. He lifted me up effortlessly and started walking as his boots sank slightly each time he took a step. However, they were sturdy enough to not get swallowed by the moist soil, and grippy enough to not slip on the shiny flat plates of rock.

"You know… these are best edition sneakers. They are called Star Light Kickers," I began while admiring my stained shoes hanging off his arms.

"They're useful in your future?" YingShua presumed with a slight turn.

"Indeed. These high-top sneakers are anti-gravitational shoes with a built-in device that, when activated, the mechanism inside produces sequential air compression. It makes you feel like your weight has decreased by twenty-five percent. With that alone, I'd be gliding through these mountains," I told him proudly.

"How do you activate it?"

"The function is turned on by voice command, but it's currently out of power." A frown came over me as I pulled my chin over his shoulders. "I'm sorry for the burden. I'm only adding more weight rather than helping out."

YingShua smiled. "Since those shoes are useless here, I'm okay with carrying you. Twenty-five percent less of your weight, you'd be blown away by the wind. The last thing I need is you flying off."

A small chuckle escaped my lips. He actually had some humor in him. "Should we go down for some water?" I asked.

YingShua agreed and climbed carefully down large rocks to the rushing stream.

I hopped off his back. "This place is so peaceful."

The rapid sound of water enveloped my ears. We were surrounded with lush greenery, countless layers of trees, and heard the insects churring nearby. Leaves swayed in soft motions as I opened my palm to receive one, closing my eyes and opening them again.

"This water tastes so fresh," I said, scooping another handful of crystal-clear water into my mouth before pulling YingShua down. He squatted with arms propped over his knees and his expression turned to one of surprise when I cupped a handful for him. "Taste it."

Shy and hesitant, he held his breath for a moment before leaning forward to have a sip.

"The swelling's gone down," I said, with a smile spreading across my face as he finished.

Without much thought, I stood up and tore the bottom part of my blouse, exposing half of my belly. It didn't bother me.

YingShua observed in uttered silence. He would normally look away, but this time he didn't, as if he was unable to take his eyes off of me.

"Relax. You said you'd let me treat you." I pulled off his backpack, he set his crossbow aside, and sat with his legs crossed.

Patiently, he waited.

I soaked the white fabric with water, squeezed it, and reached back to carefully brush it over his eyes. Repeating a couple of times, his hands crawled up my arms and grabbed my wrists. The fabric slid down, revealing his lustful eyes.

Nervous, my fingers curled into a slight fist when the only thing going through my mind was his waiting lips. The burning desire drew us closer. The roaring of the current began to tune out; all my senses were stolen by his seductiveness.

Before I could remember, he pulled me firmly to him, gripping my hips and thighs, making sure he settled me right where he wanted—in his lap with legs secured around him. YingShua removed my cap, causing a spill of unwinding black hair to flow airily. A breath broke out of me when he moved me closer to him, forcing a deep pink blush to appear on my cheeks.

He began with softly touching my stomach as his curious thumbs traced the outlines of my ribs. I inhaled deeply when his mouth found my neck; he kissed it gently once—and again. I fought to resist secretly but couldn't and shut my eyes in defeat when YingShua moved strands of my hair away and ardently made his way to the side of my jaw and up behind my ears. Pausing, he murmured tenderly in short, hot breaths, "Su-Lia… I can't stop these feelings anymore."

"Neither can I…" I exhaled—lost in a trance I didn't want to wake up from.

His curious fingers brushed my collarbone, finding the opening of my blouse. He pulled the fabric down my arm and pressed his lips against the curve of my shoulders, leaving a thrill of sensation tingling inside of me. I hugged his face against me, not wanting this moment to stop.

Then suddenly, a pain rushed through my heart like needle pricks; the thought of not being with him was unbearable. "How do I forgive myself… if I leave you?" I whispered to him.

YingShua came to a reluctant stop. Decisively, he slid his hands away, and out from beneath my blouse.

"I'm… losing it, Su-Lia." He turned his ears to rest over my heart.

I drew in a wisp of fresh air and blinked the wetness away from my eyes. "I'm not afraid to be with you. What I'm afraid of is hurting you." I held his cheeks between my palms, drawing back to stare at his handsome face.

YingShua blinked downward in disappointment. The muscles along his jaws tightened when he clenched his teeth, acknowledging the truth. His desires weren't only of lust but a suffering of wanting something that may end up disappearing from his life.

The mood became still. I stood up from his embrace and opened my hands to him. "But that doesn't mean we can't take each day at a time together."

YingShua slowly lifted his head to meet my eyes, feeling more enlightened. He took my hands and rose up, towering over my small frame. "You'll always be mine, even if we have to part."

"Who else would want me," I managed to still tease.

"All the men in your future, if they know what an incredible woman you are," he said, pulling forward, cupping my face, and warmly touching his forehead to mine.

The Tiger's Feast

CHAPTER 15

We managed to get far enough away and finally reached a clear brownish-red road. Moments later, YingShua spotted a man and his two horses pulling a long wagon of hay. He stopped the Laotian farmer and begged him in a foreign language for a lift, with his palms together politely. Thankfully the man was kind enough to agree, appearing to appreciate the urgency.

"What did you say to him?" I asked when YingShua lifted me up to sit at the edge of the wagon. He then hopped on next to me.

"I told him we needed help getting to Tha Ngon to assist a lost family," he replied, tightening his grip on his backpack full of necessities meant for the Moua family.

I smiled at his response. As dangerous as the situation was, he never forgot about those in need. It was better to be delayed than never showing up.

The bumpy ride to Tha Ngon lasted nearly eight hours. For only a short while, we felt safe to continue searching for the Mouas.

"Good luck to you both," the kind farmer said, waving to YingShua and me. We were dropped off by a small village we'd have to walk through, going east.

We decided to see if some of the villagers had any information and a few said the Mouas had come by to ask for some food, but were refused because even the village only had enough for their own families and couldn't spare any. They told us that they too had headed east.

I turned to notice the half-naked kids playing in the streets, and stray cats walking along the village homes. The children's hands and faces were stained with dirt like they hadn't bathed for days. Their thin skin stuck to their ribs, and each time they inhaled, I could see their bones surface.

"Do you have a spare towel I could have?" YingShua asked a random middle-aged woman sitting in front of her bamboo home. She wore an old tan T-shirt and was trying to finish her paj ntaub, rose cloth.

"If you want food, we don't have any, but we can spare towels if you need," she said, going inside before handing one to YingShua.

"Thank you. We are grateful," YingShua told the woman and took her by surprise by handing her a small bag of dry cow meat, along with a couple mangoes we had picked along the way.

The woman stood in awe, grabbed YingShua's hand, and said, "You don't have to. I couldn't give you food and only an old towel…" She began to sob. "Yet you still can spare some for us. We can't accept this."

"No, accept it. They look like they have not eaten for days," YingShua said, pointing to the small children—about three to six years of age—that started gathering around us.

YingShua sliced the juicy mangoes and handed pieces to each

child. They ate hastily.

"We have water if you need. It is beyond the back of the house. Please help yourselves. You seem to have come a long way," the woman urged, sending us on our way.

Further down, we found the small well and YingShua pulled out a bucket of water. He dipped the towel inside and then squeezed it.

"Here, there's dirt on your face," YingShua said, handing it to me. I wiped my face once but missed a couple of spots to the side of my lips.

Hesitantly, he smiled and pointed. Then it was just easier for him to take the rag and do it himself.

The late afternoon sun was blazing high in the sky. This time, it was my turn to raise my hands to shield his face.

While he reached to brush the towel against my lips, his eyebrows softened; followed by an intense gaze that sunk into my soul. I blinked through long lashes, losing each of my senses. Before I could remember, my palms fell on his shoulders. All my weight dropped to my toes as I lifted myself up and pecked him on the cheek.

He had gone to great lengths to save my life. The blood, sweat, and stress he went through for me—how could I not fall in love with a man who waited patiently for me time and again?

YingShua blinked with stunned eyes and stood frozen for a while. "Su-Lia…." he said eventually, turning away. His hand came down to rest by his side. "If only you knew how much I'm hurting right now."

"I don't understand…" My heart started pounding with a feeling of rejection.

"Because I am poor and live a life of danger. I only know how to protect you... but promising you a future almost seems impossible. Even so..." he said, turning to face me again with heavy eyes, and bringing his hands up to caress my face, "...the more time I spend with you the more I can't imagine seeing my future without you. So, it hurts to live each day not knowing when I open my eyes if you'll still be next to me—smiling the way you do."

I held YingShua's hands and replied, "Past or future, I'll always smile because of you."

The pain in his eyes was replaced with warmth. He pulled me into his arms and rested his chin above my head. "It hurts to keep you and it hurts to lose you. I can't decide which way to keep you safe anymore."

Deep in his embrace, I clenched my teeth while fearing at any given moment I could wake up in 2078. We had no choice but to accept what is today and what tomorrow might become.

Further east we took a steeper mountain trail. There, we entered another forest but one not as crowded and thick as before.

YingShua glanced around to determine which of the three different trails ahead we should pick. "It's likely people came this way," he said, pointing to a broken branch. He shook his head with a worried expression. "They could be in danger."

"Let's hurry then," I said, similarly concerned.

We were aware that the location was a bit more guarded but not sure how dangerous it would be. The harsh broken branches and fresh chips of tree bark looked like they were leading down the path to the left, so we hastily made our decision to go in that direction.

Not long after, we heard a child's voice talking from above. "Up there," YingShua said, pointing to higher ground. It looked like we would have to climb up a much rockier trail in order to get there.

When we arrived, the child ran to us. "Please, my dad is unconscious."

YingShua slipped off his backpack and we both propped the man gently against a nearby tree trunk. He slowly opened his eyes like he remembered what had happened. His senses appeared to be coming back. "Please, take this boy with you. He is only five but he's a good child," he managed before coughing and causing blood to splatter onto his shirt.

"Father, please don't leave me alone," the boy kept on pleading, but his father could no longer hear him.

"The men in black clothes took my whole family away from me." The boy sobbed through deep sniffles before continuing, "Everywhere we went was dangerous."

YingShua delicately shut the father's eyes and made a trembling fist over his knees. "If only we had come sooner, sir."

"Dad, please rest peacefully," the boy said, caressing his father's hands one last time. The boy laid his ears against his father's chest and then looked up with lost eyes, like he knew this was really the last time.

I pulled the boy into my arms to let him cry while holding my breath. I stared up through the canopy of trees and prayed silently. *Please, let us make it out safely…*

Minutes later, we looked around, knowing there were more members of the Moua family to be found. Twenty feet away we noticed the oldest son and the wife laying lifeless in knee-high weeds.

YingShua's face filled with anger. The wounds on the bodies were of deep cuts by deadly blades, along with several gunshots to the mother's chest and legs.

"Don't look," I said, covering the boy's face. I then asked him to turn around while we both helped bring the bodies quickly to where the father lay, and bade them farewell. We didn't have any incense but prayed to the spirits of the land to watch over us as we continued our journey.

YingShua lifted the child onto his back and gently patted the boy's head. "From here on… you'll travel with us. Your father, mother, and big brother will be with you in spirit, so don't be afraid."

I followed behind the boys and made one glance back at the bodies. Through this journey, I'd shed so many heart-wrenching tears I felt numb by this moment and couldn't even cry anymore. Had we found the Moua family earlier, maybe they would have all survived, but there was nothing more we could do to change what had already happened.

"What's your name?" YingShua asked the boy after a long while of maneuvering through the forest.

The child sniffed and answered in a raspy voice, "My parents named me TuPao."

"TuPao?" YingShua smiled. "Believe it or not, my father's name is Pao too. It's a good name your parents gave you."

"How did you and your parents end up in this area?" I asked out of curiosity.

"My uncles left us. We lost our way and ended up trapped in the area. Everywhere we went, we saw Pathet Lao soldiers. We couldn't go back to our home because we came too far, and we didn't have anywhere else to go. Mother and Father only said we'd wait to see if anyone comes by to tell us where to go," the boy explained between hungry breaths.

After an hour's walk, YingShua said it was safe enough to stop. He let the child down and sat him on a log before reaching to me for his backpack. "Eat this and fuel your belly. You'll need to be strong to travel with us." He handed TuPao two oranges we had picked along the way. "This is all I have left but we'll find more food as we go."

YingShua handed me the crossbow. "Use this if you need to."

Traveling this way with YingShua, my gut feeling was that he knew something was coming. He always remained cautious and made sure he calculated our escape route if anything should happen.

I knew without him saying a word; he wanted to make sure he didn't scare the boy so soon after losing his parents. YingShua turned slightly around, looking back at me as I quickly caught up next to them. "Stay close."

Within seconds, we heard whistles from afar and we were running before we could think. YingShua quickly pulled TuPao into his arms and held the boy tight. "Close your eyes and cover your ears," he whispered, and the boy did just as he was told.

The faint sound of an animal seeped into the forest. My heart sped.

"I'm sorry, but we had to go this route. We're heading to an area where we could run into wild animals, but this could be our only escape," YingShua said with a glint of worry in his eyes, but I had to trust his judgment at a time like this.

The danger YingShua hinted at struck fear in me because animals, especially tigers, were the last thing I wanted to hear after the cliff incident. I gripped onto the crossbow tightly.

"There you are!" The shout was followed by a loud gunshot into the sky, startling us. From behind us four of Captain Blong-Cheng's soldiers were heading in our direction. They started pulling out their guns, and when we looked up to the front, the captain walked out from behind one of the trees.

"Su-Lia, hold TuPao. I won't let anything happen to you both." TuPao was still covering his ears and his eyes were closed.

YingShua glanced to the side and that was when I realized he already knew that the only way to escape was to jump off the pathway.

The trail was narrow and led through what was more wood than jungle. Sharp thorns scattered the road and broken branches threatened to be just as piercing if anyone were to roll down the steep hill. We'd be lucky if we made it down without injury. A bead of sweat cascaded along my jaw and dripped from my chin. It was only a matter of time.

"Let us go," YingShua demanded, shielding us. He pointed his black tactical boots to the left, confirming my thoughts. I paid extremely close attention to his silent gestures and realized he was trying to buy time to give me his instructions.

"Why should I? I've seen you at the Mekong River once before. You should've died with the rest, but you lived long enough to come burn my camp. Years' worth of goods burned to ashes all because of you and your scumbag friends. And you," the captain said, turning to look at me, "you're Su-Lia. The girl who ruined my face—just who I've been looking for."

"Let me go!" I shouted, trying to rip my arms away from soldiers who had just grabbed hold of me.

TuPao's eyes popped open, realizing what was going on. "Su-Lia! YingShua!"

I held TuPao tightly in my arms. "Don't touch him!" I snapped at them.

The captain tilted his head slightly and walked past YingShua, over to me. The soldiers pressed my shoulders down with their guns. My knees hurt against the rocky, copper soil.

YingShua turned around and I shook my head slowly at him to not come forward in case he got himself killed.

"You're quite a fine looking virgin." The vile words made me sick to my stomach. The captain took my chin into his grip and came close to speak to my face.

"You see this scar," he said, bringing his cheek so near that I couldn't see anything but it. "You're going to pay for this with your body."

The captain reached for my face, and I looked away, stretching my neck as far as I could from his perverted hands. My eyes shut when his palms dropped to my shoulders. I bared my teeth, shaking in anger. Hugging TuPao tighter, I maintained a brave front despite the fear lurking inside my heart.

Slowly, the captain slid his dirty fingers along my collarbone and up to my neck. He brought his nose close and inhaled a big breath of my hair, grinning. "You smell nice too."

"Don't. Touch her," YingShua growled loudly, his eyes poised in anger. It was clear that, just like me, the ill intentions of a man so corrupted he would work to betray his people—killing, stealing, trafficking, and taking innocent girls for pleasure—heated him to the core.

I opened my eyes to YingShua's voice. The fist at his side trembled. Veins surfaced from his tightly built arms.

Before we could all react, TuPao immediately grabbed the man by the leg and bit him hard.

"Oh, you stupid brat!" The captain leaped up angrily and kicked the child so hard the breath was knocked out of him.

"TuPao!" I cried out and crawled quickly to pull him into my arms again. "Why did you do that?" I sobbed and cleared his hair out of his face.

"I'm. Okay." The child was in so much pain from the impact he could barely speak.

My head jerked back to see the captain had already turned to YingShua and was crashing his hard knuckles across YingShua's face, causing him to stagger off and fall backwards. His elbows hit the ground.

"That's for destroying everything I have!" The captain stomped on YingShua twice but at the third attempt YingShua caught his foot and twisted it, making the captain lose balance and tumble over.

Two soldiers attempted to grab YingShua but he turned around holding two sharp pocket knives and slashed their wrists. The soldiers wailed in pain and grabbed their open wounds which had blood gushing out.

Then before the soldiers had time to react any further, YingShua somersaulted between them and sliced deep cuts behind their knees. Crippled, their bodies fell to the ground, writhing in agony.

Blong-Cheng stepped back to point his gun at YingShua but that didn't seem to scare him. YingShua's fist smashed into the captain's jaw before he could dodge. A bone-cracking sound disturbed the air as the man's body went crashing to the ground. His gun flew out of his grasp.

YingShua speedily leapt into the air and struck the crawling Captain with his knees, heavily digging into the spine of the traitor's back. YingShua pulled back his sharp dagger and fiercely stabbed the captain's right hand, causing the man to cry out in agonizing pain.

I watched in fright, seeing YingShua truly hot-headed for the first time. His face became poised with a hatred I'd never witnessed before.

"These hands should be cut off," YingShua said between panting breaths, baring his teeth. The fire in his eyes flashed. "You'll pay for touching what's mine." Pressing the blades deep into flesh and bone, dark red streams started pooling from the captain's hands, staining the soil beneath as he struggled.

YingShua hadn't finished with the captain when two soldiers appeared and hit him with the ends of their guns before grabbing him by both arms. They kicked YingShua's legs and confined him to his knees.

Blong-Cheng got up with blood dripping from his wounds. He curled a corner of his lips and went to locate his weapon.

Picking up his gun and swiftly sprinting back, he connected his thick military boots to the side of YingShua's ribs. The pain from bone fracturing caught at YingShua's chest and he grunted in a deep wheeze. Seconds passed before he could breathe.

The soldiers laughed as the captain went on with the beating.

"Stop! Don't hurt him anymore. Please. Just let us go." I sobbed in anguish.

Then without warning the situation changed:

Behind the Captain, a moving shadow appeared. My expression turned as pale as a ghost at the sight of what I'd wished never to encounter again. Another tiger. This time, even larger. A full-grown adult male, twice the size of YingShua.

Watching with wide eyes, my hands started shaking. I covered TuPao's face, "Don't look." The boy tried to resist but I held on tightly. He was too young to experience such a sight.

YingShua looked up from where he lay on the ground, spat the blood and dirt from his mouth, and managed to scoff, "What? You've never seen a tiger before?" He rose to his feet in panting breaths and backed away quietly.

Captain Blong-Cheng slowly turned. Horror consumed his expression. The tiger growled and snarled as it slowly came closer, baring its razor-sharp fangs. Before long, a second pair of fierce amber eyes glowed from the shadows, appearing next to the larger tiger.

The situation had gone from bad to worse.

As YingShua expected, the tigers appeared shortly after gun blasts in the air. Tigers weren't scared of gunfire but rather found interest in what threatened their territory.

YingShua turned around to look at TuPao and me. "Su-Lia…" He sounded exhausted but managed to nod a gesture of hope. A slight smile spread across his face that gave me all the wrong signals.

"No. I'm not leaving you," I said, shaking my head. I wouldn't be able to bear the pain of being without him.

"Captain, we need to kill them now!" one of the soldiers shouted. The visibly shaken men looked like they were ready to run for their lives.

"TuPao, wait here," I instructed decisively, sitting the child behind me and grasping the crossbow a distance away.

It was now or never.

Making sure my aim was absolute, I shot the first bolt and it pierced one soldier in the leg. Reloading in haste, the second twang cut the other man's wrist, freeing YingShua.

The captain turned back with a hesitant grin, surely knowing his end was nearing. He immediately pointed his gun at YingShua and pulled the trigger.

In that same moment, the beasts tore through the air at frightening speed. The smaller one ripped through multiple soldiers, biting and clawing them to their deaths. The larger tiger had pounced at the captain, knocking him over and pinning him down with his huge weight.

"Ah! Save me!" Blong-Cheng pleaded but the tiger swiped at him like he was nothing. Sharp claws raked across the captain's face as YingShua jerked to the side and dodged the flying paw. He turned to run towards TuPao and me but suddenly staggered, swaying a little.

Disoriented, he raised his eyes to meet mine, and that was when I saw he had been shot in the shoulder.

Gasping with worry, I raced to him and caught him swiftly in my arms.

"No, don't close your eyes, please." My hands covered the bullet wound as blood coursed down my arms. His black cotton top was stained red.

"Now…." YingShua gasped, and with the last of his depleted strength, he forced TuPao and me to leap off the steep hill. Instantly falling, we tumbled through tall skinny trees as rocks jabbed at parts of our bodies, and leaves were plowing from the ground as we passed. My consciousness was already going.

"Kuv Niam thiab kuv Txiv (Mother and Father). Thov tseg kuv txoj sia… (please spare my life)." YingShua's last words echoed in the dark silence.

Lost in the Right Direction

CHAPTER 16

"Have you had enough rest?" a young boy's voice sounded.

Freezing air sent shivers down my spine. An effulgence of moonlight beamed into my vision, causing me to wince.

Slow to come back to my senses, I first noticed little arms wrapped around the boy's long, slim neck. He carried me on his back and continued walking.

"Where is this place?" In front of us, far into the horizon, lay massive fields of wheat that moved gracefully like they were worshiping the tall mountains in the distance. Dark blue painted the sky like silk. Blankets of clouds moved like turtles across the pearly moon.

"Did you forget again?" the boy responded. He bumped me back up to re-secure his grip around my legs. "You wandered off again."

"How did I do that?" Then I noticed the pink, monkey-print pajamas I was wearing. Pulling away with furrowed eyebrows, I jumped off his back. "What am I wearing?" Velcroed around my neck was Kong—my copper, furry stuffed animal.

The boy turned around and it was the image of YingShua fourteen years ago. Glowing light traced his figure. He looked down at me in slight surprise.

These moments were in the beginning of our childhood, I thought subconsciously. And I was reliving it in a dream.

I pulled my fingers in front of me, feeling parts of my face. It was soft and little again. My cute toes wiggled in the gravel beneath. I only had one pink slipper on. "I'm six."

He stared at me perplexed. "I know. You told me yesterday. I like your name—Su-Lia Chang."

"Thank you. My mommy said Su-Lia means 'as sharp as a sickle blade and always willing to pursue greater strength'. I am a fighter."

"That's special," the boy answered. "Do you remember my name?"

I tried thinking as hard as I could. "I don't remember your full name, but I remember the first part. It's Ying."

"Shua… YingShua," he told me.

"Yes! YingShua Pha, I remember now. What does that mean in Hmong?"

"My parents said at birth I held my father's pinky with winning strength and my voice cried loud and powerful, so they named me YingShua."

"Your parents gave you a nice name. I'm happy to have made a friend."

The boy said no more. Then a throbbing headache had anxiety trailing up my skull. I clutched at the knots in my hair, feeling annoyed; messy hair was not my favorite thing.

"Are you looking for your hair tie?" YingShua opened his palm. My eyes widened and I quickly pulled my hair into a loose ponytail.

"Don't talk in your sleep like that. It's scary," YingShua said, the comment

seemingly from nowhere.

"Like what," I asked, not registering.

"Kuv Niam aws... Kuv Niam aws... los nrhiav kuv os... Mother, mother, come find me." YingShua reiterating my mumbles made goosebumps surface on my arms.

"Stop. Don't scare me. I miss my mommy, that's it," I argued.

YingShua chuckled. "You're like a ghost sometimes, you know? I woke up in the middle of the night and you were gone. It took me a while to find you, but I eventually did. Why do you wander at night like that?"

"Because I'm scared. The last time I closed my eyes, I got lost. The bad people from the village can come get us and I don't like creepy trees."

"There are bad people everywhere, but the trees are good. The trees hide us. Where are your parents, by the way? And where are you from?"

"My parents are from The States. I live in North Carolina."

"Did the American soldiers bring you here?" YingShua asked in a serious tone.

"What American soldiers? I'm really not sure how I got here. I went to sleep and woke up looking for my mom. No one looked like her so I'm worried."

"You shouldn't be visiting during a time like this," suggested YingShua. "It's no time to travel, yet."

"My mother never said anything about going away on vacation, but my home could be nearby." Glee spread across my face. "At least, that's what I hope."

"I hope so too," YingShua answered, and crouched down to wait for me to get on his back again. "If you're tired, I'll carry you."

I climbed on. "Where are we going?"

"As far as we can from those who want to hurt us," he said, looking up at the night sky. "Wish I had a choice to find my parents."

Silence filled the air. I waited for him to say more but he didn't. "Did they leave you behind too?"

YingShua nodded as I gazed at his back. His soft-looking hair touched the nape of his neck. "You'll find them," I said, smiling.

"Never... will I find them."

Darting my eyes, I realized quickly. "So, you are alone?"

Before I got an answer, a sudden motion in the air caught my eyes.

"Look!" I pointed in excitement. Large insects started popping in and out of the wheatfield. "Grasshoppers!"

Seconds into the moment, bright yellow and orange lights rose like gentle stars into the peaceful night. Our walking along the path quickly turned into dancing, and we waltzed with the fireflies as the grasshoppers jumped along in rhythm with our movements. YingShua twirled me around in circular motions before running towards the still mountains where it felt safe.

Finally, he came to a stop, panting. With a big smile he turned to me and patted my head. "I'm no longer alone. I have you now. Will you stay, Su-Lia...?

"Su-Lia...?

"Su-Lia...?"

Rain touched the ice-cold surface of my skin. My eyelids twitched, eyeballs quivering beneath, trying to wake me up from a dream that was already leaving my body.

A breath broke out of me like someone had punched my

stomach. There was nothing in sight when I parted my eyes, but I could feel leaves rustling beneath me. Darkness consumed the air. Sharp thorns stuck to my arms, sending agonizing pain, making it difficult to move.

From hovering trees, drops of liquid fell onto my face and flowed into my mouth. I gulped and tried gathering my thoughts. My chest raised and descended.

Then the last minutes before falling came crashing back to me as tormenting memories.

"TuPao? YingShua?" my voice echoed. Just as I tried getting up, flinching in harsh gasps, I realized the stabbing sensation throbbing from my left leg.

A two-inch tree branch had punctured my thigh. As miserable as it felt, I still managed to wrap a tight grip around the piece of wood. I squeezed my eyes shut before pulling it out. My cry of pain cracked into the otherwise silent night.

Red streamed down from the open wound when I rose to my knees. The foreign area was pitch black but that didn't stop me from moving. I peeled the prickly thorns off my arms and crawled through the wet ground until I gathered enough strength to pull myself up. They couldn't be far from here.

In no time, the pain in my legs had numbed and I limped on, unsure if I was heading in the right direction.

"YingShua. TuPao," I called over and over again. It was fifteen minutes before I shortsightedly tripped over a tree vine. I landed by a body sprawled on the ground. "YingShua?" Clutching at his shirt, I reached for his face to feel and confirm.

It was him. Irritation hit me when I couldn't locate the backpack; we were without any source of light. "Answer me… please!" Feeling along YingShua's body, I found TuPao braced in his arms. "Still breathing." A relieved sob broke from me.

"Su-Lia… is that you?" YingShua whispered shortly after. He grunted when he tried raising his head, but I carefully grasped his shoulders and settled him back comfortably.

"You're still hurt. Don't move." By now we were all soaked from the rain and God knows how long we'd each been laying in mushy dirt, layered in wet leaves. One hand rested at the side of his face while the other sat on TuPao's chest.

YingShua caressed my fingers and squeezed. "If I don't make it…" he managed before a raspy cough forced him to pause for a moment, "leave me here… keep going with TuPao."

"Shhhh. I don't want to hear that. I'm not going anywhere without you or TuPao."

The air grew muggy after the spell of rain. YingShua took a hard swallow. "Su-Lia…" Tears streamed down his face, melting over my fingers as he spoke. "You're the most amazing girl I've ever met." Inhaling, his voice cracked, "The only girl… I'd risk my entire life for."

Tenderness filled my heart—so full the fluttering in my chest rushed up and down my throat. I put his hand to my cheek and my tears gushed down his knuckles. "Thank you for fighting to come back to me."

And at that moment, I came to realize how much more I'd grown to love YingShua. When I return to 2078, where in *my* world will I find him? Must our strange fate be complicated with such divided destinies when we only want to remove the barrier of time. That alone would mean we can be together. But if our encounter was not destined then what is this? Aggravated in the moment, I kept questioning if this was a trial in my life where I had to fight for what I wanted in my future? If so, I was ready.

Before long, I felt a small struggle in YingShua's arm. "TuPao?"

"Su-Lia? YingShua?" TuPao got up, hair looking a mess as he rubbed his eyes.

"You're going to be just fine." I sniffled away the emotions and hugged TuPao with my other arm.

He nodded and touched a spot on his head. "There are bumps and they hurt," he said, before moving his arms tentatively. "I feel pretty bruised too."

I couldn't help but smile. "Glad your limbs are all still attached. Thanks to him…" The stars had favorably shifted over us, and I was able to see YingShua's good looks despite the condition he was in.

YingShua put on a slight grin and told TuPao, "I'm glad you made it down with only a few bruises."

"I'm going to call you Tij Laug, big brother, from now on…" TuPao announced. "I owe you my life."

My head turned to TuPao, marveling at the sudden decision to take YingShua as his *older brother*. Although not bound by blood, becoming part of each other's lives for eternity was a beautiful acceptance to come out of such adversity.

Morning finally arrived.

"It didn't completely fill up but there's some in here." There had been no source of water nearby. Luckily, TuPao had segmented a few bamboo tubes and, through the night, was able to collect rainwater to help us stay hydrated.

After handing me the tube of water, TuPao sat next to YingShua, gripping at his shirt.

"He's not well," I told TuPao in a troubled tone. YingShua looked weaker than he had the night before. The curves of his mouth were cracked. Dried blood stained the edge of his lips. The corner of his forehead had started to scab from all the flesh-tearing beatings he received from Captain Blong-Cheng. A purplish-green bruise had appeared on his left cheekbone.

Raising his head from my lap, I parted his lips with a thumb and poured crystal clear fluid into his mouth. "You have to stay with TuPao and me."

"Tij Laug," TuPao said, shaking YingShua's arms while sniffling, "we can't go without you."

It took a moment before YingShua fought to regain his senses and finally answered, "I'm a lot tougher than you think, little guy." Reaching out to pat TuPao on his head, we both caught each other's eyes. He realized he was lying in my lap. "I'm sorry to have burdened you."

"What burden are you talking about?" I told him, although my back was stiff from leaning against a hard tree.

"You didn't sleep again," he said in a serious tone, the truth of which had undoubtedly been revealed by the dark circles beneath my eyes. A sleepless night for me, but in a good way that I had been able to watch him rest.

Wincing slightly, YingShua rose to a sitting position. The bullet wound was a bloody sight. I touched it and he twitched his shoulders.

"This looks painful..." I told him.

"My right arm doesn't move well but we can't sit here all day. It's not safe," YingShua warned, attempting to get up. He looked dizzy and touched his palm to his head. After panting for a few seconds he held his breath to steady his breathing. His jaw muscles flexed in and out, feeling agitated that his body was weaker than he thought.

I pulled him back to me and crossed my arms around his neck and chest, placing my cheek against his. "Don't push yourself. I'll think of a way…"

It was hard for him to rely on me when he was used to doing things independently, but I wanted to reassure him in any way I could.

With the thick fog that had surrounded us beginning to dissipate, I had a better view of the surrounding area.

"What is this place?" TuPao asked, having followed my gaze.

The forest looked tangled and mysterious, and yet different and enthralling:

Sunlight beamed through dense cumulus clouds. Behind us was nothing but mountainous rocks covered in green moss. Up ahead, various shades of brown and grayish vines intertwined neighboring trees. Clingy plants draped from long stretched branches, coiling in lush, green leafy threads. Bright cherry-red orchids graced the landscape.

How did we end up here? a voice asked from within.

Later on that day, TuPao stayed with YingShua while I went to survey the area, hoping to find materials to weave into a sheet of bedding to transport YingShua in. While he was lean and well built, he weighed more than TuPao and me combined.

I'd never crafted anything like it with my own hands before, but it was worth a try. With YingShua's medium Hmong knife, I was able to chop a handful of sturdy rattan fibers, ten smaller stems of bamboo, and an armful of large ferns.

"You were able to carry all that?" Visibly impressed, TuPao stood up.

I nodded, dropping my hands to my hips and blowing my bangs. "I'm not sure where to start but let's do this."

TuPao analyzed the pile of materials and began giving instructions. "First, we should connect all the sticks of bamboo together as a border. Next, we'll take the strings of fiber and crisscross wrap each connecting corner. Make sure the fibers are secured tightly. Take more stems of bamboo and connect it from side-to-side and weave the ferns through each slot. We'll need more ferns to give Tij Laug a bit more cushion. The rattan fibers can break easily, if used for the sled handle. Let's use larger tubes of bamboo and actual wood vines for sturdiness."

Mind blown, my mouth felt like it had dropped to my feet. "And how do you explain knowing all that?"

The child was only five and yet he knew far more survival craftsmanship than me. He was like an intelligent wiseman living in a small body.

TuPao smirked. "My dad was able to build just about anything. I have watched him since I was born. I know a lot more than you think."

Grinning, I quickly answered, "I'll go grab the rest of the materials and we can start."

"I'll start it for you," TuPao said, and he began setting out the bamboo sticks so he could measure their profiles.

In no time I was back and TuPao had already finished the borders and center connections of bamboo. Thick layers of ferns had been weaved, as per his design, to close off any openings that may cause discomfort to YingShua's back.

When the sled was complete, we stared at each other in relief and contemplated the early evening.

TuPao and I helped turn YingShua onto the sled. Tossing the wood vine rope over my shoulders, I began pulling with all my strength.

"Let me help you," TuPao said, running up to my side and taking the ends of the rope in his grip. Although he had little might, he was still allowed to feel like he was doing a great job.

The vines had a tough surface, and in minutes, my shoulders were already burning, but I still kept going. There were no villages nor even a single person to ask for help.

Black crows flew across the shadowy night, inviting bone-chilling goosebumps with their sequences of coos and caws. Tall, hairy grass tingled my feet creepily. I became afraid snakes or even earthworms would crawl up my legs. Mosquitoes started biting and our skin was getting irritated.

An eerie howl of wind from behind breezed through, and as we went deeper into the forest, the barrier of mists began to separate, revealing a body of vaporizing water. The pool rippled like satiny emerald diamonds.

Healing

CHAPTER 17

It was really a hot spring, with a giant rock formation surrounding the pool. We spotted a cave passage towards the right.

"TuPao, look," I said, pointing up ahead. "Let's hurry before it gets too dark. We can take shelter there."

TuPao nodded brightly, gripping onto the vine rope even tighter. "We're almost there."

The small might and big courage the boy had brought hopeful anticipation in so many ways. I squeezed the vine handle, dug my feet into the cold ground, and kept moving.

YingShua was in and out of consciousness the whole time. Pulling harder to get over the more elevated areas caused him to grunt from the strain it placed on the infected area of his wound.

"Su-Lia, please… you can stop," he gasped, showing more concern for my discomfort than his own.

I ignored him and kept my gaze focused ahead. My palms stung from the scratches made from rubbing against the rope, but I continued pulling. Stubborn to a fault, all that I could think of was how to save his life.

After a while, TuPao and I stopped to catch our breaths.

I paced back to check on YingShua and raised his head for some water. "Hang in there…."

He managed to grab a hold of my hands before I got up. "Your shoulders… does it hurt?"

Beaming, I placed his hands to his side. "Compared to your wound, there is no pain."

With that, I stood back up, secured the rope, and went on.

"Su-Lia… your shoulders are bleeding," TuPao said when we finally made it by the edges of the natural pool. Beneath us were hard gray slippery rocks and scattered green moss.

I ignored the comment and changed the subject, eyes surveying the glass-like fluid as it rippled gracefully. "TuPao, hot springs are a natural way of recovering wounds. Where I am from, advanced medication helped as well but, with too many side effects, people considered using natural healing processes as a long lasting alternative."

The worried look on TuPao's face lingered as he stared from me to YingShua, "You are not from here?"

TuPao's question caught me off guard. After a long pause, my eyes softened, and I gave him a smile. "Let's just say I'm from a faraway place but for now this is my home."

TuPao curved his index fingers under his chin. He looked up at me, eyes filled with curiosity. "Now that you mention it, I've never seen anyone with red and greenish hair."

"It's called hair dye. Colors of a person's hair can resemble their unique characteristics or their mood."

"What do your colors mean?"

"Green is an everlasting sense of freedom. Red," I said, bending down to caress TuPao's arm, "is to always stay courageous."

TuPao marveled. He dropped the rope and raised his hands to his hips, "Then I want red!" and proceeded to take the vine handle once again in his grasp. "Only a short way to go." His little body moved and so did mine.

"You *are* a tough fighter," I managed as laughter broke out of me.

Before long, we were only steps away from entering the cave opening. A flight of bats came storming over us, screeching loudly.

"TuPao!" I tugged him back so I could shield him. The colony rumbled past my ears, throwing my hair into a mess.

Looking up, more bats came as I picked up the five-year-old. In a twist, leaping backwards, my body landed over YingShua with the child next to him. I squeezed both YingShua and TuPao's heads against mine; my eyes shut, hands holding them tightly.

The air in my chest felt constricted and I wondered how much longer it would be until all the bats passed. Fortunately, it wasn't long until the sound of wing-flapping could no longer be heard.

"Are they finally all gone?" TuPao asked with his eyes still shut. Both his fists were balled against his chest.

My head rose up slightly. The pool was in my sight again as coils of steam rose calmly into the night. Glancing back into the noiseless, pitch-black cave made me feel oddly safe. Its massive presence over the inviting water made the area feel more welcoming than it was threatening.

With my nod of approval, TuPao rose up to walk around the area, making sure no animals or danger was in sight before we settled in.

I turned back, remembering to check on YingShua as he struggled to regain consciousness. My fingers combed, brushing his hair away from his face, and I gazed at him intently.

YingShua parted his eyes and sharpened his focus. "I haven't been able to see you this clearly since we fell down here."

Smiling with relief, I pushed back up and cupped his face with both my palms. "How's your sight?"

A slight line curved at each end of his lips. His free hand caressed the back of my neck, pulling me centimeters away from his face. He blinked and answered quietly, "My strength is slowly returning. Till then… I'm in your care."

His voice tickled my ears. Heat burned across my cheeks. The breath in me became short; his endearing nature was hard to avoid and I only grinned back.

Then we heard little feet running back to where we were. TuPao stopped. He covered his eyes and turned around. "Sorry Tij Laug. I've interrupted you and Su-Lia."

I pushed at YingShua's chest, attempting to break from his brace but he grasped my arm and held me in place. "You are not interrupting us, TuPao," he said, watching me with teasing eyes and causing me to look away in deep embarrassment.

TuPao turned to face us. "I'll start up the fire inside then," he said, pointing—wanting to get past us.

"Wait, wait." I raised my hands to stop TuPao. He was too young to try to start a fire on his own. I glanced back at YingShua and told him, "Be good… you're still recovering."

Standing up from laying over YingShua, I patted the dirt off my legs, and walked over to TuPao. "I'll do it…"

TuPao stared at me for a moment before smiling. He handed the materials to me willingly. "Stay here with YingShua," I said before walking away.

A while later, TuPao came to check on me. "Su-Lia? It's been a while. Have you got it to work yet?" He was holding a small burning wood torch in his hands.

My mouth slightly dropped. This child was not to be underestimated. "Well, maybe I should have let you start up this fire," I answered in a titter.

He came closer and looked at me as I sat down in defeat. We both observed my sad pile of twigs and the small wisps of gray smoke that rose from it.

I brushed the back of my hand across my nose, sweeping my bangs to the side.

TuPao pointed and laughed, "Not only are you making a messy fireless pit, but you'll need a bath in the hot spring too."

I chuckled, shaking my head in agreement. TuPao came over with his torch. "Step back, I'll just light it this way," he said, proceeding to toss it into the pile of wood, soon causing it to ignite.

We stared around us to get a better look of the cave. It was not very deep after all. The space was surprisingly large, like a regular village home, but with no other passage tunnels as I had imagined. The vaulted rock walls stood high above us. Our shadows stretched from one end to the other, connecting our figures.

"What would I do without you?" I glanced over to TuPao, and he raised his chin up proudly.

"I think he's waiting for you…" TuPao clasped his hands to his back and gestured his shoulders towards YingShua behind him. He was leaning against one side of the cave entrance, gazing at the pool.

"If you're not tired yet… you should soak in the hot spring. It'll help you recover faster," I said, standing before YingShua, with one hand behind me and the other outstretched, waiting to receive his.

He looked up, seeing me glowing from the moonshine. Cool wind hummed through my hair. I blinked as my bangs returned, settling over my eyebrows.

YingShua glanced away and replied beneath his breath, disappointment evident in his tone: "I've been useless in the last two days."

I scooped his fingers up from his knees, causing him to recoil slightly in surprise. "You'll be feeling more recovered after this."

YingShua rose with the help of the cave wall and I tossed his arms over my small shoulders. We slowly started walking towards the body of water. My thin fingers gripped at the side of his firm waist, guiding him with the little strength I had.

"Careful. Watch your step. It is a little slippery." We tip-toed along the shiny plates of rocks, the smell of sulfur becoming stronger. Not a pleasant odor but one that smelled like it could be healing medicine for YingShua's wounds.

We walked deeper into the emerald-green pool, the ripples forming a sequence of rings that spoke of our progress through the warm, steaming liquid.

Our hands were locked, fingers intertwined—making sure we went deep enough to soak every open wound of his body.

YingShua's back was against the smooth edge of the pool. His tall figure stood before me with unwavering eyes, his concentration on me alone.

I gazed and nodded, quietly waiting for his approval to remove his shirt, but his eyes only dug deeper into mine. He unlocked his fingers, releasing me—respecting our distance but a slight wave ushered me back and he caught me, pulling me closer to him again.

The throbbing in my heart was at the point of exploding. I had no idea what I was doing, but in no time, I had already pushed his black cotton shirt up over his stomach, revealing his defined abs and the fleshy masculine chest that rose and descended.

The shoulder with the bullet wound had limited movement but YingShua still did a good job with his other hand in peeling off his shirt and releasing it into the water. He brought his eyes back to me while his built, veiny arms returned to circle around my back, touching the ends of my ribs.

Dodging his intense stare that always made me lost and speechless, I tried speaking under hot breaths, "This warm spring is healing to our bodies." I scooped the water from one side of his arm and poured it on his shoulders. Caressing his wound carefully, my hands traced the outlines of scars across his back given by thorns and sharp objects. With another scoop, I washed away the blood stain around his shoulder blade, bringing my fingers over his tensed biceps.

YingShua blinked and brought water to my face, rubbing dark spots off my forehead and nose. "You couldn't start that fire?" he asked in slight amusement.

I brushed my arm across my forehead feeling a bit embarrassed. "I've still got a lot to learn. But—"

Before I could finish my sentence, his lips covered mine. My eyes popped open in surprise, but I didn't refuse, allowing myself to be drawn into the warm trance. At this point, I had zero strength to climb myself out of his arms.

My fingers crawled up and circled around YingShua's neck as his shoulder muscles flexed at the closing contact of our bodies. The twirl in my head set off waves of contentment, suggesting our feelings within were mutual.

He had lips that were invitingly tender, curious, and in some moments, possessive—it was a losing battle against him. He explored in ways that teased my nerves and sent butterflies in and out of my stomach, stimulating an intense craving that had waited far too long.

I could feel the heat run through his body as he lifted me up—a strength that came from nowhere—and shifted me around, back against the inner walls of the pool. Pulling his mouth away reluctantly, he rose over me with widespread shoulders, panting as one hand clutched the smooth curve of rocks beside me. A questioning look fell upon him as if he was afraid what he had done was wrong.

Emotions ran through me and every inch of me wanted him. I nodded slowly, staring at him to answer his expression, and caught his lips again, running my fingers up his dark, wet hair. He squeezed my waist tighter than he ever had before, as if he hoped I'd never leave.

"Su-Lia, I've never wished for anything in my life…" he whispered between breaths. "My only wish… is to have you by my side."

I opened my eyes to his words and, while I knew our love was not promised, I surrendered to the strange fate we had, and murmured, "I want every lifetime with you… Even if it means parting tomorrow. The moments with you are enough."

YingShua released the buttons of my blouse, and just as he peeled the drenched fabric from my body, now seeing the partial bareness of my chest, he pulled away with concern. Assessing how deep the rope had cut through my skin, he brushed a thumb over the scar and said with a frown, "I've been your biggest burden…"

I glanced away, staring at nothing. Unsure what words would comfort him, I turned around, wanting to run away suddenly. Afraid I'd disappoint him with all my scars.

"Su-Lia," he gasped after me, catching my wrist with a splash.

"If I told you I did it to save you—it would only be half the truth." Mist passed us as I spoke, behind which a hesitant but brave smile formed. I turned slightly and raised my eyes to meet YingShua's, causing his to widen. "I've loved you all this time… even before I realized I did."

The courage it had taken me to speak those words was met by the satiny bareness of his chest rising in short breaths. But before I could pace out of the pool, he caught me in his embrace and held firmly. Dropping his lips down to each of my scars, and then bringing his chin over my shoulders, he answered my confession, "I've loved you since the first time I carried you on my back fourteen years ago."

With that, he turned me around and crashed his lips onto mine again—his kiss unyielding and deeper.

"I'm sorry…" He pulled slightly, studying my expression. "I've never kissed a woman before. Forgive me for doing what burned inside of me." He gently brushed his thumb over my swollen lips.

My mind was still lost but I managed to answer, "Don't be sorry. This is my first too."

"Come inside!" we heard TuPao call out to us. "The cave is warmer now." His lips curled in an expression of guilt, like he had eavesdropped on us for God knows how long.

YingShua brought his gentle chestnut-brown eyes down to me again. Then, at the corner of our focus, we saw scattering lights swaying through tall grasses.

"Fireflies!" TuPao ran out of the cave to catch the breathtaking scene.

"Perhaps these creatures are a reminder to see our inner glow. If we hold on to our wishes, it will be granted as long as we believe the truth of our existence. Whether in the past or future." YingShua squeezed my hands from beneath the water. I took a moment to make a wish I would keep only for myself:

If fireflies do grant wishes, may this lifetime be ours to keep.

The Belly Trap

CHAPTER 18

The cave ground was unlike the moist outdoor soil and soft grasses. There were sandier areas but some footsteps found unlevel, hard, bumpy surfaces—some even cold to the touch.

TuPao slept between YingShua and me. The fire continued burning, preventing the surroundings from becoming too cold, but frequent howls kept waking me from my sleep.

"You can open your eyes…"

My body responded the instant I heard YingShua's voice. As usual, he had slept with an arm folded beneath one side of his face, but he was now behind TuPao who remained in the same position he'd adopted the moment he closed his eyes.

"How are your injuries?" was the first thing I inquired about.

"Better…" He blinked and let out a loud exhale, rechecking himself. "If the bullet had shot through the left side, it may have gone through my heart." His fingers tapped lightly at his chest with a look of relief that lingered.

Swallowing hard, not wanting to remember the moment, I replied uneasily, "You fought very hard for all of us… we wouldn't be alive without you."

YingShua shook his head. "At that time, the only thing that went through my mind was making sure you and TuPao were safe. Death used to be a thing I'd wake up to in the middle of the night, not knowing if I'd be alive to see the next day."

He turned onto his back and tucked both his palms under his head. "But having you in my life changed those thoughts." He nodded to where TuPao was breathing soundlessly. "Now, having both of you, I've become desperate to stay alive."

"Then live… for us," I encouraged him.

He kept his regard at the ceiling of the cave where shadows danced with an orangish glow from the fire. "Su-Lia…"

Hearing YingShua's voice was always soothing to my ears. Speaking calm words of comfort always helped me sleep, but this time they worried me.

"If the day comes where you have to return to your world… marry a good man. Someone who belongs in your future. Who will protect you, live for you, and wait for you, as I did in *this* past."

There is no man other than him to fit my future, I vowed secretly.

My vision became clouded and I turned away—not allowing YingShua to see the fluid that coursed down my cheeks. The taste of salt and sweetness melted over my crusty lips.

I didn't answer—couldn't answer him yet. It was true we could be cast apart at any given moment. Comfort was the only thing I could offer him.

The atmosphere became quiet, and it stayed like that until I was able to get my emotions under control.

"YingShua... do you believe that when stars fly across your world, they also cross mine? The stars belong to the galaxy—not our worlds; they have no time."

A long pause followed, as if he was searching for hope in what he was hearing. I understood that the more he grew to love me, the more the thought of letting go was starting to suffocate him. It made my safety of utmost importance to him.

Rolling onto my back, we both stared at the same space in the shadowed ceiling. As hard as it was, I would stay brave for him.

"If there's nothing we can hold on to in both our worlds... let us both become the stars and defy time. Should I part from you, you better keep fighting to stay alive. As you've always waited, I'll *always* find my way back to you."

YingShua slowly turned his head and raised his arms across TuPao towards me. The warmth of his palm was like a spell that cast all my worries away. His hand trembled softly as it rested over my eyes.

I curled my grip around his fingers and told him, "If you refuse to let me see your smile then don't ever tell me to marry another man."

"I won't say it again," he promised. "Now sleep. You've said enough..."

The comforting words were what he wanted to hear from the stubborn woman who loved him. The woman who also believed in a love that could never be—should be, and will be.

"TuPao?" I had woken up the next morning to no sight of the

boy. A further look around revealed YingShua was missing too.

A dread of fear came over me, hoping they were not in any danger. Getting up, I noticed a binding around my left leg, where I had pulled out the piercing branch a day ago. The fabric was the same shade of beige I remembered from TuPao's T-shirt beneath his black Hmong top.

The pain from the wound was barely noticeable but one of the boys had been thoughtful.

I walked out of the cave entrance to a burst of brightness. It was still early but I could already hear the hummingbirds chirping and buzzing, racing through the air.

Where could those two have gone? They were good at keeping themselves busy, for sure. Or wait! Were they in some kind of danger? I couldn't allow myself to overestimate the safety in this lost forest.

Pacing much faster through dangling tree vines, and swaying strings of leaves from my face, I kept my eyes open for any sign of YingShua and TuPao.

The burbling sound of rushing water in the distance led me onto another trail. And before long, I was stepping on sharp black rocks of different sizes. I stood and surveyed the area. There was still no sight of the boys.

Then, retracing my steps, to my left, the sound of movement startled me. It was as though someone was coming through the forest or, worse, someone was following me.

My chest raced. Scared of what I couldn't see, I listened as the sound became louder, like it was fast and dangerous.

Without thinking, I had already started walking faster and faster, but now broke into a sprint.

I could hear sniffing, followed by grunts, and then a loud-pitch squealing came. I realized then that something wild was headed straight in my direction. Sure enough, within seconds, a large, hairy creature with a pointy pig nose came thrashing from between two bushes.

The scream from my throat was so loud all I saw were streaks of green leaves and tree trunks passing as I kept on running—not knowing if it was after me or just running with me.

I watched as the wild boar galloped faster, and just as I saw it passing, banana leaves caught my feet, stopping me in my tracks. Looking down, I observed the unstable ground and within a split second the twigs broke beneath me and I instantly fell six-feet beneath.

A trap?! my mind screamed as I rubbed my back, feeling like my tailbone was injured.

I sat for a short while but stood up when hearing running feet approach.

"Su-Lia?!" I saw TuPao's head pop over the lip of the hole I was stuck in.

"TuPao! Hurry, help me out of here." I jumped up, raising my fingers to him.

"Hold on!" TuPao shouted and he disappeared.

I waited impatiently, worried also YingShua was not with TuPao.

A while longer, a tree vine rope was tossed down at me.

"Su-Lia, grab that and try to climb up. I'll try to pull the best I can too."

Grasping the weaved vine that TuPao had put together, I pulled while pressing my feet against the walls of dirt. My shoes slipped every time I tried.

"Su-Lia, you must kick into the dirt as you climb, so you can create steps to make your way up," TuPao called out.

Then it registered. With each step, I created foot dents into the walls. He was right: it definitely made it easier.

Nearing the top, a sense of relief filled me, but it soon switched to panic when I heard the wild screeching approaching again.

TuPao stepped back. His face appeared worried, and he reached out to me. "Su-Lia, hurry! It's coming back."

Heat ran through my head but I fought to remain focused. I kicked my last step and finally reached the top.

"Go, go!" I called out to TuPao when realizing the boar, the size of a 150-pound normal pig, had dodged the trap and was coming right at us.

"Back towards the trap, Su-Lia!" TuPao said and I nodded as we circled around trying our best to get the animal to run into the trap. "That's our meal today!"

Meal? I thought. Then I realized TuPao must have been out early to hunt. The trap was his and YingShua's doing. They were full of surprises every day.

We approached the area once more. "Let's split in separate directions right before the trap," I instructed TuPao, and he agreed.

Heading off, a quick glance behind revealed the animal had chosen to chase me, avoiding the hole dug for it.

"That didn't work!" I called out to TuPao who ran to the other side of the trap.

Circling back around, I saw YingShua skidding to a halt. His eyes enlarged at the sight of me and, an instant later, he lunged forward, catching me in one arm. In the same fluid movement, he rammed a strong foot into the boar, forcing it to crash into the trap.

"Tij Laug!" TuPao called out enthusiastically.

YingShua still had me by the waist, and I had to ask him to set me down on my feet. He proceeded to walk around the squared hole and told TuPao, "You did good. Glad I chased it back."

TuPao looked at the angry animal who hastily ran around the trap, squeaking and grunting. "We all did good! You should've seen her earlier," he said staring over at me, amused as he crossed his arms.

YingShua glanced down at my dirt-covered legs. Even my hair was in knots, which I hated. "Did you fall in there earlier? Where did you hurt yourself?"

I threw both my hands behind my back, covering up my tail bone. YingShua tried peeking over my shoulders, but I stepped back and walked away. He blushed and blinked elsewhere, pretending he didn't notice with a faint grin.

"TuPao, did you do this?" I pointed to the wrap around my thighs as YingShua walked up behind me.

"Tij Laug only had one shirt to wear so, since I had two, I lent it for him to bandage your legs," TuPao said. It made me smile—they both were just like brothers.

YingShua looked up to observe the tall, soaring trees. A small act of innocence when he had been shy about wrapping my legs in the middle of the night.

I slipped my fingers into his hands, surprising him. "Thank you…" I said, smiling away as we all began to discuss what to do with our catch.

"That was one aggressive wild boar. How did you both manage to dig that hole?" My eyebrows arched, staring at the hairy animal who was now tired of going around in circles and headbutting the wall. It lay on its side and breathed heavily.

"The hole was already three feet deep when we found it. This morning, Tij Laug and I only had to dig a little more. We laid long, breakable tree branches and covered them with banana leaves to camouflage the trap.

"That's quite clever. Who would've known I'd be your first victim," I joked and YingShua and TuPao tried really hard not to laugh along.

We spent all afternoon preparing the boar. TuPao and YingShua helped each other set up a meat smoking wood firepit; two Y-shaped tree sticks four feet long with a sturdy stick hung between.

The meat was washed clean at the stream close by and sliced into strips to hang over the smoke.

"How do we eat all this?" A hand wrapped around my knees as I settled next to TuPao, who was sitting on a log attaching shoulder handles to a basket he had made from bamboo.

"We don't," YingShua answered. "We'll bring the rest home."

"This is for all that meat." TuPao placed the basket down and pointed to a handful of banana leaves he'd picked to wrap the leftovers in. "Since you said you were not from here," he started, "do you know what this is called?"

YingShua looked at me like he was taken by surprise. TuPao knew I was a foreigner. "Those are Hmong baskets called *Kawm*. Of course, the ones I've seen in the future are much sturdier. But what you've made is an original. It's authentic and from this era."

"Did you say future?" TuPao asked in a surprised tone.

I acknowledged and YingShua sat quietly next to me, turning the meat. TuPao was young but he was a wise little man who I knew would understand.

Scooting closer to TuPao until I was shoulder to shoulder, I began, "My mother has one from my great, great grandparents who lived during this time. It's been passed from one generation to the other. Bamboo is such a resilient grass. The many things I've seen you build are amazing."

"Do you use bamboo in the future too?"

I nodded. "I must say yes, although the craftsmanship is no longer done by hand but by mass producing machines." Staring down, I opened my palms. "I've only learned through being here how hard it is to use my own hands for everything."

YingShua took my hands into his, spreading my fingers out to get a closer look. The calluses across my palms were already rough to the touch and still looked pink. "You have to be mindful and not be impulsive. You've hurt yourself," he commented, centering his eyebrows, and moved on to see more small scabs by my elbows and a splinter in my index finger.

I didn't argue, knowing life had been a little rough since I'd come back.

TuPao stared in awe at his brother and asked in YingShua's place, "When you return to your *time*… will you forget him—I mean *us*."

I shook my head slowly while staring at the fire. Smiling, I replied, "I would *never* forget *you—both of you*."

A stillness descended but I broke the silence by throwing arms around both YingShua and TuPao. "But who's saying I'll be leaving soon?"

We all tried to grin it off. The thought was unimaginable after everything we'd gone through. What had seemed normal in my future would now feel so foreign without them. In the same way, it would be different without me always causing them trouble.

"Su-Lia, I want to live in the future too. Maybe that's where my parents went. What if I can meet them again?"

I frowned before managing a quick, hesitant smile. Such a wishful thought of a five-year-old but I would allow him to hope. "TuPao, your parents could already be in my future. When people close their eyes, it's not forever. You'll meet again."

"Really? I can't wait for the future then!" TuPao beamed and I shook my fingers through his hair.

"TuPao, you're very strong for a little guy. In your future, what's one thing you'd like to learn?"

TuPao looked lost in thought, looking up to a sky now full of clouds. Then he nodded, "I'd like to learn English. Father said English in the future will be the most important language because it gives you unlimited opportunities.

"I'm going to keep fighting for my future. Red is going to be my favorite color from now on."

YingShua and I watched TuPao as he tried writing with a stick, as I had taught him. He carefully carved the first few letters of the alphabet in the brown soil.

Our gaze caught in the middle of TuPao's happy moment and YingShua pulled out a knife to slice a chunk of cooked meat. He handed pieces to TuPao and me first. "Here, this part should be ready."

"What about you?" I asked, accepting the meat into my grasp.

"I'll wait for the next bit to be cooked," he answered and turned another chunk over.

Tearing off a portion from what I had, I raised it to YingShua's lips and repeated his own words to him, "*Eat this so you won't starve.*"

His serious expression turned soft when I gestured again with teasing eyes. Giving in, he took the meat between his teeth and chewed slowly while looking away, shy and speechless.

A Familiar Love

CHAPTER 19

"Mother… father… Please don't go." The soft, desperate plea shortly transitioned into harsh panting breaths.

Being a light sleeper, my ears rang to the sound of his voice. "YingShua…" I rushed to his side, one hand on his forehead, the other gently resting on his chest.

"Don't leave…" He continued to shake his head. "NO! SU-LIA!" The shout burst into the night, startling me into landing on my behind with a thud.

Short of breath, YingShua jerked his head and realized it was me beside him. He hurriedly grasped my arm, helping me back up, and apologized. Still distracted, he turned away to avoid me.

I understood his actions—nightmares were the worst. They not only mentally haunt you but create illusions that steal your sense of peace.

Then it came to me. It was only right to bring him out for some fresh air, so I tapped him on the shoulder and prompted him to follow me. At first, he appeared reluctant so I grabbed his forearm and pulled him to a stand.

"Come with me…" I gave him a reassuring look and he followed as I walked ahead.

Before reaching the entrance, YingShua tugged at my fingers. As I turned to look back, he wrapped his arms around me. He held firmly, squeezed like he was silently praying for my safety.

I clutched at his arms, listening to him breathe as he spoke, "Su-Lia, I really thought I lost you. There was so much fire. I couldn't save you."

The air that was stuck in my chest slowly came out. He had taken me by surprise but I managed to answer from within his embrace, "I didn't ask… because I know what it feels like to not want to remember them. It's dark and soul-draining."

"I felt like dying," he said, gasping. "It was like walking through the final moments of seeing how my parents burned to their deaths. I couldn't enter our home no matter how many times I tried. The flames were fuming hot and our home had broken into pieces. It was a repeat of the situation except it was you whom I couldn't save."

YingShua pulled back to search my eyes. "I worry every day, Su-Lia, wondering when I can live in peace. All I want is to keep you safe."

I clutched at his shirt and tapped lightly at his chest—right above his heart. "The safest place for me… is right here. That will never change. I've become stronger than I used to be. I also want to keep you safe; whether it's your mentality or your physical being."

YingShua relaxed his jaws, looking more appeased, and he raised a palm to touch my face. "Please be strong for a few more days. I promise to get you home safely…"

He observed the stone intently before taking it into his grasp.

He spread his thumb over it. "Our time is at the mercy of this… Keep it safe," YingShua said in a strange tone I didn't understand.

He let go and walked past me out of the cave. "We've been here for two days. I'm feeling much better thanks to you and TuPao."

I watched his tall-standing figure from behind for a long moment. Although I noticed the tone in his voice had changed so quickly, it didn't bother me, especially because I agreed that the stone was to be kept safe. Who knew what could happen next.

YingShua turned back and instructed: "We'll set off in a few hours. In the two days here, I've come to conclude it's better we leave as soon as possible. It's strange that the forest is this peaceful."

I nodded and woke TuPao up at the rise of dawn. We wrapped a few pounds of meat in thick banana leaves and stuck them all in the *kawm*. YingShua pulled the handles over his shoulders as TuPao and I stared at him from behind with readiness.

"Tij Laug, are we finally going home?"

YingShua replied, "You'll have more than just me to look up to. There's Meng, Nujai, and Yue who are like my family."

TuPao's eyes grew as he skipped ahead of us. He took out the small Hmong knife YingShua had given him and chopped tall vine thorns and plants to make way.

Luang Prabang was three days of trekking away from Tha Ngon. The fogs of the deep forest felt like going through a maze: thick like empty smoke and at times tingly to the skin.

YingShua held onto TuPao with one hand and me with the other. With some of the ground proving very soft, there were moments when my feet sank too deep but continuing to hold onto YingShua's forearm for support enabled him to pull me out pretty quickly.

The trail out of the fog lasted about two hours.

Upon reaching a dark brown road path, an overwhelming storm of wind and a dense flood of locusts flurried past, striking us with disbelief as we peered through the eye-stinging dust. Our ears filled with a deafening, shrill high-pitched noise followed by loud screeches and chirps. We couldn't figure where the gust of nature had come from so spontaneously.

"Wow… look!" TuPao said, pointing just as the flying dirt and leaves cleared away.

Bewilderment filled our eyes, witnessing what must have been thousands of creatures bouncing all over the area and yet all seemingly heading one direction—down the hill.

The disappearing thick mists revealed an enthralling sight of soft pink petals of blossoms that withered in front of our stunned eyes. It was an overwhelming scenic view of an orchard of peach trees that embellished the land.

YingShua slowly let TuPao down. He too was flabbergasted at how we had ended up in such a place.

"What blessing or curse is this?" I asked warily beneath my breath.

YingShua shook his head, eyes following all the creatures with deep curiosity.

We continued to walk, enjoying the vibrant colors surrounding us. The air sang past my ears, fluttering the ends of my hair as I twirled around to smell the fresh nature. In every direction in the distance, the mountains of Laos soared tall into the sea-looking sky.

As always, YingShua walked slowly, making sure he was able to capture every glimpse of happiness across my face. My smile spread wider than it had on any previous day. Even my insides felt light, like a bird with spreading wings.

The rough days had been tough but the beautiful days were breathtaking. A wishful thought of staying in 1978 crossed my mind as I came to a stop to face YingShua from afar.

The man standing before me belonged to me. He belonged to my future and my past. I spread both my arms to him and waited with a warm smile.

YingShua's eyes slowly moved to meet mine. He beamed as though also understanding our hearts were one and, before I knew it, he was sprinting towards me.

A life with him was what my heart promised. Forever was only possible if it was with him. YingShua's silky hair motioned from side to side as he snatched me into his arms, picking me up with force. He circled me around several times as we laughed our hearts out.

"YingShua…" I said as he let me down. I moved a piece of his hair out of his face, and he brushed a blossom petal off my nose. "Let's make this lifetime ours. I want to spend the rest of my life with you."

YingShua looked at me intently. Happiness glowed from his face like it was also what he wanted. If I could have felt his chest, I'm sure I would have found his heart racing too. Then a moment later, the tenderness in his eyes was replaced by hesitancy and a hint of worry—like he suddenly didn't feel confident.

"Su-Lia," he said, caressing my face. Anxious, I searched his expression for understanding of what was causing his worry. "I've been praying daily. I wish to be able to see… see you as my wife. Watch you become the mother of my children. And have a life together being happy just like this. But—"

"There is no but," I told him, covering his lips. "I don't care what conditions we have to live in. After all, we've been through so much. I'm not concerned. So don't be afraid."

Clearly, unable to provide an immediate response, YingShua glanced over to TuPao who was waiting for us at the end of the orchard. "I've never been afraid... I just hope you won't be disappointed in me."

I shook my head. "I'm happy as long as I'm with you."

"Hurry, I think I see a village from here," TuPao called, jumping and shaking his hands in the air.

"Where, TuPao?" I asked after we had dashed over to him. I dropped my hands to my knees to catch my breath.

"There!" TuPao said, pointing west.

I turned my head and YingShua was already a few steps in front of me, observing. Shortly, he commented, "There are no people in that village."

"Really?" TuPao and I said in unison.

I used my hand to shield the sunlight from my view. "We'll have to go through the village to get past the mountains." We all agreed and walked down the hill of the peach orchard.

There wasn't an entrance as such, except for two logs laying on the ground. One step beyond them, and into the village, revealed ground that felt strange. An uncanny feeling lingered from within the soles of my feet. The hairs on my skin rose but I remained calm, knowing we were only passing through.

I reached out to grab TuPao's hand, but something had caught his eyes and he started chasing it.

"TuPao! Wait."

"Look, Su-Lia!" TuPao pointed to an old ball made of rattan that lay on the ground. He picked it up and started kicking it.

My expression softened. He was having fun and there was no one in the village so I thought there was nothing to be afraid of.

This settlement must have suffered a lot... The ten houses no longer looked like homes, and the ashes evidently had blown away over the years. Even the wind felt dry and unhappy. But I could sense that at one point the town had been lively with colors, children, and loving families.

I turned back to say something to YingShua but stopped when noticing the lost look on his face. "Is everything okay?"

YingShua kept moving, scowling like he was collecting thoughts in his mind.

A moment later, he came to a stop. His eyes paced from one spot to another. Then came an expression of realization.

"Tij Laug, do you know this place?" Even TuPao must have noticed YingShua's curiosity.

We both kept following and watched as YingShua entered a burned down home that only had two connecting sides left. The rest of the structure had been broken down by fire. Inside the home was mostly ashes. It was hard to tell which room was which, but YingShua knew.

He bent down to spread his hands across a spot, straight across from the entrance. It looked like a bed and black crumbly blankets. "Hatkiang... was my home. Here was where my parents lay together in their last moments."

Shocked, TuPao and I glanced at one another with wide-eyes and stood back, allowing YingShua some space to himself. He grieved silently. The pain in his heart burned across his eyes no matter how strong he tried to be.

Then he walked over slowly to pick up a small pot, opening the lid and closing it with a clack. With a sadden grin he said, "Mother used to cook *kuas dis*—rice porridge—in this pot for me when I was sick." Then he moved further back and touched a part of the wall. "My father's favorite spot to hang his gun after he came back from hunting."

YingShua later led us out the broken door, where we found more crickets hopping on the roadway. TuPao was already trying to catch the creatures but they all moved so quickly he failed each time.

"Mother, father, if *this* is your doing… thank you for bringing us back here," YingShua said, putting his palms together and praying silently with closed eyes. Finishing, he took my hand and walked towards TuPao.

At the end of the village the crickets disappeared into the tall grasses, and there we saw two piles of rocks. Seeing some small flowers growing around them, I stared up at YingShua.

"This was where I buried my parents," he said, answering the questioning look on my face. "It took me four years before I could come back to give them a proper burial. After the Americans left the country, it made it very difficult to return since our people were being chased from one place to another. When Nujai and Yue found me and took me in their care, years later I felt confident enough to come back to see the remains of my parents. I was only fourteen at the time."

YingShua crouched down to touch both his parents' graves as he spoke, "Mother. Father… I already know that you led me here again today; I can hear your voices through the chirping crickets— your guidance has not gone unnoticed."

He opened a hand and a cricket landed on his palm. Then he turned to TuPao and me to give his insight. "As Hmong, we are always surrounded with spiritual guides. Those are our ancestors and our loved ones. If we pay close attention, the trees, insects, animals—even the wind—speak to us, but most times we ignore them because we're only human.

"I, too, have put some thought into the last few days. The two tigers surprisingly hadn't attacked us—only Captain Blong-Cheng and his men. Instinctively, animals don't decide if you're good or not, they just attack.

"The forest was also too quiet. No places during this time go undisturbed by humans or animals. We were blessed with several pounds of meat to eat and to bring home to the others.

"Thank you, mother and father, for protecting us all this time," YingShua said, holding my hands next to him and squeezing. "Today, I've come with a special person. A girl who came from the stars; the future."

My head jerked towards YingShua, surprised at what he was saying. He ignored me with a smile and continued, "She's not only an amazing girl but she's strong, smart, and beautiful. She's everything I've asked for in a wife. Please give us your blessing."

Then my insides trembled when I saw him bend down to his knees before his parents' graves.

"Mother. Father. Today, I promise to love Su-Lia all my life. There's no one in this world that can replace her to be my bride. No matter which side of the world she is in, I vow to love only her. I will wait for her until the end of my life."

YingShua's words poured like heaven over my heart. In that moment, my ears heard nothing but his voice, repeating those vows like it was our wedding day. He later bowed twice to his parents, with fists and knuckles indenting the soil each time his head reached the ground.

Love is truly a journey. Spiritual love that comes from the deceased is on another level. It comes in ways that the world cannot offer such blessings, protection, and revelation to the living.

My mother's sweet face flashed across my vision. My heart hurt, missing her dearly but I gathered the courage to still be happy with my choices. The road ahead was not promised in 1978 but I was content to make each day count.

After two days of walking, we finally reached the Monkey Trail. That meant we were only a day away from home.

"Over there!" we heard a voice shout from afar. That voice. It could never be mistaken. It was Meng's.

TuPao got scared and hid behind YingShua, but YingShua lifted TuPao and sat him on his shoulders. We all started running towards the voice. "Don't be scared. You'll like Meng and Nujai."

"YingShua, Su-Lia!" First, we saw Meng then Nujai and Ia catching up from behind.

"Hey man, we were getting worried, so we came back here to wait for the last two days," Meng said, throwing an arm over YingShua before noticing TuPao. "Oh, looks like you brought a little guy with you." Meng reached over to take TuPao and flashed a big smile as he settled him down on his feet.

TuPao looked up at the tall men standing around him and didn't speak until YingShua gave him a nod to introduce himself.

"My name is TuPao. Nice to meet you. Are you the other brothers my Tij Laug told me I would meet?"

Nujai and Meng stared up at YingShua with excitement. They all agreed at once and, one by one, shook TuPao's hand.

"My name is Nujai. You can call me Tij Laug Nujai, and he is Ti Laug Meng." The two men exchanged glances that suggested they wondered where the boy's parents were, but YingShua only acknowledged their expressions like he'd tell them another time.

TuPao gave a gleeful grin and squeezed his eyes happily as the guys held his hands. Ia walked up and I introduced her.

With the men's introductions out of the way, Ia approached the boy. "TuPao, this is one of my good friends, Ia," I said.

"I'm happy to meet you too," he responded.

Meng stopped to observe YingShua, his eyes dropping to the ragged shirt. "What happened to you?" He began searching more thoroughly, inspecting all the healing scratches and wounds. "Was it Captain Blong-Cheng?"

Nujai scowled from Meng to YingShua, suddenly angry as well. "He did this to you?"

"He's dead..." YingShua said stony-faced before blinking away. He continued walking.

"You killed him?" Meng questioned, eagerness in his tone. He hurriedly followed.

"He deserved it. The tigers had him."

Both Nujai and Meng froze for a split-second. Mention of tigers would give anyone pause for thought.

Then Meng scoffed like he felt the same way YingShua did. "Eh, sounds like an awful death."

Nujai nodded in agreement and stopped YingShua in his tracks. "Give me that," he said, pulling the basket of meat off his shoulders. "Let me share your load. After all, we're brothers and you've not fully healed."

Ia wrapped her arms around me tightly. "You've gone through a lot. Let's go home…"

Meng picked up TuPao and tossed him onto one of his shoulders. "Amelia is going to be jealous."

"Who's that?" TuPao asked.

"His pet monkey," I answered.

"You mean *you're* going to be jealous, Meng. Amelia is going to love TuPao," Nujai stated. YingShua only smiled and everyone else laughed.

With that, we made it home safely a day later. TuPao met Yue and Mainong who welcomed him with a warm meal.

The Unspoken Truths

CHAPTER 20

YingShua and I got to meet the new addition to the family, baby Leng. He had a lot of hair for a newborn.

I held the infant in my arms for a short while before passing him to YingShua. He held Leng with careful hands and brought the baby closer to his face, squinting at him with a grin.

"Don't startle him," I joked.

YingShua glanced my way before returning his attention to the infant. "Because things are always more beautiful when seen closer."

I scooted next to YingShua, bumping him on the shoulders. "Do I look more beautiful now?"

Caught off guard, YingShua became flushed and answered beneath his breath, "Yes, near or far, your beauty never cease to amaze me."

While still being flattered by YingShua's words, a knock interrupted us. By the entrance was Leng's mother. She came in with a pile of folded clothes. Mainong handed me a stack and YingShua the other.

"This is for me?" I marveled, admiring the silk and paj ntaub stitches. Unfolding the crop top and skirt. I observed all the finely handmade designs. Both the outfits had matching green and red trim. Along the neck were Hmong flower designs alternating with triangle-like shapes. The sleeves were mid-arm length and made from see-through chiffon.

"I love this fabric."

"I figured you'd like the design since you usually wear air-flowing clothes," answered Mainong.

"Too many layers is so hot in this weather. I prefer shorts, a light top, and good sneakers." Staring over to YingShua, I told him, "I can't wait to see you in your new clothes."

YingShua only grinned, flattening the vest against his chest to make sure it would fit. His outfit came with a nice pair of black trousers, a red sash belt and a vest with matching red and green trims.

"How long did it take you to make this?" I asked.

"Not long. YingShua especially chose these colors for you for a special occasion," Mainong said, taking baby Leng back into her arms.

"Oh, what does that mean?" I asked.

"Nujai and Ia have decided to get married," YingShua told me. "Your clothes are getting worn out, so I asked Mainong to alter my mother's outfit to fit you."

With a look of awe, I hugged the clothes and told YingShua, "I really thought I had lost it but you still had them. Thank you."

"I found it while searching for you after the tiger incident."

At the time, I had dropped all my belongings while the beast chased us. It was an incident I never wanted to ever remember again.

"It's such a special piece of your mother's. I will cherish it. I am also so excited for Ia and Nujai too."

Mainong's eyes gleamed, and she grinned before saying, "Ia also asked me to come get you. We're going to go do laundry by the stream."

"That's great," I said and then turned to YingShua. "I'm going to wash your clothes today. What do you plan to do while I am gone with the ladies?"

Before he could answer, Meng knocked. "He'll be with us. We're going hunting." Meng cocked his head towards the front door. "We're leaving now."

"Go, hurry. They are waiting for you," I told YingShua.

The rest of the men were already outside talking to one another. TuPao and Nujai were leaning against a wagon of horse hay with their arms crossed.

"Be careful while you are at the stream," YingShua said to me as he went to join them.

"Don't worry. I'll be fine," I replied, following Mainong to where Amelia was coiled around TuPao, tickling his neck.

"You're so furry! I really like you."

Meng smirked as his eyes followed the child. "They get along quite well. TuPao is a good kid. I could tell he came from a good family."

"It was unfortunate…" YingShua lowered his head. The gloom over his expression darkened.

"Listen, we can't save every situation. The kid has a new home now. We'll help you take care of him," Meng told YingShua and shook his shoulders to lighten his mood.

Nujai chimed in and added, "TuPao is our family now, my good friend. You made the right decision to bring him home."

Then Yue came from behind and placed a hand on YingShua and said, "Doesn't this remind you of how Nujai and I found you?"

YingShua turned to notice Yue and exhibited a brighter face, like he was recalling his childhood days.

TuPao ran around the front yard. Amelia chased him and jumped back onto him when she caught him.

Yue hooked his hands behind his back and walked out in front of us. We all followed as he began telling the story:

"You were just as bright as TuPao, except you were a much more careful child. You didn't quite trust anyone. Especially during days like these, who knew if anyone would have trafficked TuPao for money? Gladly, it was you and Su-Lia who found him.

"In Hatkiang, where your original hometown was, I used to stop to rest between missions. Your parents were always willing to give me a place to sleep as the village keeper.

"I am grateful to your parents whose kind deeds went a very long way for me. Who would have known that months later when I came through the territory again, I'd learned how quickly they had passed away? The home was so badly burnt it hardly looked like anything was left."

Yue turned to face me as his eyes bounced back to Nujai and

YingShua. "Nujai and I searched home after home to see if anyone was alive. No one answered except we heard a mourning voice at the far end of the village. It was ten-year-old YingShua."

Nujai added, "We found him lying on the dirt ground, legs curled against his stomach inside the home. The place reeked of burnt flesh as we stepped through the entrance. YingShua's face was pale like he had been starving for days, and his clothes were torn, old, and dirty. Thorns pricked his feet, but he was so devastated he hadn't even noticed."

Taking YingShua's hands, I squeezed them and met his eyes. "Was this after we met?"

YingShua nodded slowly. "I was alone for days before Yue and Nujai came by. I had no place to go, just like TuPao, except to come back to the village."

"YingShua was reluctant to leave his home behind, but when we promised to come back with him to give his parents a proper burial, he agreed." Baby Leng started to fuss and Yue quickly said as he took his child from Mainong, "This is why we save lives. A child's life is very precious. If we can give hope and our people a chance to live—why not?"

"And then, five years ago, YingShua, Nujai and Yue helped me with the American soldier who passed away after his plane crashed. Learning that there were people out there who also knew of Captain Blong-Cheng and fought for our freedom and people, the Unit came to be after the Americans left the country." Meng had slipped in his part with a wide-spread smile. Amelia jumped from TuPao's hands onto Meng's shoulder. Its tail swung back and forth.

Yue placed his other hand on Meng and then on Nujai. "I'm very proud of these boys. They carried on my purpose for our land and our people. I could have gathered everyone long ago to Thailand, but Captain Blong-Cheng was too cunning. If he was able to betray his own family and friends, he'd hand over anyone to save himself."

"Why do you sound like you have some kind of connection to him? You know a lot about him," Meng said.

Yue paused with a long face before answering, "He was my father's best friend. They fought in the war together."

Everyone exchanged glances like it was the first time anyone knew.

"Yue, how come you never told us?" Nujai asked, his expression one of deep interest.

"You were too young at the time to understand betrayal. I wanted you and mother to live carefree while I kept you both safe. All that mattered was that he was a dangerous man.

"We almost got ourselves killed by the bastard when he came to the village one day. Blong-Cheng was a traitor from the beginning when he kept on leading the communists to every village he knew, pretending he was going to get them to safety or to Thailand. He did just that with us, saying my father sent him to get us—and we believed him."

"What did you do to escape?" I asked, remembering the same situation during the Mekong ambush.

"Father always taught me to never trust anyone except Mother and my own brother. I was around the same age as you boys at the time. Blong-Cheng was a manipulating liar who got his way with the enemies, but I knew he was bad blood when I saw his bowie knife on the second day of traveling.

"Father had shown me that anyone who came in the Pathet Lao logo of blue, red, and gold are enemies. The logo was engraved on the sheath of his knife. Blong-Cheng did a good job hiding it until he had to use it to cut through a few wood vines to untangle our path. From there, I questioned if I was going to save Mother and Nujai or if we were walking to our deaths, knowing we were wrongly betrayed.

"Disturbed the whole day till night, I managed to find an opportunity to write in the dirt quickly so Mother would be informed. Then that evening, we poisoned our food and shared it with him so Blong-Cheng would go to the woods with a stomach ache. It worked perfectly in our favor several hours later. While he was gone, we took off and ran as far as we could and managed to escape.

"I wanted to find the most secluded area where army trucks could not drive through. With only very narrow trails, we've lived here for the last decade. Father never came back from war and till this day his whereabouts remain unknown. Mother remarried another man and left for Thailand years ago."

"Blong-Cheng deserved to die a terrible death. The tigers did it perfectly," Nujai commented angrily but with a hint of satisfaction. He no doubt remembered the events that happened to Ia and wrapped his arms around the girl.

My mind drifted off, imagining the story as Yue resumed telling:

"For ten years I secretly fought against Blong-Cheng, making sure my whereabouts were unknown to the communists.

"There were many moments I felt like giving up but didn't. I study Blong-Cheng's corruption, plans, and motives through disguising myself as Pathet Lao and Vietnamese soldiers. I had stolen uniforms and weapons from the deceased and wore them to get close to the camps.

"From there, when I gathered enough information, I'd convey it quickly to any targeting village and I would be the one to lead them to safety.

"The duties changed to YingShua after I met Mainong while helping her family, but she ended up staying back in Laos with me to settle down and be my wife."

"YingShua is just like Yue. He always made wise and clever choices, which is why Yue left the responsibilities to him. It's very dangerous but YingShua does it with a passion," Mainong said with a proud face.

"So does this mean it's about time for Tij Laug to get married too?" TuPao said out of the blue.

The whole group glanced at YingShua and me, sending our faces boiling with embarrassment.

"TuPao, how did the story turn into us getting married? That's very off topic. Not yet," I answered hurriedly, glancing from YingShua to the ground, feeling very shy.

YingShua only grinned from me to TuPao and reached to brush the boy's little nose with his curled index finger.

"Are we going hunting yet?" TuPao stood beneath the tall men, and everyone looked down at him with beaming faces.

Yue reached to wiggle his fingers over TuPao's black hair. "Let's go see who can catch the most squirrels for dinner tonight."

The men and TuPao went their own way. Mainong now had Leng on her back, wrapped in a nyias—baby cloth wrap—and we stood together staring at the men as they disappeared into the vast, dense green forest.

"Do you… love him?" Mainong asked after a while, regarding me with firm eyes as if she knew I had a look of awe.

"Do you really have to ask?" I quickly dashed back inside to grab the basket of dirty laundry, a little flushed in the face.

Mainong followed me and took my hands into her grasp. "I know that YingShua loves you…"

The words stopped me in my tracks. I gazed patiently with interest as she nodded her head seriously. "For years he sat up there," she said, pointing out the front door to where a tall mountain superseded the hill overlooking the home. "The moment I saw you, I knew you must've been the person he was looking for."

I watched the image of Mainong stepping away as my vision fluxed into a blur. Where has the time gone? Our childhood once came as dreams. But to YingShua, it had been his reality all these years.

A while later, we arrived at the stream. Ia was back to herself again. A free spirit with the brightest smile that quickly transferred to the faces around her.

"You could guess who these clothes belong to," Mainong said, moving a basket in front of me. She was right—there was no mistaking YingShua's clothes, especially the black shirt with the sleeves torn off. It did cause me to wonder why he'd want to keep such a ragged item. It should've been thrown away long ago, but he kept it and still wore it often. Even an old top was special to him as long as it was during those times he spent with me.

Ia waved in my face to get my attention. "You look like you've been lovesick ever since you and YingShua returned."

Pulling a bundle of clothes over my chest I asked the girls, "Is it that obvious?" I was innocently surprised by the comment.

Both women shook their heads, grinning. I looked away and proceeded with my laundry duties. Later we brought the clothes to the backyard of the home and hung them in layers along four clotheslines.

While taking a rest to drink some water, both Mainong and Ia exchanged glances.

"TuPao said you came from an interesting place—is that true?" Mainong inquired with a look of interest. Ia tossed the last of Nujai's pants on the clothesline and took her seat next to me.

"Yes, I always thought you wore very unique clothes." They both looked down at my feet. "Your shoes are really different too. No one sells those kinds of attire here."

I glanced down to my white cropped blouse, black high-waisted shorts, and touched my sneakers together. If I wanted to stay, it was only right for them to know the truth.

Drawing in some air, I exhaled and began, "If I told you I live 100 years in the future would you both believe me?"

The girls' jaws dropped at once.

"The future?" Mainong gasped and almost spilled her cup of water. Her eyebrows furrowed like she didn't understand. "Is it miraculously possible?"

"Wait, you mean there is a future that is another world unlike here?" Ia's eyes fixed excitedly on mine. She took my hands, clearly keen to hear more.

"If you live 100 years in the future then how are you and Ia the same age?" Mainong said, turning to me trying to make sense.

"I was born in the future and not here. We are from different dimensions of time and space." I pulled my knees to my chest. "This stone is magical…" I continued, grabbing the necklace and unwrapping the pale-yellow plant fiber to reveal its sapphire and golden profile. A deep pink glowed around the surface. "It resonates with my spirit, allowing me to exist here."

"That is incredible. I've never seen this stone before. It feels…

rather lively and warm." Ia rolled it over her fingers while staring. "It's so pretty, like it has a life of its own."

"YingShua's parents gave this stone to him as a gift, and it brought us together. I only remembered this place as dreams, and some were terrible nightmares. After fourteen years, everything turned out to be real events."

After telling more about my findings of Destinite, Mainong observed the mineral for a few seconds. "The elders once talked about wandering spirits; souls that can exist in different times. But very few can travel in a physical form. Who could have thought something like this was possible where magical stones can bring you back in time or send you to the future."

I raised my gaze to see Mainong's hopeful face as she finished, "You must really be destined to be with YingShua—even being worlds apart."

My heart raced. Mainong always knew what to say to strengthen my hopes.

"It's so hard to imagine a future during times like these," Ia said, sighing.

"The future is amazing with many soaring glass-like buildings. Everywhere you walk, you'll see the reflections of the whole city. Lights there are always glowing in colors of bright blue, pink, and purple. But I must say, I am a girl of nature. I enjoy being able to breathe outside of the city. Seeing the vast stars, being in the tangles of forest, and hearing the outdoor animals make their unique noises. There is a future, I promise you both."

"I can't wait for all this to be over then!" Ia said, standing up and startling Mainong and me. "What interesting things do you do in the future? Do you raise animals and farm too, but in a futuristic way?"

Mainong shook her head, wanting to hear too.

A chuckle broke through my lips before I could answer, "Oh, there are lots of fun things to do. So much food to eat and celebrations are always happening."

"This makes me look forward to Leng's future," Mainong said. "What about your family? Do you miss home?"

The white, blue, and tan blankets billowed on the clotheslines. I raised my head up to the sky and answered in a long sigh, "I've thought about home many times… I miss my mother, my two girlfriends, my college campus and even my comfortable bed. The life in my future is very carefree and all I ever remember worrying about is studying for my exams in school."

"Did you find the bolts?" We heard Meng's voice calling from a distance and we jerked our heads towards the front door.

YingShua's back was turned against us, walking towards Meng as if he heard part of our conversation.

I stood up in confusion and went to the entrance. I called out his name, but he didn't turn back. He kept walking with his stack of arrows and handed it to Meng who had a long bow in his other hand.

"The boys must have come back to grab the bolts," Mainong said with a grin.

My eyes paced from Ia to Mainong. "I wonder if he heard me earlier?"

"You called out to him pretty loud too. Maybe he didn't hear you," Ia answered.

He heard me, I was sure of it. "Ia, we're going to the woods too."

"What? The woods. For what?" Ia asked not comprehending the motive.

Mainong came behind us with soft pats on our backs. "Go along now, girls. Don't cause trouble for the boys."

I grabbed Ia's hands and we both hurried in case we lost sight of the men.

A Waiting Home

CHAPTER 21

We took a route past the easy-flowing stream. YingShua and Meng were quite a distance away, but we followed far enough to not be seen.

Half an hour passed before we came to a stop. "We should've brought some water," Ia gasped, trying to catch her breath.

"Sorry, I didn't think it was this far out," I answered before looking around in concern. "Ia, I think we lost them!" We hurried again.

We really were in the middle of the woods but, luckily enough, we heard familiar voices, so we followed the sound.

"Hang on!" Ia hissed and spread her arms out as she listened carefully. "That's Nujai's voice but why is he angry?"

Carefully, we moved closer until we could hear more clearly. "I

think he's mad at YingShua," Ia first said.

"This is not like you, YingShua," Nujai commented.

My eyes widened at hearing YingShua's name. I wanted to get up and see what the problem was but continued to listen.

"What can we do to help?" Nujai added.

"Have you told anyone else?" Meng questioned.

"No…" YingShua's voice was quiet, as though he was ashamed.

Ia and I glanced at each other with confusion. Ia clutched at my fingers as we sat low, crouching behind several bushes.

Meng grunted in frustration, and we heard a few sniffles. "If this goes on, who knows if you'll ever be the same again…"

Was the situation that critical? The words threw my insides under flames. Had something really gone wrong?

"What's this about?" I shot up without realizing and startled the men.

YingShua eyes widened at the sight of me. Beaming light glared down from the thick layers of trees.

I glowered at only YingShua, wanting to know what it must be that he was hiding, but Meng coughed and turned the situation around.

"YingShua was just missing his shots at the squirrels," he said, his hand landing on YingShua's arm and his gaze switching from us to Nujai.

Nujai noticed Ia and his frown quickly turned into a smile. "You girls did good following us here," he said, changing the subject.

Confused, I walked up through the opening in the bushes with

Ia following behind.

The men looked at one to the other hesitantly as I walked up to YingShua and stopped closely in front of him. He blinked downward to the ground.

I tilted my head beneath YingShua's to give him a warming look. "Do your eyes hurt from the sunlight?"

YingShua stepped back a little, like he was caught off guard. A pink blush crossed his face as he stared more intently into mine. After seconds he managed to say, "I'm… quite beautiful today."

Everyone froze and Meng was first to burst out laughing. "He means, you look beautiful today."

A look of amusement glowed all over my face—his sight might be good after all.

Then I stepped away and challenged YingShua: "True or not, it will depend on you." I pointed to a nearby tree. "I'd like to see you shoot that dark looking target on the trunk."

I had deliberately selected a skinny tree that, at thirty yards away, would take some skill for an arrow to not miss it. Midway up the lean trunk was a small coil of darkened wood that made a good target spot.

"I'm just as good at archery as you are, Su-Lia. There is no need to prove my skills," YingShua said, grinning.

"Then why are you hesitating?" I crossed my arms and waited, noticing his fist tighten around the grip handle of the wooden bow.

"I'm not," he answered quickly.

"Then let's see how good you are." My goading was sufficient to see YingShua take up a position ahead of me.

The atmosphere became tense. Everyone around us held their breaths while YingShua prepared himself.

Standing a few steps away, I studied his face, his posture, and even admired how soft his hair looked so charming against the bright afternoon.

YingShua's arm muscles bulged as he raised the bow and drew the string back towards his cheek. Before long, the bowstring popped with a loud crackle. The long arrow blazed through the air, penetrating the improvised target perfectly.

Everyone exhaled and Nujai and Meng both jumped with delight.

My upper lip arched, looking up at YingShua teasingly. "You did good…"

I received the bow and arrow from him and walked past Ia as she raised her eyebrows, wondering what I was planning to do next.

Positioning the bow and arrow, I wanted to test my skills.

Seeing Meng and Nujai stare at me intently brought me amusement.

A little further away, a bird landed on a tree branch about twenty yards up. I drew the bowstring back towards my face, closing one of my eyes to analyze target, range, and crosswinds.

"Yes!" Ia cheered while Meng and Nujai clapped their hands when the bird fell from the tree.

I took two more arrows from YingShua's stack and fired them where I saw two squirrels climb down separate trees.

"You helped us cut our time in half, Su-Lia!" Meng picked up the animals from the ground and sprinted back.

"Wow, I didn't know you were that good at archery," Ia said, jumping to my side in amazement.

"Looks like we'll have a combination of food for tonight and a feast for the wedding," Yue said, as he and TuPao caught up with everyone.

"Look!" TuPao raised both hands before him with two strings of stacked carp they caught. Yue carried the weaved bamboo basket behind his back with some herbs and greens they had picked.

"This little guy is great at fishing," Yue proudly commented as the men all talked amongst themselves.

"So that's where you both went," Ia said aloud.

YingShua approached me. "You and Ia go back home. We're going to prep the meat and wash it before we return." He took the bow and arrow from me and smiled before turning away. "Don't worry, I can *see* you just as good as day."

I beamed back at him wordlessly. He was good at worrying me, yet also good at reassuring. He was the man who understood even those things that went unspoken.

Ia and I walked for a good half a mile. The soft swirls of pink, purple, and orange sky from the reflection of sundown was seen from the deeper woods. "I could've sworn I heard voices coming from over here."

"Su-Lia, I usually know the way back, but I think we came a little too far. I can't tell which way we've been," Ia commented. "Maybe it wasn't a good idea to insist on coming back ourselves."

Nujai had offered to escort us home, but we told him we'd be just fine. A claim that was now appearing to be wrong.

We continued going through the woods, hoping to find a familiar trail that might put us back on track.

Two hours later, what looked like trees became creepy tall figures with long bony hands, wanting to grab us at each corner we turned.

"Oh gosh, what did we get ourselves into?" Ia whispered as she tightened her grip around my arm.

I had learned to be quiet in the jungle, where creatures can hear you and come fetch you. My heart was thumping but I did my best to not let the thought scare me.

"We'll get out of here," I assured Ia. It was my fault and so my responsibility to get us back home safely.

"Tigers, bobcats, snakes, or worse: phim nyuj vaim," Ia hissed.

"What's that?" I asked as we walked slower than normal. A scary feeling crawled through the hairs on my scalp. Was she talking about bigfoot? A bear maybe?

"There's been stories in the woods. People who lose their lives mysteriously while traveling through haunted jungles. Phim nyuj vaim are tall monkey-like creatures of the woods. The elders say they are shape-shifting demons who can transform into other animals. Their feet do not face forward like normal—they point backwards and… they eat people's organs."

I felt like vomiting at the thought. Tigers, reptiles, and even earthworms were scary enough. Demons were bone-chilling, especially if you can't see them.

"Shh-shh…" I silenced Ia at hearing a sudden howling. We both stared at each other as panic rushed upon our faces. We debated without words if it was time to start walking faster, run, or stay hidden in the dark shadows of the woods—hoping whatever the thing was, it didn't notice us.

The howl sent spine-tingling sensations down my back, churning my stomach like my intestines were already being eaten by this thing. I couldn't decide if the howl was just a random earthly creature or if it was really a phim nyuj vais. Whatever it was, it was not far from us.

Then it jumped! Long tree branches shook and leaves hit our faces. Landing from one tree to the other, we struggled to follow its movement until its voice echoed louder, like it was already right above us.

"Should we run or hide?" Ia gasped, panting like her heart was about to pop out of her chest.

"Run!" At the drop of my response, we both took off at once—hand in hand, no one would let go. Then, suddenly, we heard tailing footsteps closing in on us and it sounded like multiple creatures were now gaining speed.

"Ack!" A large spread of sticky spider web stuck to our faces. We hurriedly peeled it off as fast as we could but then Ia fell to the ground with a loud thump. Leaves were cast aside, accompanied by a thick puff of dirt that came flying into my face.

Our grip broke from Ia rolling her ankle over a missed step. I grabbed her forearm and pulled her up. We both sprinted again, towards the only light we saw ahead.

A frightened squeal broke out from both of us when one of the shadows flashed past. A second later another appeared and grabbed Ia, separating us.

Just as I turned to look ahead, trying to find a route to escape, a large arm snatched me, jerking me sideways and off the pathway. My body slammed against its firm, panting chest. "It's me, YingShua!"

he hissed loudly, returning me back to my senses.

Shaking like I'd seen a ghost, my eyes parted and looked up at him breathing down at me. "YingShua?" I almost cried but held my tears back in a choke, feeling relieved at his worried yet calming face.

YingShua sighed. "Had you run off this track, I wouldn't have been able to save you." He pulled me away from him and steadied me to a tentative stand. I was still getting over the shivers but managed to look behind me.

The trail was cut off; a dead-end cliff that, in our panic, we had failed to realize we had been fast approaching. The moonlight made the scenery ahead look deceiving, like a light at the end of a tunnel.

"Are you both okay?" I heard Nujai's voice and turned around.

"Nujai!" Ia cried out. "We were so scared." She held Nujai by his neck and cried against his shoulders as he patted her back.

YingShua held my hand tightly, knowing I must have been extremely frightened, and we slowly walked back.

"We saw you girls turning the wrong direction when you got to the trail. We came after you, but you disappeared. You had a good scare," Nujai told us. I could see he was trying not to grin.

"We didn't chase you. You and Ia just started running. Were you that afraid of phim nyuj vais?" YingShua asked in a serious tone.

"Well, the howling was scary," I argued. "I've never seen one before, but if it eats humans, of course I'd be running for my life."

"I've traveled the jungles all my life. The howl was an old night owl. You both heard wrong," YingShua corrected.

"Don't wander off into the woods again. Next time there really could be a phim nyuj vais," Nujai warned Ia but she only pouted. Her ankle was in pain, and she was exhausted, so he lifted her onto his back and we all started walking through the woods again.

YingShua stayed behind me as usual, making sure the way was safe for everyone. He had an eye for everything and anything.

The home was only a quiet thirty-minute walk up the hill. We passed the stream again and YingShua touched a red string tied to a short branch sticking out of one of the trees. "Whenever you get lost, just look for one of these. It'll lead you back towards the main trail and back to the house."

I walked next to him and admitted, "I wouldn't have brought us out here had you not ignored me earlier."

He blinked away and looked up ahead. He didn't seem to want to answer but must have known I wasn't going to give up.

"I came back to grab the arrows, since Meng forgot them," YingShua began. "You miss home, don't you?"

"Was that what you were worried about?" A frown loomed over my face.

YingShua stopped and let out a sigh before caressing the curves of my shoulders. "Su-Lia, it only occurred to me today that you have family and friends who must be worried about you. You've been missing for over a month now. How do you think I feel about that? I'm keeping you from a perfect life that belongs to you."

"But it won't be perfect. Not without you," I argued, staring off into nothing. The spirit in me felt weakened.

YingShua was good at testing my resolve. But I understood. He was a man who was used to losing things in his life, even after fighting his very best, and he had to face the practicality of accepting the truth that exists.

Nujai and Ia walked past us quietly, no doubt sensing the tension between me and YingShua. "We're going up ahead. Ia needs to be treated."

YingShua heard Nujai but his fixated pupils only glowed the reflection of me. Then he took my arm and raised it for us both to see. "Look at you... weak muscles to your bones. You're pale and even thinner now than you were a month ago. Even your appetite has changed. Worse still," he continued, reaching to touch one corner of my eyes with a thumb, "you've not slept well. The bags beneath your eyes are darkened by stress. I've made you this way because I wanted you to be by my side."

Speechless, my mouth couldn't move. It was a true judgment after all. But it wasn't long until I stubbornly contended, "I'm staying for as long as this stone entitles my existence."

YingShua clenched his jaw and urged again, "Have you not thought about your mother who's alone? She needs you."

Both my fists clenched as I answered him in a firm, unwavering voice, "My mother would understand."

YingShua's hands dropped down to his side again. He stepped up, aligning his shoulders to mine and stated, "Life here is not for you, Su-Lia. You deserve more than this. This is being selfish."

"Selfish?" I snapped in disbelief. My eyes followed him as he passed and I retorted, "Is it selfish to want to be with you? I *also* only have you here."

YingShua turned his ears to the fury in my tone. His broad back was against me, arms tensed with soft, deep breaths like he felt defeated by the validity of my statement.

He waited. And I gazed, feeling a sense of anger that coursed through the blood vessels inside my throbbing head. Calling my decision selfish had made me truly upset at him for the very first time.

Then without much thought, I stormed to him and stopped abruptly with a gasp, "You didn't wait all these years just to tell me I deserved better." I grabbed two handfuls of his white top and pulled him down as my lips covered his in great frustration; torn between the life we both wanted and what we knew would come to an end one day. But in that moment, nothing else mattered.

My back arched as his hands grabbed my hips, pulling me tight against his body. He too was maddened when he pressed back, wanting more as our kiss deepened.

Clinging my arms around his strong neck, I invited the heat of his mouth to taste, feel, and lead. He shifted his head and I turned to fit him, taking his bottom lip between my teeth hungrily and letting go when he leaned forward to nick mine in return. YingShua's fingers then raked through the strands of my hair, taking a fistful behind my head and grasping my neck, imprisoning me in his hold with dominance.

His nature alone defeated my sensibility, yet I refused to stop and caught his mouth again, encouraging his control. Then he pressed forward, forcing me to take steps back—far enough until my body was pinned against a tree I had no idea was there. One of his palms raised to flatten over the textured trunk next to my head as our lips broke between breaths and united again.

I brought my hands over his breathing chest, feeling his heart race before moving down to gripping the ends of his shirt against his stomach. My fingers daringly traced the outlines of his ab muscles beneath his shirt, feeling them tense under my touch.

"You'll really have to marry me if this goes any further..." YingShua calmly said in a flirty tone, pulling away with a grin while stiffening his posture to hold me in place.

I stared up to YingShua with relieved eyes, thinking an exchange of our lips can be such a sweet reminder of how much we deserve one another. "I'll have no one but you... and I'm not ready to let go."

The words caused the sea in his eyes to gleam endlessly, as if he too felt the same way. He watched me adoringly for a long moment before pulling me back to him. "Su-Lia… you may live a poor life with me. Some days you'll struggle more than others. You'll be forced to survive in ways that you may regret further down the road, but I promise you that I'll do everything to keep you safe."

"I've been in your life since childhood. I've never regretted this journey with you," I told him, and he hugged me again.

"After Ia and Nujai's wedding, I want to show you a place I picked for our home."

My pupils increased, hearing words I'd waited to hear. My eyes fixed solely on him, overfilled with joy. "I want a garden of flowers and to be able to see the mountains of Laos every morning when I wake up—high enough to touch the clouds with my fingers but still to be able to smell the fresh rice fields of wheat when they're ready to be harvested."

YingShua drew back to see my expression, grinning down to me. "Granted. It will be our home for you to always come back to."

The Wedding Day

CHAPTER 22

The day came when Ia and Nujai stood outside while Yue happily conducted the rooster Hmong ritual called 'Lwm Qaib'[1].

"Come on in. Now that you both have decided to join hands and start your life together, Mainong and I are very happy," Yue said, taking his seat next to Mainong. "Nujai, although mother and father are not here to join us on your wedding day, be at ease. Your sister-in-law and I will make sure your marriage is completed; that we all feast a joyous day celebrating till night, and you will always have your best friends who are just like your brothers and sisters."

Nujai and Ia stared at all of us gathered behind Yue and Mainong. We all cheered with excitement from across the room.

---

1 *Lwm Qaib—pronounced Lw-Qai—is a ritual practiced in the Hmong culture. When a bride is brought home by the groom they would stop at the front door, facing towards the home, and wait for an elder of the home to motion the rooster three times around their heads to sweep away any bad omen from the newlyweds. Then another three times to bless and welcome good fortune to their marriage.*

Then Yue turned to Ia to acknowledge her, "We couldn't have asked for a better sister-in-law. The day Nujai brought you home injured, I knew it must have been love at first sight."

Ia blushed, glancing at Nujai, who grinned.

"However, I'm saddened that your only family left was your mother, and she is unable to join us. But from now on, Mainong and I will be just like your parents. We will watch over both of you so your marriage is strong, solid, and you will prosper in everything that you do." Yue gestured to Nujai to bow to each of their ancestors.

"Isn't there usually a Mej Koob, wedding negotiator? Maybe four?" I whispered to YingShua.

"In actual traditions there are. There is also supposed to be a *phij laj*—the groom's best man—and a *niam tais ntsuab*—the green lady, who follows the bride everywhere to ensure she does not run away—but the nearest village is a few hours away so this is as simple as it can get."

Inhaling with eyes enlarging, "I like this a lot better," I told YingShua. He arched an eyebrow.

Answering his expression, "Once in the future, I attended a wedding of a friend and there were two sets of Mej Koob, one for each side. The future culture is much different. We've mixed a lot of the Hmong culture with American culture. The celebrations are very large, like the entire town is invited."

"Sounds like many things have changed in 100 years," YingShua commented.

"On my wedding day, I don't need any green lady to watch over me." I stuck my nose in the air and YingShua gasped a quiet laugh. "What?" I asked.

"Why is that?"

"Because…" I hooked my index fingers into YingShua's hands, "how could I run away from such a handsome man?"

YingShua blushed calmly and grinned, looking ahead as we both resumed watching Nujai continue to bow several times to the ancestors, each time to his knees while pressing his knuckles to the ground.

"Isn't that what you did in Hatkiang?" My eyes enlarged remembering the scene.

YingShua nodded. "Nujai has Yue to do his wedding for him and all of us who can witness this day for them. I don't have parents or family except for everyone who lives in this home. But that's really all I need as long as I've already received blessings from my parents." A hint of sadness lingered in his tone but it left just as quickly when he felt my hands.

"We'll grow a family together…"

YingShua turned to catch my gaze, his eyes glass-like. He was touched. "I've already promised you before my parents' grave."

Warmth hugged my cheeks like a shy girl. He had. I tapped my face and attempted to turn away so I could hide my embarrassment but YingShua held my wrist in place. "Why are you running away?"

My mouth parted but no words came out. Then out of nowhere, TuPao appeared, peeking up at us as we stared down. It broke our grip.

TuPao tugged at YingShua's black trousers. "Tij Laug, I think we have a problem."

YingShua and I exchanged glances before crouching down to listen to what TuPao had to say. "The chickens got away," he hissed, and we jerked our heads. TuPao pulled YingShua and me by our fingers and took us out to the backyard.

TuPao shouted, "Su-Lia! Not sure who left the back gate open but grab those three over there!" He pointed towards the yellow bamboo gate to our right where all the lemon grass plants were.

TuPao lunged ahead of us and caught two large white and black feathered chickens. He secured them beneath the arch of his arms with satisfaction, but then frowned, knowing there were still three chickens loose, flopping up and down as they made their way out of the yard.

YingShua lunged over to help TuPao put his two back into their cage.

Without much thought, having never had to catch chickens before, I turned to grab a bamboo basket by the doorway and ran after the others.

I jumped over Mainong's garden of peppers, cilantro, and other assorted herbs before getting to the open gate. I leaped over in an attempt to cover one of the chickens with the kawm, but it jumped out of the way and my palms splat into a puddle of mud. Dirt splashed all over my face.

My eyes opened and shut in disbelief. I had thought chickens to be slow. Apparently not when they are being chased.

I regained my feet, wiping away the clumps of dirt from my face.

YingShua called out to me but I was too focused on chasing the other three around the home.

"Not the cows!" I rolled my eyes, stopping to catch my breath before running off again.

When I reached where there were two cows eating, I saw that the chickens had already hopped onto the stacks of hay. The sun beat down on me as I pushed a hard swallow down my throat, mustering the courage to climb up the five and a half feet mass of dry straw.

The chickens clucked and chattered amongst themselves as I began climbing up. Slow enough to not startle the cows but my hands ready to snatch at least one of the feathered creatures.

"Gotcha!" The others fluttered off, landing gracefully onto the ground and walking off as I stared from above, feeling partly accomplished. The red-brown chicken I had grabbed squawked, flapping its wings frantically.

I squinted hard, clenching my teeth and feeling a little dizzy all of a sudden, but hearing YingShua call out to me brought me back to my senses.

"YingShua! What should I do?" Nervous and unsure how long I could maintain my grip on the aggressive bird. Feathers were flying around me and some even stuck to my hair.

YingShua and TuPao stopped below me. "Su-Lia, you did good," TuPao said, opening a long cloth bag that was meant for the chicken. Behind his back was the bamboo basket.

YingShua was smiling until he noticed the exhausted look on my face. "Here, hand me the chicken first, and I'll help you down."

He received the wings to hold it in place, then wrapped his fingers around the two legs and settled the chicken into the bag. Using a thick brown thread to secure the top, he placed the bird inside the bamboo basket and slipped it onto his back.

YingShua then turned around to help me down, but my legs gave way. An instant later, he caught me in his arms. Crouching down, he laid my body against his thighs for support and tapped my cheek a few times.

I raised my hands to touch YingShua's face. "That chicken is going to taste really good tonight."

His look of worry slowly faded and, with an arch of his lips, he managed to smile at my joke. "You had me scared there for a moment," he said, gently blowing the stray feathers from my hair. "Just close your eyes. I'll carry you back."

There wasn't enough time to refuse, and he was lifting me with both arms before I could insist quickly, "It's okay. I can walk."

He glanced down. "Don't worry. You're no heavier than baby Leng."

My mouth arched at his unrealistic comparison. Then a question came to mind as I touched his exceptional arms, "Where did you get these from? Carrying things seems to be your best hobby?"

He flashed an attractive grin before answering, "The years of going on missions brought these arms. During the war, we helped the Americans carry and deliver heavy weapons from base to base. Some campsites can't be reached by army trucks due to the dangerous narrow paths. We worked for them as weapon transporters up the high peaks of mountains. Planes couldn't fly over some areas due to heavy enemy occupancy, so transporting during the night was the best time."

"You did all that while I was gone?"

"Ever since I was sixteen," he said. We reached the house and he set me down.

"Where have you been? And what happened to you?" Mainong said, having come to the door.

"The chickens got away," TuPao replied, looking down at the ground a little guiltily.

Mainong giggled, putting the back of her hand against her mouth. "It was my fault; I was watering the garden this morning and forgot to close the gates. I can't explain how the chickens got out though."

TuPao looked up and admitted, "I wanted to play with the rooster. But it got out of control and all the chickens flopped out."

Meng chimed in, "You like cockfighting?"

TuPao shook his head quickly. "My father didn't allow me to take my favorite rooster with me when we had to leave our village." A deep frown formed across his face.

YingShua picked up TuPao. "I'll help you train one, but we can't use this rooster. It's for the wedding. I'll buy you a fighting one in the future."

TuPao cheered up as the group stood around him, teasing and laughing about recent events.

"Should we bring the rooster out for another wedding ritual?" Yue teased from behind when he noticed both YingShua and I standing at the door.

YingShua's first reaction was to glance at me, where I stood blushing.

"No, today is Nujai and Ia's wedding," YingShua answered. I helped him bring down the bamboo basket of chickens.

Mainong and Ia took me with them to help prepare all the food hunted the day before, along with the chickens. All afternoon I was learning how to cook up a small feast for the wedding as the men settled themselves with fresh rice wine, fruits, and snacks.

The evening came quickly. I finished helping Ia with the dishes and swept the floor where everyone was eating and even outside around the home.

"Su-Lia," Ia said, taking the broom and dustpan from me. "You've worked hard all day. Let me finish up."

Ia walked off with the broom and I pulled a chair to rest on. The men were in front of the home, sitting out in the night with a large bonfire. The air smelled so good as the freshly cut scent of wood burned twirls of sterling smoke into the velvet night of twinkling gems.

My body weakened against the bamboo wall of the home. I kept on gazing at the red-orange fire glow, mixed with the dense jungle, until the silhouettes of the men started fading away. The sounds of voices, insects, and even the wind began to tune out, and in no time, I was gone.

"Su-Lia, it's your wedding day," Mother's voice sounded in my ears, causing my eyes to part.

"Mother? Why am I here?"

Mother had a worried expression. "What are you talking about, my daughter? Aren't you excited? You've waited all your life for this day."

"I have?" I pushed the blankets off quickly, remembering YingShua's face.

"It's really our wedding today!" I got up in haste and went into the bathroom. Patting my cheeks and sliding my palms down my hair, I stared into the mirror in confusion. "Wait, but YingShua lives in the past?"

When I walked out, Mother was already leaving the house. "I'll be back. I have to go pick up your wedding dress."

"My wedding dress?" I'd never even seen my wedding dress.

Something was really wrong here and nothing was making sense to me. I picked up the phone and called Jinnee. It took only four rings before her voice came on the other end of the line.

"Hi, Su-Lia. Ready for your big day?"

"Is it really my wedding day?" I answered nervously.

"Are you feeling okay? This doesn't sound like you."

I gripped the phone a little tighter, trying to find the right words to say. "What year is it?"

"2078, April 16th. It's Saturday and it's almost 9 A.M. right now," Jinee said in a giggle, like she knew what I was going to ask. "I'm almost there to pick you up. We have to go get our hair done."

Before I could answer, Jinee had already hung up. A knock came at my door, and it startled me for a second.

Slow to open it, I waited and heard Jinee's voice: "Su-Lia, I'm here!"

As the door swung open, it was really Jinee. She threw me a big hug. "Why do you look so scared?"

"I'm not scared, really." I thought quickly, curious if Jinee knew who I was marrying. "This sounds extremely weird but who is my groom?"

"Well, it's your childhood sweetheart, YingShua Pha of course."

My mouth dropped.

"Hurry, let's go." Jinee packed my bags and dragged me to her car as I tried slipping both my shoes on. "But wait, wait." I looked at my clothes and I still only had my pajamas on. "I haven't changed my clothes yet."

Jinee tossed her head and laughed. "It's okay. You're going to change into your wedding dress later anyways."

I agreed and went along. Everyone seemed to know about my wedding day except me.

The scene abruptly changed, and I was already in my pearly-white wedding gown with a deep pink bow that tailed along with the length of the back. A high neck wedding dress laced with pearls and a shoulder of soft feathers that dangled in threads of shimmering beads cascading down my arms. The beads swayed side to side as I walked down the aisle.

The groom wore a well-fitted pearly-white tuxedo that had pink Hmong designs outlining the trims of the arm and black shoes. I wasn't able to see his face yet, but the figure was just as tall as YingShua's five-eleven.

The feelings of blissfulness started filling up my chest. Nervous, I was really marrying the love of my life. Walking further and further, the closer I got, the darker the floors became, and the lights started to shift away from me. The people who came to attend our wedding started to disappear one by one.

Mother gave my hands to my groom. His were cold to the touch, sending doubts and fear that tingled against my skin. These hands were not YingShua's, I thought quickly. And just as I tried to pull my hands back the groom immediately tightened his grip.

"Mother! This is not YingShua." I jerked my head back but my mother had faded away.

"Su-Lia, please marry and live a good life," I heard her voice say.

"No Mother, this is not the man I'm supposed to marry!" Although the vocals vibrated in my throat as I screamed at the top of my lungs, not a peep of sound came through.

Snapping my head back, I saw it actually was YingShua. "Su-Lia, what's wrong?" He reached out to touch my face.

What was going on? Am I going crazy here?

"YingShua?" I grabbed him by the arms and looked into his eyes, making sure it was really him. "Why are you in my future? How did you come here?"

A deep frown consumed him. He held onto my hands and hugged me before disappearing into the dark.

"I'm only here to say goodbye…

"Goodbye…

"Goodbye…"

A Losing Past

CHAPTER 23

"No... No... Not yet!" My eyes popped open from the dream. The bitter feelings left, and my spirit felt reattached to my body. I really thought I'd gone back home. It was still 1978.

Then, faintly, the moments of YingShua laying me in bed settled in. A warm towel had been put against my cheeks and across my forehead. His fingers had traced the parted pieces of my bangs that rested airily over my eyebrows and he had smiled slightly. The next thing I'd heard was liquid being squeezed into a bowl of water, followed by gentle touches against my skin.

Words he'd said lingered in my chest while my light sleeping memories sank in. "Su-Lia, please rest... you'll need a lot of it. As you once said, this is all a dream. You'll be going home soon..."

With a deep scowl, I wondered why he would say such a thing or if I'd only dreamt it. I peeled the blanket off me and rushed to the door, where I ran into Mainong who was visiting me with a bowl of chicken soup and rice.

Gasping, I asked her, "Where is YingShua?"

"He's outside with the men," Mainong said, muddled then insisting, "Eat first. I brought this soup for you."

I looked down. The aromatic green herbs caught my senses. The sight of the freshly killed and boiled chicken was irresistible. With two slurps and taking the large chicken leg, I quickly thanked Mainong and excused myself. Her eyes followed me in confusion but she appeared content enough.

Outside, searching, I didn't see anyone until Ia and Nujai came into view. "Su-Lia? Where are you going?" Ia asked.

"YingShua was just right there," Nujai said, pointing in Yue's direction, who was cooking meat over the fire. "He's, uh, gone."

Anxious, a rush of worry weakened my legs, but my feet kept on walking. Where had he gone?

My first stop was at the steady stream. He was not there. I let my thoughts settle in before noticing the small hill where we had sat to watch the stars. There. I could see his silhouette from a distance, staring down at me.

My legs quickened and, before I knew it, I was sprinting. His words repeated louder and louder in my head. This was not like him.

The wind rumbled through my ears, coiling through each strand of my hair, and I was already there.

YingShua stood up slowly as I made it to the top and stopped before him, panting for air.

The moonlight gleamed through his charming eyes as he gazed at me, waiting. The orange and red fire glow background outlined his strikingly attractive figure dressed in his silk Hmong outfit, trimmed in red and green.

"What's with the chicken leg?" he called out.

Then I remembered and looked at what I had carried with me all this way. "I had forgotten to eat it because of you."

Confused, YingShua chuckled and then commented, "You look amazing tonight."

It didn't register with me until I saw the gorgeous outfit YingShua had Mainong refine for me. I hadn't had the chance to wear it yet. A breeze weaved in and out of the dark see-through fabric around my arms.

Beneath my fingers, every thread was perfectly sewn into its unique design, with bright red and green trim. The top fitted perfectly and wrapped across my chest, buttoned down one breast to my ribs with silver elephant foot designs. The dark red and deep purple skirt ruffled across my thighs with more unique prints of flowers, and vine-like stitches with exact sequence designs that trailed down the dress apron. The tail of my red sash belt flowed behind me.

"You dressed me?"

"I had Mainong and Ia change you into clean clothes since you worked hard all day. You deserve to feel as beautiful as you first came."

"As I first came?"

YingShua nodded before hugging me and pushing one side of my hair behind my ears. "Your cheeks used to be rosy—fuller—and your eyes had shades of soft pink, orange, and brown paint over them. Your lips used to be glossed, and every time you spoke, I wanted to kiss them because they were full and chatty."

"And you've grown chatty recently," I teased him. He lay my head against his chest before stepping back to bend down to my eye-level. "Remember what I told you yesterday?"

"After the wedding, we're going to visit where we'll start our life…"

His eyes searched deeply into mine before looking aside. He took my hands into his and we both walked slowly down the hill.

I meant to ask him about his words during my nap, but his presence alone made me forget all my worries. It was just a dream, I convinced myself.

"We're going on a walk," YingShua informed the men.

TuPao ran over to us with Amelia in his arms. "Su-Lia, are you feeling better after resting?"

Amelia reached her hands to me, and I caught her surprisingly. Her soft tail tangled around my arms. "Now do you like me?"

Then I turned to TuPao and put a hand to his shoulder while holding Amelia in the other. I inhaled the crisp burning wood scent into my nostrils and answered, "Very refreshed now."

The monkey squeaked a high-pitch sound, then pecked me on the cheek which made my eyes pop open. "That's a yes." I laughed and she jumped back into TuPao's arms.

"You both look great." TuPao beamed with two thumbs up, before twisting around and running back to Meng's side. He grabbed a fish and held it over the fire while the other men cooked more pieces of meat to celebrate the rest of the wedding evening.

Nujai and Meng noticed us and stood up from their places. Nujai waved. "You both go on ahead. We'll finish cooking the meat."

Meng's hands landed on his hips. "YingShua, your wedding is next!" he shouted, and poured more rice wine into his mouth.

My eyebrows arched, forgetting the men had been drinking. I had a second look at YingShua, and his cheeks were warm and rosy.

"How much did you have?" I asked before it dawned on me why he was so talkative earlier.

YingShua answered, "Don't worry. Rice wine won't get me drunk." He turned left and pointed. "We're going that direction…"

I peered past the usual hill that oversaw Yue's home, and behind it was another mountain that soared into the vast dimness. Soft lights of pink and green radiated around it. "Is that where you're taking me? How long is it from here?"

"It's an hour's walk to get there and another hour will take us up to the highest point of the mountain. You'll get to see the clouds by morning."

"You're really serious about this?"

He nodded and we then started walking.

An hour passed and we finally reached the familiar vegetated grounds of the mountain.

"This was where we spent our first night in the hut. It was a cold, rainy night but we both still managed to make it to morning," I said, recounting moments I'd never forget.

"Yes, and since then you learned how to starve," YingShua responded, smirking.

A burst of laughter broke out from me. "And you knew just when to feed me."

The other side of the mountain was high but had flatter ranges to walk on and, from there, the night was almost as bright as day due to the natural bloom of magenta, neon green, and purple that billowed like curtains across the vast heavens.

I had to stop midway up the elevated roadway to admire the

sight. YingShua stood next to me, staring as I said, "This is like an exact reflection of my city, as if my world is floating in the sky. These same colors drift through the streetlights and levels of buildings at night."

"That is the same sky I stared at for fourteen years," YingShua said, looking down at me with gentle eyes.

"If only the aurora in the sky was really my world, I'd be looking straight at you too," I told him with a grin.

Then we continued stepping upward along the narrow path until we reached the top. The higher the elevation, the stronger the wind blew. Warm air still hugged our bodies as we finally made it onto the flatter terrace of the mountain top. It was the perfect spot chosen to start our life together. As soon as I saw the sight of different peaks of mountains soaring all around, I knew the area was high enough to see, feel, smell, and touch.

"YingShua, this is everything I've envisioned! It's the most stunning view I've ever seen." My heart thumped as we continued walking right up to the cliff edge.

The ground falling away before me gave a wonderful feeling of walking on air. I closed my eyes as the serene ambience of Laos sank into my soul. Then I remembered and pulled out my poorly stitched heart-shaped paj ntaub charm I had worked so hard to make as a gift to YingShua.

Mainong's voice resounded through my mind. *The Hmong Heart symbolizes love, family, and prosperity.*

Staring down with happiness, my thumbs pressed the soft cotton filling inside the charm. Around the heart, deep pink and dark green crisscrossed flowers were stitched, and in the center read:

S *heart* **Y**

I squeezed it with bliss. Just as I was about to turn around,

YingShua grasped me against his torso, curving his back downward until he could find comfort. His arms wrapped tightly around me.

YingShua pointed slightly to our right. "That's where our home will be. There's no garden of flowers but you'll have them."

I clutched his arms with one hand. "That's perfect."

"Behind us is a field of rice wheat we'll harvest yearly. Below is the main creek. I'll teach our children how to fish. And when morning comes and the rooster is crowing, you'd wake up to the mountain breeze and touch the moving clouds."

"I can't wait…"

Then he pushed his cheekbone against mine and asked, "Su-Lia, what are your biggest dreams you see in your future?"

"My biggest dream?" It took a moment for me to articulate the right words, but they came out as my heart spoke. "I've always dreamt of becoming a gallerist. Display and share with the world all my artistic inspirations. Maybe I can even open up historical museums and exhibit our culture and history. Most of all, I wish to have a peaceful family and live in the midst of nature just like this… What about yours?"

I tried turning to look at him, but his other hand kept my jaw in place like he had something important to tell me. "Su-Lia… in my world, dreams have never existed. At least not for me. But when I met you, I started dreaming of having a life with you. Recently, I've even imagined what our children would look like and how well you, as my wife, would take care of them while we live on this peaceful mountain.

"But since returning back home," YingShua continued, squeezing a fist against my collarbone, "day by day, *hope* turned into just a word as the vision of my future became dim. The darkest days in my life are coming and I refuse to put you through it."

I swallowed hard. Every root of hair in my skull screamed fear as his words rang through my ears; scared what his words meant for us.

"Have you ever stopped to wonder why I'd only walk behind you?"

I shook my head slowly to answer him.

"It was my way to protect and love you senselessly. I'd listen to your every step; I'd smell the scent of flowers that flowed through your hair. When in front of me, occupying my vision, you are the center of light in my world."

Wet drips of tears fell onto my arms. They were not mine but his. "What does this mean, YingShua?"

YingShua held me firmly in place, refusing to let me move until I had listened to what he had to say. "Trust that no matter what happens, that we'll be the stars in each other's sky." His hands moved my chin towards him. He parted his mouth slightly before pressing it against one side of my lips and whispered:

"I promise you my next lifetime, so I can love you dearly."
(Cog lus rau koj lwm tiam, kom tau hlub koj os, mog.)

Startled, the crackling sound of rupture sent signals to the core of my bones as the last of his words echoed. A deafening screech pierced through my ears, followed by a twisting pain in my temples. For a split second, my vision became distorted.

Then as I lifted my eyes, like a rewinding tape, every piece of reflective fragment flashed the memories I'd spent with YingShua in 1978: scenes of our last passionate kiss, his tender touches to every word spoken, and all our sacrifices. They vanished before me.

It struck me so hard my face crumbled in despair. Shimmering sapphire and gold particles withered, ascending to the midst of the night.

"YingShua!" I tore out of his arms, glowering from the centered space of my chest. Facing him, my head shook side to side, refusing to believe what just happened. The stone was destroyed!

My heart cried harder than it ever had, like all my hopes and dreams were taken from me.

"Why... now?" I demanded, through a stricken throat filled with tormenting pain. Fluid filled my vision.

"Forgive me…" YingShua said, so softly I could only see the movement of his trembling mouth as his gaze met mine. A thin crimson stream of blood coursed down his fist. The spirit that used to live in his eyes was no longer there. He hated himself.

I burst into anguished tears, catching a glimpse of my translucent hands desperately reaching out to him one last time.

The heart charm fell from my fingers as YingShua spotted the gift. A look of remorse stole the life from him. "Su-Lia!" He immediately lunged towards me with grasping arms, but the gravitational effects happened so fast, the world I came to love exploded into a futuristic vision of flying aircrafts that trembled the ground beneath my body. Sirens screamed from a distance in glaring colors of red and blue.

Droplets of rain bounced, one by one, off my dirt-stained face while ribbons of black hair spilled over my neck. The wet earth beneath me hugged my arms in a cool, sticky sensation. My hands twitched at the touch of weeds curling between each of my fingers.

"Where did she come from?" the high-pitched tone of a boy standing above me asked.

It was followed by a woman's raspy voice, "Poor girl. Where is her family? Did someone hurt her?"

Yes, my mind answered… *He* hurt me. Did YingShua one-sidedly decide this for us? How could he? The aching hadn't stopped despite the transition of time. Neither had the tears that kept trickling down the side of my face, only to disappear in the rain.

"Make way! The paramedics are here!"

I saw nothing but distorted images of people, while the sounds I first heard became mute and dark. My mind played the final moments of our parting as feelings of betrayal shredded my insides again and again. The pain was deep, like a fire that was meant to burn forever.

'I promise you my next lifetime, so I can love you dearly', my mind scoffed. What next lifetime when you decide this yourself? Leaving him was inevitable but… did it have to be so soon?

The life inside of me was gone. My mind was nowhere to be found, no matter how much I searched. My toes and fingers were numb, yet I cared no more.

Foreign hands examined my condition as my jaw trembled. "She's bleeding. We have to get her to stop biting her inner lip."

Another male figure came into view and managed to unclamp my bite. Then he took a flashlight to my eyes, checked my pulse, and called out, "Get her into the emergency helicopter, now!"

People gathered around like gray shadows against bright lights. At the count of three, my thin body was lifted from the wet grass.

The metal blades of the helicopter sliced through the dark gloomy sky in slow motion as my thoughts continued:

'My darkest days are coming, and I refuse to put you through it.'

That's absurd. Why not fight the hardship together and be each other's light?

'I promise to get you home safely…'

He had his mind set all along. I knew… but denial was easier.

I should have paid more attention to the depths of his words. He understood that staying in 1978 was inconclusive but that was only half the truth. His heart couldn't settle for me to live in darkness with him.

I was selfish…

And he was selfless…

My eyes whirled and any consciousness left in me disappeared into an opalescent pattern of haze.

Ending the Beginning

CHAPTER 24

"YingShua, it's so hot and I'm hungry." A splitting view of sunlight touched my lids as I opened them. The top of my head burned from the scorching sun as we walked between the two mountains seen the night before.

My hands were about to fall off his shoulders. He caught my wrist and pulled it back over his chest, holding it in place.

"Su-Lia, hang on…" YingShua tipped me back up so I'd stay steady on his back, cheeks against his neck. "I think I see a house over there," he said, pointing.

But I didn't have enough energy to lift my head. The hunger in my stomach wouldn't stop either.

"Hey, we are here. Open your eyes." YingShua had already sat me down beneath a tree where the breeze tickled my arms and cooled the sweats along my slender neck.

Hands against my stomach, I pressed both fists into it so my belly would stop making noises. Then I would exhale a few times and the growling would subside for a short while.

YingShua waved his hands in front of me slowly to fan the heat off. Then I smiled when realizing how admiring the boy looked as his hands motioned up and down. The night before had been dark but the morning proved his voice was not only caring but everything about him was genuine.

Warm beige was the color of his complexion hidden beneath soft, darkest brown medium hair that curtained over his almond chestnut-colored eyes.

"I'm okay, YingShua. I'm heavy, aren't I?" I sat up against the tree trunk to get comfortable.

YingShua paused and tittered, "Yes but I wouldn't leave you behind."

"Do you think we'll find my mother today?"

"I hope so. But let me go ask for some food first. Stay right here—don't go anywhere." YingShua ran off towards a row of three bamboo homes, topped with golden bundles of dry grass and reeds made into triangles of thatched roofs.

The first two homes were vacant, giving him the chance to search for anything that looked like food.

After a while of waiting, YingShua finally rounded the far corner of the third home and came running. "Su-Lia!" A small pot was in his grasp as he came closer with a gleeful look. He pushed his hair away from his face before settling the pot down in front of me.

"What is this?" I asked, craning my neck to see.

"They left a pot of yellow squash. This was all I found." He grabbed the small oval spoon inside the pot and scooped blocks from the bottom. As he was about to put them in his mouth, he stopped and glanced at me, noticing my swallow.

"Here. You eat first," he said, serving a spoonful of the yellow mushy squash into my mouth before I could refuse.

"That's old people's food. Stuff Mother, Grandma, and Grandpa would

eat," I mumbled through chewing—disappointed, thinking it would be sweet. "It tastes... so bland."

Then I gazed up at YingShua who replied in a frown, looking away, "At least you have old people to eat with..." He fed me what was left of the chunks and lifted the remains of the liquid to his mouth, before wiping the wetness from his lips.

YingShua found a spot next to me, and he propped one knee up as the other lay flat on the ground. He leaned his head against the rough surface of the tree trunk. Then it dawned on me he had recently lost his parents. I must have hurt his feelings.

One of my hands reached out to him but I stopped halfway, thinking I should just shut my spoiled mouth.

His hands then rested on his stomach which made me glance at the empty pot. "Oh no... I ate all the squash. I didn't mean to."

YingShua curled his lips even though his eyes remained shut. I thought he was upset. The air blew into his hair as leaves came swaying down to our laps.

"I'm glad you have more energy now. That way you can stick with me."

I crawled over to him. "But what if I have to go home? Mother won't let me stay here forever. She must be very worried by now."

His eyes opened to meet mine, widening at the sight of my big six-year-old hazel-green eyes staring at him from only inches away. A blush surfaced around his cheeks. He dropped his hands down to push back against the tree, turning his head to the side.

Then I stood up in a twist with more energy and heard him exhale roughly and cough a few times.

"Where are all the cars, planes, lights, and big media TV?" I asked, turning back to YingShua when I had the chance to survey the terrace before us.

"I have no idea what all that is… Again, you are in Laos." YingShua crossed his arms against his chest as if he wanted to be able to rest.

"How far is Laos from America?" I asked, touching a finger to my lips. Past the rustling trees towards the blistering light of the day, an eagle swayed in the vast blue sky, its wings spread.

YingShua must have realized I wouldn't stop talking because he stood up and his eyes followed the eagle's flight. "The Americans got here by plane so your home must be far away."

"But we drove a car to get to the woods for our family camping trip."

"What's camping?" YingShua asked with interest.

"It's when you stay up late at night to watch the stars with your family," I told him with a beaming smile. "Ouch… my back itches," I declared.

"What's wrong?" YingShua asked, hurrying to my side, searching for where the pain was.

"It hurts right here…" I pointed to my left shoulder blade, and he peeked down the back of my pajamas.

The bandage had fallen off. "How did you get yourself hurt?"

"Mother spilled hot water on me by accident when she was prepping chicken for an event a few days ago." My eyes became watery. "Maybe I was naughty and my mother abandoned me."

"She wouldn't," the boy assured and proceeded to assess the burn site.

Then turning my head to the side, I asked, "Why did you not abandon me?"

The question caught him off guard. A moment later he breathed and looked me up and down. "Because you're weird."

"Weird?"

YingShua laughed. "Who carries dead animals around?"

I looked at the ground behind me and saw he had carried my stuffed monkey animal the entire time. "It's called a plush toy," I corrected and stomped to pick it off the ground.

"Whatever it is. It's useless. It doesn't talk."

I walked around to face YingShua with a widespread smile. "How do you know? You tried talking to it?"

"Of course not, I knew it was fake," he replied unconvincingly, his eyes bouncing from one place to another.

Bursting out in laughter, I picked up the stuffed animal and squeezed it. "He's not real, silly." I pushed the red-brown monkey before his face and wiggled it side to side. "Meet Kong."

"It has a Hmong name too?" YingShua beamed as he watched me throw the stuffed animal several times into the air and catching it.

"No, Kong is an American name." I stuck the Velcro hands together and tossed it around my neck. "Should we keep going?"

"Wait," YingShua said, and I watched him take out his Hmong knife from the side of his hip and cut a slit at the edge of his pale red sash belt. He pulled hard, tearing off a long piece of fabric, and wrapped it around my shoulder to cover the infected area. "Leave this here," he said, patting it, "until I can find an aloe vera plant of some sort. It's good for curing burns."

"How do you know?" An eyebrow of mine raised with curiosity.

YingShua looked ecstatic. "My mother was always good at medicine. It was what she used to treat me. At least that's what I remembered."

Then before long, the sky was covered by stratus clouds which then led to rain spilling down on us. We both cheered, glancing at one another, as rain always felt fun and exciting.

YingShua hurriedly sprinted to the closest spiral of a banana tree and broke off the largest leaf he could reach. I waited for him, seeing his curtain hair now flat against his face. His black T-shirt was stuck to his skinny frame and he pulled his trousers up to prevent them touching the soaked ground.

Seeing YingShua walk on bare feet made me look down at my own. I still only had one pink rubber slipper on. I kicked it off my feet, feeling like it was useless without the other and we both ran together, twirling in the rain.

"We could have snuck into those vacant homes, YingShua," I said, panting, when we stopped a mile later.

Catching his breath, he answered, "The house smelled really rotten, like dead animals had come to make a home in it."

"Ew." I made a disgusted face before giggling again. "But anywhere is livable with you," I added, throwing my nose into the air.

YingShua looked back at me. "We'll hide out here for a bit until the rain stops," he said, indicating towards the lengthy bamboo woven bridge we'd just used to cross over a long pond. He held my hands the entire time we ducked beneath the bridge.

I couldn't stop myself from shivering while we crouched, waiting for the rain to pass.

YingShua noticed and searched my face. "Su-Lia…" He put a hand on my forearm and wiggled it.

In and out of consciousness, I sneezed and told him, while cuffing away the moisture from my nose, "I just feel cold and my eyes are itchy."

A frown weighed over his face. "Could you have caught a chill?"

I exhaled and a small cloud of vapor escaped my lips. "Look, I'm breathing smoke from my mouth."

YingShua looked like he wanted to chuckle but his face quickly turned serious again.

My body felt weak and it collapsed against his shoulders. YingShua moved my jaw against the ball of his shoulder as he wrapped his arms around his bent knees. He sat as stiff as he could like he didn't want to disturb my sleep.

A while later, my eyes parted and I found myself leaning against the round stilts of the bridge. YingShua was gone.

The rain had stopped and I crawled out to search for him. The other side, which was quite a way since the bridge was long, probed into more crowds of jungle, greenery, and stands of trees. Behind me were soaring limestone formations of rocks.

"Su-Lia!" I heard YingShua's voice as my eyes paced from one area to the other.

"Up here!" he shouted a little louder, causing me to raise my eyes to the top of a twelve-foot formation of limestone. From there YingShua was waving his hands in the air enthusiastically.

"Why are you up there?" I called back to him in a weak voice, feeling fatigued.

On top where soil and grass crowded, was one large wildly grown aloe vera plant. Thick, green spiky leaves curved over the rocks.

"Look! This is what my mother used on me." YingShua quickly unsheathed his small Hmong knife and sliced a couple of pieces, shoving them inside his shirt.

He then climbed down the tree he had used to scale the limestone, jumped off and tottered upon contacting the ground. Rolling down to his back, he wailed in pain, "Su-Lia, hurry! I think I got thorns in my feet."

A look of panic hit my face and I hurried to him. "What do I do?" My little hands grabbed a foot then the other.

"Right here," he said, pointing to a stick of long prickly thorns that had punctured the sole of his feet in multiple places.

Grabbing it without caution, I flinched when the sharp thorns stung my fingers. Grimacing in frustration, I tried again—although now also bleeding.

Then it dawned on me to pull from the edges of the branch for better grip, and I slowly managed to remove it from YingShua's feet.

My stomach felt grossed out by the size of the thorn that punctured the center sole of his foot, it was half a thumb deep.

YingShua seemed already relieved and he sat up with a groan, rubbing his bottom from where he had fallen hard on his tailbone. "That was painful." His wrist and the side of his arm had long lines of red scratches from the impact.

I flung the thorn needles away at seeing how hurt he looked. "YingShua! Don't die yet! Mother will find us and we'll be safe."

Visibly baffled, YingShua then relaxed his face as he extended his hand over my head and wiggled my hair. "Don't cry. I'm not going to die from this."

Hands pressed against my eyelids, and he allowed me to sob in his arms for a few minutes before caressing my shoulders back so he could see my face. "You'll heal in no time. So will I."

Then his eyes enlarged at the sight of the fear in my face. "You really look like a bloody ghost now," he said before breaking into laughter.

Settling back, I raised my fingers in front of us in confusion. He wiped streaks of blood off my face as his shoulders shook with amusement.

The freezing, bitter night came. Beneath the bridge, we hid in the stillness of the dark. My tiny body wouldn't stop shaking, to the point where my teeth jittered. I waited for YingShua while he scouted the area to find a better shelter.

After a while, I heard splats of mud before his head popped underneath the bridge and he reached his hands out to me. "I found our house for tonight."

"We have a house?" I marveled, sniffling with a small cough.

We climbed back up the grassy, muddy hill and in the distance was a very poorly made shelter built with bundles of branches and twigs leaning diagonally against a massive tree.

"That doesn't look like a house," I pouted.

YingShua stopped and stared at it before answering, "This looks like someone has already been by this area and left this shelter here. See?" he said, pointing. "They even left some of their belongings."

We searched through a black bag with a small zipper and found old, smelly rice which we hastily ate. Then searching deeper, YingShua pulled out a handful of rags, beneath which was a small green iron compass.

He opened it. "What's this?" YingShua held it up to the sky to get a better look.

I received it from him and told him, "Oh, this is a compass! This is what Grandpa used when we went camping." I raised my eyes to meet YingShua's. "This might help us find my mom and my grandparents!"

I almost jumped out of happiness but YingShua hushed me. "We don't know who's lurking around in these jungles, so we have to keep our voices down."

Then he skipped over to lift a few large oval banana leaves he'd already laid on the ground. "Su-Lia, come help me cover the sides."

We both proceeded with covering each pile of sticks, creating a few layers of banana leaves to make sure the rain wouldn't seep through.

I wiped my nose across my arms, staring down at YingShua who was already making a space to rest.

He gestured for me to sit between his legs, having made them into a triangle shape.

I raised an eyebrow but noticed the stick of plants he pulled out from his ragged T-shirt. I sat comfortably in front of him, underneath our small shelter, placing Kong on my lap. Its fur was dirty and wet.

Frowning, I asked YingShua, "Will we ever find my mom?"

"You will. I'll help you find her," he assured and applied gooey substance across my burn before re-bandaging my shoulder as best he could.

"Now sleep…" he prompted and switched spots with me, making sure I was closer to the tree trunk, where it was warmer and more protected from the chilling wind.

I watched as YingShua lay next to me, his back against the wilderness.

"Will the bad people come get us?" the small voice came out of me as I held my breath and pulled Kong over my chest.

"I won't let that happen." YingShua closed his eyes but I wasn't ready to let him sleep yet.

"I miss my home… I miss my mother, grandpa, and grandma." I blinked tears out of my eyes and sniffed.

YingShua pushed himself to a sitting position and he choked at the sight of my pale lips. He must have realized I was running a fever because he touched my forehead in concern.

It took both my little hands to cover his, and I pulled it down over my eyes to comfort me. Tears soaked his skin but he never removed the hand.

Later on, in the middle of the night, I was woken up by the sound of my mother talking from a distance.

I raised my head up slowly, wondering if she really had come looking for me.

Glancing at YingShua, I saw he was sleeping soundly.

Without a thought, I crawled over his legs and out the tree shelter, sprinting off with the compass in my hands.

"Mother?" I called out with Kong in my arms. Every time I looked up, there were only trees, but in the dark jungle they looked like witches' claws that wanted to grab me.

Scared, I continued moving faster. Twisting around, regret filled my insides, I didn't know which way to go back to YingShua.

Then, suddenly, foreign voices saying words I didn't understand sounded in the night. They added to my worry. I didn't know if they belonged to bad or good people—whether to run towards them for help or to run away from danger.

I stood still and covered my ears, frightened.

"Su-Lia!" I heard a sharp hiss to my right—YingShua had already found me, and he was panting for air. He quickly hushed me and said, "The people walking through this pathway are another group of travelers."

"Really? Let's go with them," I said insistently.

YingShua disagreed and, just as he pulled me to his side, a deafening cry came from one of the women followed by a rush of bodies thrashing through the shadows of the jungle.

YingShua covered my mouth right away and pulled me aside to dodge the running crowd headed straight in our direction. But in doing so his injured foot gave way. He threw me out of his arms and impacted the hard ground flat on his chest.

Just as I gathered myself back up, my first step felt extremely light—like my body had lost contact with the ground. The noise in my ears became quiet and all my senses escaped my body, like an invisible force had flung me into a whirl of spinning colors.

YingShua's voice vibrated through my ears as my eyes felt heavy. Once closed, I couldn't open them no matter how much I tried.

"Su-Lia…"

"Su-Lia… please wake up. Mom is here…" Mother's quivering lips brushed against my thumb as she held my hand tightly against her cheek.

A seep of cool, fresh air continued to flow directly into my nostrils. My chest rose and descended. The center of my vision sharpened, seeing a beeping holographic medical device monitoring my vitals. Over my mouth was an oxygen mask.

I felt weak but managed to move my fingers.

"Su-Lia?" Mother's head popped up, her eyes bigger than I'd ever seen them. "You're finally awake." She looked awful; her eyes were red and puffy like she'd been sleepless for days.

The Only Man

CHAPTER 25

Mother hurried the doctor and nurses to examine me. Dr. Eric Hang was my family physician and in his mid-thirties—one of the few doctors that was favored by all the nurses. He had short black hair that was usually freshly cut, which complemented his professional appearance under a light blue mask and his white coat.

"Dr. Hang, is she going to be alright?" Mother asked impatiently as he beamed like he too was glad to see me awake.

He went through his clipboard of notes and checked off a few things before returning his attention to me. "Su-Lia, you're indeed very healthy," he said, removing the oxygen mask from my face. "You just needed this long rest to restore your energy. May I ask what happened—if you can talk about it?"

Mother nodded hurriedly and was at my side again. "Yes, tell us. Where have you been, my daughter?"

The muscles of my jaw moved but nothing came out of my mouth. I kept my face devoid of emotion because it was easier to pretend I was okay. Every time I tried to speak, the sound stopped at my chest; my heart ached each time I was reminded of the past.

The three nurses waited with Dr. Hang for a long moment and, with my face now stricken, Dr. Hang said, "It's okay. If it was dangerous, you're now safe."

He gave orders to one of the staff and added, "Nurse Mel will start your discharge documents. You may leave as soon as tomorrow." Before long, everyone left except mother, shutting the door behind them.

The back of my knuckles pressed against my eyes that were already drenched in tears—unable to remain brave any longer. I sat as my sobs intensified. The louder I cried, the harder it was to breathe.

Mother noticed right away and came, gasping, "What's wrong honey? Calm down... you can tell me." The sound of my crying voice was the first thing mother heard from me since my return.

"My heart hurts... so much, Mom." It took several attempts before I could coherently finish the rest of the sentence: "We will never meet again..."

"Meet who, Su-Lia?" She caught my fingers in her grasp. I tried to prevent her from uncovering my face but she was insistent. She lowered my hands and revealed a pair of puffy, swollen eyes.

Tears continued to spill, drenching my vision. Mother's figure was blurry at first, but she reached to wipe the tears away. I was able to see her clearly for the first time in a long while. She held my cheeks in the warmth of her palm before asking, "Who made you this way?"

"No one, Mother. I went further than I understood, knowing this day would come—he wanted what was best for me."

"A man? He hurt you and left you in the middle of nowhere? How is he a good man?" She pulled back in disgust. Then she asked, "Who are his parents?"

"He has no parents," I answered through a croaky voice. "And he did nothing wrong. This is my own problem." I was unsure where to start but felt it was important she knew what had happened.

"YingShua is from the past. Time traveling is REAL, Mother," I said, my voice trembling. My mother shuddered and sat in her chair beside the bed. "I went back and lived through a time when our people were pursued and killed after the Vietnam War." My fingers crawled up to my temples as dark memories sped through my mind. The smell of ash, blood, and voices of devastation forced me to squeeze my eyes shut.

"Who would believe me…" I said in a soft tone. I bent my knees to my chest beneath the lavender gown, rocking until the trauma was replaced with a different thought. "But I was never alone. I met a boy… who came in progressions of dreams for fourteen years. He was alone in his world and became the man I fell in love with."

Her mouth flapped open like she was lost for words, but she otherwise remained calm as I continued:

"YingShua was everything a good man could be. He protected me, took care of me, and loved me. I even declared I would spend the rest of my life with him, but he saw the future further than my own. He said the past wasn't suitable for me."

Mother pulled me into a tight hug. "Shhh… don't say any more. As scary of an experience it is… I want you to know that I believe everything. I believe you."

She sighed before proceeding, like there was something she knew that I didn't. "I'm now convinced what is happening is like a deja-vu from when you were only six years of age. You went missing for four days during our camping trip in the woods and came back with an old vintage compass in your hands. I didn't think much except that you may have found it in the woods. I am thankful to him for allowing you to come back to me."

"A compass?" I had to seek confirmation since it was in my dream just before I woke up from my coma.

"Yes… Do you remember?" Mother asked firmly.

Blinking tears as I glanced towards the city from the heights of the hospital, I replied, "The compass is from our childhood."

I swallowed back the stabbing sensation as I continued to voice my thoughts, "Time can be such betrayal. After everything we went through—he ended it, just like that."

Mother pushed a strand of hair behind my ear. She locked her gaze on me and said, "*Nothing* is ever an end if you believe in fate." Her hands stroked through the back of my hair. "Don't resent him. He did what he felt was right in his heart."

I raised my head to look at her, tightening my dehydrated lips.

"Everyone believes time can only move forward. But in this new age, you are living evidence that time waited for you. Next time… I'm sure you'll meet him again."

"There is no next time…" I said slow and composed, brushing the wetness off my face.

Before we could talk any more, Mother noticed Jinee and Kathy quietly listening by the entrance. She stood up to make room for the girls, who came in with frowning faces.

"Su-Lia…" Kathy said, approaching me with open arms.

"We heard everything…." Jinee managed to say between her own tears. "I can't believe you went through all that." She hugged me tight as Kathy landed another arm around both of us.

Like a lifeless doll, my body swayed in their embrace. Not an ounce of energy was left in me, but I managed to give them a smile.

Mother seemed happy to allow this sisterly reunion to last as long as needed before saying, "Why don't you girls take her out for some fresh air? I'm going to see if I can get her discharged sooner. I would like to bring Su-Lia back with me to Asheville."

"Mrs. Chang," Jinee said, standing, "we didn't tell you first because—"

"I know," Mother answered before Jinee could finish. "You're her best friends. True girlfriends will keep each other's secrets. But if ever she is not well, I'll rely on you both to be open about it. After all, Su-Lia is my only child and you both are like daughters to me too."

"Yes, Mrs. Chang," Kathy and Jinee both said at once, brushing the wetness from their faces. They held each of my hands and squeezed.

A short while later, Kathy trundled in a wheelchair so they could take me out for a breather, but I wanted to walk on my own. She glanced at Jinee in slight surprise, but I ignored it.

"Su-Lia, you're a little different," Kathy commented.

I glanced at the girls without a word, knowing what she meant. The majority of New Hickory, North Carolina, was built with what we also called speed walkways—everyone tended to use them but walking felt better for me.

The surface of the porcelain floor felt ice-cold on my feet. Cool air-conditioning hugged my legs as I walked through the long hallway.

"You forgot to put your shoes on…" Jinee followed from behind with my slippers, her yellow sweater falling off one side of her shoulder.

"I'm okay. I'd like to be without them."

"Fine. I'll see you down there," Jinee said, hopping on the moving walkway.

"I'll walk with Su-Lia," Kathy called out before shaking her head. "That woman is never patient."

A gust of rose scent came flowing through the automatic sliding doors as we exited the rear of the hospital into the garden. The air definitely smelled different to what I had become used to. It was clean, crisp, and not as moist, humid, and musky as the jungle.

In the center was a rectangular fiberglass water fountain. It sprayed and spiraled water from the ground into two spherical metal structures which glowed an electric blue.

Jinee arrived a moment later and handed us each a cup of tea.

"So, you were being thoughtful," Kathy commented amusingly.

"Well, it's best to have tea in the garden, right?" She winked and turned—her pearl hair accessory glinting in the light of the blue fountain.

We all sat on a floating white bench, facing the sunset. The pink of early evening fused with the honey-kissed rays of sunlight that ascended from the horizon.

Being April, the tree branches were blossoming into violet buds and the green grass grew from the rich soil vibrantly. The age I lived flourished in so many colors and ways… but the norm in my life still lingered with an empty space.

"Does time really heal?" I asked serenely. Both girls exchanged glances.

Kathy first answered, "I believe it does. But the question is… how long will it take?" She caressed the curve of my shoulder.

"I disagree," Jinee said, her back stiffening. "Time doesn't heal love. You can only heal from hatred, grudges, and betrayal. Not from love."

"Why are you suddenly talking like you've been heartbroken?" Kathy asked.

We looked up to watch Jinee pace in front of us. "Why do you think I could never commit to any man?" Her tone had become sad. "Love was what hurt me too. Even I have not healed, no matter how much I've tried to patch it up. Nevin passed away five years ago due to leukemia—it wasn't his choice."

"Yes, Nevin was a good man," I acknowledged, remembering the boy's cheery personality each time we visited him at the hospital. His ash-blond hair had quickly disappeared when he went through chemotherapy. So much of his spirit lived in his green eyes and he had closed them too soon. He only looked like he was having a long sleep when we attended his celebration of life.

The frown on my face sank deeper. I placed my fingers on my breastbone and it felt tingly, like the necklace was still there. Dwelling on this separation felt awful.

"I'm sorry, Jinee. I never knew…" Kathy said quietly.

"It's okay. I never talked about it. But this isn't about me. This is about Su-Lia…" Jinee grabbed my hands in hers. "We'll help. Even if we have to figure out how you can go back to him, we'll do it. You won't heal until you see him again."

I shook my head. It was indeed a wishful thought. "If that was possible, I would have returned already with the magical stone that connected us. There is no more Destinite. YingShua destroyed it and sent me home."

The girls' mouths dropped, cheeks twitching.

"I can't believe he did that," Kathy said, slapping her forehead. "It's really over between the both of you."

"Yes. And without my permission too."

"So… no more going back?" Jinee asked sadly and Kathy stood up.

"No more. It's the end." The hardest thing to accept was the truth. "However, that doesn't change our love. He'll still be the only man…"

"Does that mean you'll always be a virgin?" Jinee asked semi-seriously but with an accompanying grin.

"Even if it means staying a virgin—it is what it is," I replied to the humor, despite appreciating Jinee had only been trying to make the situation lighter.

Kathy almost spat out her tea, but managed to gulp it down before rolling her eyes. We all stared off towards the half-sunk sun as the day dimmed to night.

"Su-Lia, honey," Mother said, having caught up to us a while later. "Are you ready to go home? Since you are on a short leave from school, come stay with me until you have to return to campus."

"I'm ready, Mom. I miss home, and Grandma and Grandpa."

"Oh look, monarch butterflies!" Jinee said, pointing at a swarm of butterflies dancing by the wine-red bushes of roses. One flapped right passed us. With its sheer orange wings, patterned with black veins and white spots around the edges, it fluttered and landed on one of the roses. The butterfly lowered its wings gracefully and rose back up with dignity.

"They represent spiritual transformation," Kathy whispered, clearly keen not to disturb the insect.

Mother added, "It also means to look forward to a new beginning. I gave you your name for a reason—you'll always be fighting for the best in you."

Back at Charlotte Arts Academy, Mother waited in the car while Jinee and Kathy came with me to the dormitory to grab my belongings. A month in the past felt like I'd been gone from here for years. Not much had changed except for the school adding more rooms to the west wing.

"Are you extending classes through summer to get caught up?" Kathy asked as we stepped inside my dorm.

"Yes. I've missed so much school—I'll have to work hard," I replied.

"Mr. Benz kept your belongings and gave them to us," Jinee said, pointing to the wall next to my bed; my book bag and wallet were exactly where I'd left them, hanging on my coat hooks.

I grabbed my laptop, charger, and packed a few pairs of shoes into my pink and black duffle bag. "Did they also turn in my phone?"

Jinee answered, "Oh, yes. Your mom has it but it's broken. She's already bought you a new one."

Kathy packed up my paint brushes, carving tools, and foldable wooden easel. "You're going to need all these to help you ease your mind while you're away."

A happier look spread across my face as the girls helped me take a few more things to Mother's SUV. After closing the trunk, we exchanged tight hugs. "Thank you, girls, for everything…"

"Hey, why are you acting like we'll never see each other again?" Jinee said, pulling back. "We're taking you out when we visit this weekend."

Kathy nodded. "Did you forget it's your birthday on Sunday?"

"It is?" Life was really getting away from me. April 17th was just four days away and, for the first time, I wasn't looking forward to celebrating my birthday.

Mother drove us from campus through the streets of Hickory and onto the highway, headed towards Asheville—my hometown.

Out of the corner of my eye, I could see her glancing at me. "The green compass is at home," she said, answering my thoughts.

She knew me best. It was the only thing I had left of the past. *Dual Destiny* was on my lap and I planned to finish it to see if there were more answers I could find.

"That looks like an interesting book."

"Dual Destiny…." I responded calmly.

"Dual what?" Mother asked, before looking into her rear-view mirror and grimacing.

Red and blue lights streaked past. A police drone flew ahead, recording a crash in the other lane. My head turned indifferently to the scene as I continued:

"It's about a supernatural phenomenon where one's spirit shares a unique connection with stones fallen from the stars." I sucked in some fresh air after lowering my window to let the breeze touch my face.

"A supernatural cause. I see. Sounds like a fantasy."

"This is actually real. It's about the last recorded case," I replied.

Stillness lingered between us before Mother commented, "Is this something related to what's happened to you, Su-Lia?"

"Yes… I was born with the same gift. I can manifest between separate times but only with the existence of Destinite," I explained with a frown.

"That is truly unearthly. I've never heard of this before—sounds a little scary, in a dark magical way."

In a little over an hour, we were finally back home. Asheville was surrounded by colossal mountains and the city lights streaked the noisy traffic in blue and pink.

Downtown's asymmetrical buildings were all reflective and the vibrant scene was added by the music spilling out from clubs and the noise of drunk people.

"You never liked the street noises. You always preferred peaceful nature and the blue ocean," Mother remarked happily. "Grandma and Grandpa will be excited to see you. Grandma's currently preparing dinner for you."

Hearing about my sweet grandparents reminded me to be thankful for the life I had.

A New Age

CHAPTER 26

"Su-Lia…" Grandma had hastily opened the door but froze when she saw me. Her eyes grew worried as she pulled me in to wrap her arms around me.

"I've missed you, *Tais Tais*," I muffled through Grandma's knitted sweater before noticing Grandpa walking to the door with his cane.

"Darling, you are finally home," Grandpa said, stroking my hair lovingly. "We were so worried about you. Your mother has already told us everything. We are glad you are safe."

"I'm just happy to be home." I snuggled into both of them.

Grandma took my hands and ushered me to the kitchen. On the table were my favorite dishes: steamed pork dumplings, egg drop soup, and what I came to love while living in Laos, boiled chicken and herbs.

After washing my hands, I sat quietly at the table as everyone watched me with care. Grandma grabbed one of the large chicken legs from the soup and placed it on my plate. "Eat this so you won't starve yourself."

These were the words YingShua used to say to me. The chicken leg was what Mainong made for me. I missed everyone from the past, especially YingShua.

I took a bite and chewed slowly until the images of mother and my grandparents became clouded in tears. Thoughts of the past continued to play as I eagerly consumed spoonful after spoonful of rice.

I missed those watchful eyes that never left me. As long as he knew where I was, he never turned away.

I missed the way he spoke to me. Every word was of care, concern, or because he loved me.

Most of all, I missed his touches. The gentleness in how he held me, and especially those lips that kissed me madly—making my legs weak.

Trust that, no matter what happens, we'll be the stars in each other's sky…

Before I knew it, I had already eaten four plates of plain rice. I was still stuffing mouthfuls until Mother stood up and caught my wrist.

Tears flowed down my cheeks as I looked up, realizing all the food I'd eaten while in my trance.

Grandma and Grandpa sat in awe.

Brushing the wetness from my eyes, I told them, "I'm just thankful… and hungry."

Their expressions softened and Grandma said in unrealistic humor, "Then keep on eating, child. You have to stay strong and healthy. We expect you to outlive your future kids."

I coughed, tapping a fist at my chest, and Mother quickly poured me a cup of water to flush it down.

Forcing a smile, I assured them, "Don't worry, *Tais Tais* and *Yawg*. I almost died many times during my time in 1978. I've escaped fires, bullets, tigers, and even boars, so I'll get through this too."

Mother and my grandparents sat in stunned silence. Grandpa's spoon fell out of his fingers.

"Oh, my poor child…" Grandma said, rising to hug me and caressing my shoulder.

"Our Su-Lia is truly brave and strong…" Grandpa said despite his worried expression.

"Yes, whoever gets our Su-Lia is the luckiest man alive," Grandma added, tapping the table. "She's got a great heart, is smart, and incredibly gorgeous."

Mother turned to me with a whisper, "If you're full, honey, then shower and go get some rest. We can take it one day at a time, okay?"

My grandparents were trying very hard to make me feel better. I covered my mouth while attempting to cough the rest of the itchiness out of my throat.

"Alright Mom and Dad, let the poor child go to sleep. It's been an extremely long day," Mother urged, allowing me to excuse myself from the kitchen.

"I'd like to meet this young man one day," Grandpa continued, now talking to Grandma as I passed them. They stared off, beaming at me like they were glad my mood was looking better.

"He must be exceptionally handsome to steal our Su-Lia's heart," Grandma commented to Mother, and I exhaled after sliding behind the living room wall to listen.

YingShua had wonderful features… every inch of him was perfect.

"He had his reasons, Mom. She's definitely safer here," Mother answered.

The lavender oil that mother loved lingered in the air as I stepped up the stairs to my room. It had been months since I last returned home from college.

Mother always made my bed and still washed the sheets, even when I was away. It was her way to have a clean bed waiting for me. My sky-blue pillows were fixed nicely over my white blankets, and Kong, my stuffed animal, was still lying against the pillows.

I sat at the side of my bed before deciding to lay down. My thoughts continued:

Maybe I'll rest and close my eyes. If I could dream… would that bring me back to you as it did before?

I had been trying this for days but could no longer dream of YingShua and anything connected to our past. It really felt like it was the end…

April 17th came around in no time. Jinee and Kathy had already pulled up in our driveway and rang the doorbell.

"One minute!" I shouted from the bathroom upstairs. My hair was thrown up into a high ponytail. The tints of green and red had faded, and were now barely noticeable. My bangs had grown out a bit, causing them to curtain to the side of my cheeks.

With one last look in the mirror, I practiced smiling and fixed my black and white Adidas sports jacket. Dressing comfortably for a nature hike up the mountains was a birthday wish every year for me. Nothing was better than spending it with people I loved.

Opening the front door, a blast of cool wind freshened my face. In front of me was a big bouquet of fruit and chocolate. I received it with glee.

"Happy Birthday!" The girls dived in for hugs. It had only been a few days but they snuggled me like they had not seen me in ages.

"Here's cake!" Jinee said, bringing out an eight-inch fruit cake from her back. "It's green pandan flavor. Let's devour it when we hit the top of the mountains to celebrate."

"Thank you and that's a perfect idea, if you're willing to carry the cake all the way up there," I said.

"Oh, I got it. Not worried at all." Jinee whipped out a massive, square lunch box that had straps like a backpack. "The cake will be safe in here with all the rest of our snacks."

Then she noticed my bag full of art tools, canvases, and the foldable easel at the window. "What's with all that?"

"Catching up on schoolwork," I replied and shut the door.

"I knew you would need that," Kathy said with a smirk. What do you plan to paint for Visual Arts class?

"The city scenery of Asheville."

"Oh, it's going to look breathtaking," Jinee marveled.

"Girls, is everyone ready? Mount Mitchell will be about an hour from here," Mother said, emerging with a backpack of hiking gear and her trekking pole.

Mother tossed something at me, and I caught it realizing the army green object in my hands was the compass.

The bezel ring was black and the face of the instrument had a crack across the middle, branching into two smaller lines. I closed the compass and slipped it in my jogger pocket.

In deep thought, I walked past Mother, grabbed my backpack—which had a rolled up sleeping pad—took my easel and headed out first. Mother and the girls froze for a moment and clamped their mouths when realizing the compass made me frown. Without a word, they quickly followed me out to the car and Kathy popped the trunk open.

We all settled in quietly. I didn't know how I had already ended up sitting in the front passenger seat when the back was my favorite spot in the car.

YingShua's childhood words revisited my thoughts:

"You will. I'll help you find her.

"Have you not thought about your mother who's alone? She needs you."

In the end, he really had sent me to my mother. The week-long coma allowed me the opportunity to relive the beginning of our childhood. Although was only a few days, he was my first friend. And my first love…

"If the day comes where you have to return to your world… marry a good man. Someone who belongs in your future. Who will protect you, live for you, and wait for you as I did—in this past."

The aching resurfaced. I'd cried enough tears and had begun to hate shedding them. Every day, I'd re-promise myself to take it slowly. If only love was a physical thing that could be written and erased, maybe it wouldn't hurt so much.

The drive was undisturbed. Then it registered that I was lowering the morale on my birthday.

"I'm… sorry. I didn't mean to act out of character," I muttered, staring at my lap with a cast down expression.

Kathy glanced over from driving, "Hey, it's nothing. We've learned how to adapt to this new you."

Perplexed, I questioned with an arched eyebrow.

"Let's be honest here… you don't even look happy on your birthday, but I guarantee you, you're going to be thankful," Jinee declared.

Mother only smiled when I gazed back to notice her. She was reading a book in her lap while listening to our conversation.

After a forty-minute drive, we were already rounding the foot of the mountain. Elevation increased as we passed through the morning mists, and in no time, we were already at our destination, Mount Mitchell—the highest peak out of all the giant landforms that make up the splendor of Asheville.

"Oh, everything here is so breathtaking!" said Kathy. It was her first time up here.

I tossed Kathy a box containing a pair of Star Light Kickers; one-of-a-kind sneakers. "I got these for you. I figured you'd like them."

"What? Are these the latest edition? This costs an arm and a leg! Where'd you get the money to buy it?" Kathy opened the pearl white box with a bright blue lightning logo. The sneakers looked simple yet sophisticated in style with their silk-effect purple trims against the jet black synthetic leather exterior. The sole of the shoes had a built-in air compression device like my own.

"Easy, I sold a few of my landscape paintings. Activate them with your voice. I've already had them program your name so just say: *'Hey Kathy. Activate Light mode,'* and it should switch on."

"Oh, I've heard of these shoes before. These are amazing—it makes hiking that much easier, and you can travel longer distances without being worn out! Thank you." Kathy wrapped her arms around me until I couldn't breathe. She tossed her tennis shoes off her feet, threw them in the trunk, and hastily slipped on her new high-top kickers.

Then Kathy noticed my worn out white and red ones. "You should've bought yourself a new pair of shoes. Why did you buy these for me?"

I looked down and touched my toes. The white leather had a few wear tears and, even when I'd had the shoes professionally cleaned, the mud stains were still visible in faint brown. A part of the lace sprouted threads, but I still loved them. They had a battery life of 35 hours, so it worked just fine.

Smirking, I answered, "They were the shoes that YingShua said were useless when we were being pursued by Blong-Cheng's men. If only he were here, I'd show him how incredible they are."

I remembered YingShua's ragged cotton shirt and the reasons why he kept it. My old kickers were the same way; they were special because it stained a journey of our story.

Kathy stood in awe.

"All that running away from that horrible captain, the shoes would've kicked their behinds too!" Jinee commented, walking up to us. She already wore her pair and dropped her hands to her hips. "These shoes work wonders. It makes carrying our bags and items that much lighter. Let's do this!"

Mother giggled into the back of her hand. "If only those

sneakers can make me age backwards, I'd get a pair for me too, but I'll tread behind you girls. Just don't go too far where I can't catch up."

"This is amaaaaaaaazing!" said Kathy, who was usually quiet and only tended to speak in a monotone most times, as she zoomed yards past us up the flights of rocky stairs and in and out of the forest trees.

Jinee laughed and gave a smirk. She was better at maneuvering her Star Kickers, so she too activated their Light Mode. She set one foot back, readying herself to leap. "Here we goooooooo!" Then she was gone before I knew it, toppling off bushes, scaring the rabbits and squirrels back into their hiding spots. Leaves swirled behind them as the girls dashed from one place to the other, racing to the top.

Then it hit me. "Jinee! Wait! The cake!" I commanded my kickers and was startled when the air compression deployed and I could feel the transparent sheet of air beneath my feet. It took a moment for me to stabilize before I leapt off in dashes up the long steps of rocks.

In seconds, I was behind Jinee yelling, "The cake!"

Jinee glanced back but didn't hear what I was saying and simply gave me two thumbs up which made me roll my eyes. Just as she was about to jump over an upcoming formation of rock right before the top of the mountain, her bag's strap clamp malfunctioned and detached.

I caught the strap and managed to slip the cake cooler off Jinee's shoulders. We jumped over the crowd of rocks but Jinee missed her landing and hit the ground with a thump. I stopped in front of her with the cooler beneath one of my arms.

"Ooouuu… I think I sprained my ankle," Jinee said, wailing in pain. "Su-Lia, you did good on saving the cake. I would've hated myself.'

Kathy returned to us at the sound of Jinee's voice. "Hang on…" she said, twisting her backpack around. After removing Jinee's sneakers, Kathy applied some smelly ointment and wrapped her ankle in strapping. "You'll be fine. It isn't horrible."

"I was enjoying my exercise," Jinee said, laughing, before we raised her up to her feet, an arm around each of our necks.

Warmth caressed the back of our heads, and we turned around. The bright sun blinded our vision for a moment, as the breeze flowed through red maple leaves. We lowered our arms, our breaths taken away by the scenic view of Asheville surrounded by rich mountains.

It was a while before Mother finally made it to the top. She held on to her trekking poles as she stood behind us also admiring the scenery. "Jinee, did you hurt yourself?"

"I'm alright, Mrs. Chang," Jinee answered with a grin, but then asked Kathy to help her spread out her sleep pad so she could have a seat to rest.

I hurried back towards Mother, helping her catch her breath while holding her arms. "It's stunning. The last time I was here was many years ago."

"You were always a curious child. You loved counting the stars with your grandparents and sleeping in tents. You'd claim they were your spaceship," Mother started to explain. "This was the same place where I lost you for four days…"

"This was also where I went to sleep, not knowing I had time traveled to Laos. I met YingShua for the first time," I replied, thinking through the unforgettable memories.

"Fate is truly a place and time. No matter what happens, accept that there's a reason you two met and a reason you returned. It's to make you stronger, so you can fight for what you want in life." Mother's dark brown eyes looked into mine, and I could see she hoped her words meant something to me.

They rang true. The journey back to Laos was something that had made me develop in so many ways. Returning to the present had brought me resentment and sorrow, but in a bittersweet way that was helping me search for the better me.

"Thank you, Mother. You've done a lot to help me through this. I really thought I'd never get to see you again…" I wrapped my arms around her tiny shoulders and touched my cheek against hers.

"What? Because you'd almost run off to get married 100 years in the past?" Mother drew back with a chuckle.

"What would you have done if I never came back?"

Mother whirled her eyes to the sky and back to me, "Of course I'd spend my whole life looking for you. Even in the afterlife, I'll never stop searching. But if you really run off to get married, at least give me some kind of warning next time."

Later on that early evening, after Mother made a simple dinner of brats on a bun, grilled vegetables with shrimp kabobs, which would be accompanied by red wine, I sat painting.

The girls looked over my shoulders and pointed out, "That's not Asheville."

"What?" Then I squinted, thinking where in the world my mind had drifted off to.

"What are those?" Jinee pointed to all the old broken houses in the painting.

"They are bamboo homes in the mountains of Laos," I answered, admiring.

"Those blossoms are so graceful. Was that a special place you visited with YingShua?" Kathy asked in awe.

"Yes, it's where I told him I wanted to spend the rest of my life with him." I also thought about the promise he made to his parents.

"Oh, why does your love sound so complicated? You stay with him and you leave us forever. You stay with us and you leave him forever... Why can't we just live in one world?" Jinee was trying not to cry but she sniffled while looking down to the city of Asheville, where the early evening greeted our view.

Then Kathy pulled the fruit cake out and changed the mood. Mother and the girls stood up and sang me *Happy Birthday*. While blowing out the candles I made a wish:

"May we all dream big, live in great health, and reach all our goals in life."

"That's right!" Jinnee threw her hands in the air as her short black hair motioned with the wind. "I'm going to be a wedding dress designer!" Her voice echoed back to us from a nearby peak.

"Su-Lia, wish that you'll meet YingShua again!" Kathy said, startling me with a nudge to my side.

Then my heart became energized. I turned my head and shouted, "I'm going to meet you again, YOU JERK!" The word 'jerk' echoed back so loudly it made us burst out in laughter.

Kathy and Jinee knew just how to be the best girlfriends when my soul was consumed in sorrow. Although the pain was the same, each day became easier as I learned how to replace resentment with better memories of our time in 1978—and that was through the love of art.

We all surveyed the vast view, where orange transitioned to a deep red and partially purple evening—it was like breathing new air at the heights of Mount Mitchell.

As the natural breezes whistled in and out of my ears, I could hear YingShua's voice as I talked to him, like it was yesterday:

"Who else would want me?" I'd ask.

"All the men in your future, if they know what an incredible woman you are."

I'll always be your incredible woman. Let me shine the brightest so you'll never miss me glowing in your sky.

As I switched my gaze to the vast view of our shiny glass-like city, a massive airliner traveled across the sky. A tunnel of brightness zoomed into my vision, where I saw myself through the passenger window.

My life transitioned into 2084. It's the future and I am twenty-six.

The room filled with a boom of ceiling aircraft lights. Deep-red lipstick stained my cup of tea as I pulled it away from taking a sip. The silk of my black hair spiraled over my button-up black bodycon dress, which trailed down to mid-thigh, while my black, sheen nails rested on my lap.

Six years had gone by just like that...

"I've landed. I'll be there in an hour." I got off the phone call with Kathy, whose three-year-old was crying in the background.

The exit door popped open as black metal airstairs lowered to the ground. I stepped outside and stopped to smell the flowery air of Asheville.

Glancing out towards the terminal, where Jinee should already be waiting for me, the wind stole my red chiffon scarf from my neck. I quickly reached out but it slipped through my fingers. The scarf flew far into the air and billowed away but I only smiled, fixing my oversized pitch-black round sunglasses.

"No big deal…" My lip curled, and I stepped gracefully down with my bright red five-inch heels hitting every metal stair with a clang.

The Muse Man

CHAPTER 27

Through the gate and out onto the concourse, my heels clacked against the gloss-white terrazzo concrete floor. Even in 2084, I was still not using the city speed walkway. Walking still felt livelier.

I was certainly excited to see the girls. We separated after college and began to pursue our dreams. After the last two years of school, it took another four years working in New York City as an assistant curator for various museums, which then led to me opening up my very own art gallery. I'd dreamt of sharing my *wanderer* journey with the world and held onto that vision for six years.

Presently, my solo exhibition team members were preparing a second grand opening to the people of Asheville—my hometown.

The man who lived in the past that once fought for the life of his people had become an historical figure through my paintings. The peace fighters were a humble unit during the Vietnam War. Their earnest missions brought hope, restoration, and reconciliation for many of the Hmong, and has touched the hearts of many across the world.

My phone rang—it was one of my managers. "Miss Chang, the President of Hickory Academy of Arts and Design requests to speak to you. Are you available?"

"Yes. Please transfer her through," I told my directing manager.

"We'd like to extend an invitation to you on behalf of the college. Your success has inspired our students in many ways, so we'd love to hear about your journey and what you have in store for all the aspiring artists."

The conversation went on until I saw Jinee waiting for me in the crowded arrival lobby. She was waving her hand in the air with glee. Her hair had grown much longer and it bounced in black curls over her shoulders.

"I'll be happy to attend the meet and greet at the college, Mrs. Caplin. I'll be there an hour early as agreed at 6:00 P.M." I closed the conversation and tossed my hands up, acknowledging Jinee.

Always one to stand out from the crowd, she was wearing a bright, melon-green high-neck blouse beneath a soft, cotton, candy-pink sweater. Her legs were long and slender in white leather pants. The pink five-inch platform heels made her look taller than I was used to.

With two quick taps on the point of my toes, the heels I had on converted into red and black sneakers. Much better. I was never a high-heel kind of girl—only for business.

"I've missed you so much!" Jinee said, diving to embrace me. "You should've kept your heels on. I'd expect you to have grown a lot more, being gone so long."

My eyes rolled in humor. "Stop. I've always been this size and height."

"Well, you look amazing. I'm so proud of you and can't wait

to come join you at your grand opening," Jinee told me. Then we walked out of the airport where her car waited for us.

With a fingerprint scan, followed by her 'Pegasus' voice command, the self-operating black vehicle unlocked and raised its doors for us to get in.

"Wow, nice ride," I complimented when seeing the rich, tan leather seats facing each side of the car. The interior was slate-blue, and the windows were heavily tinted.

"It's the newest Acura Pegasus aeromobile," Jinee said, grinning. "Cost me an arm and a leg but I love it. Sit tight and enjoy the ride. I'll be your *anti-driving* captain." She saluted jokingly, and voice commanded her Pegasus to the restaurant where we were due to meet Kathy and her daughter.

The aero vehicle made a hum as its engine started, and before we knew it, the reflective dome airport was already beneath us. I was impressed by how quiet and fast we had ascended.

Asheville in 2084 was filled with bustling streets and humming skies. New, more innovative construction of homes, sustainable business buildings, and efficient public transportation had expanded Asheville into a commendable city.

Smaller aeromobiles roamed at building level, while electric cars drove through the intersecting streets and in and out of the underground tunnels. The Sky Train was people's favorite; cutting travel from one town to another in twice the time it usually took by vehicle.

In the last decade, the city's population had tripled. Even the number of Hmong residents had increased massively, while still continuing to maintain traditions and improve cultural strength among the community.

"We're here!" Jinee called out, bringing me back to reality. Her black aero car slowly descended to a parking spot on the ground.

"That was a smooth ride, Jinee. Thanks for picking me up."

I swiped my bangle watch, and the hologram device projected the time, weather forecast, and generated the restaurant menu so I could place my order before being seated. Time had become more valuable as I aged; moving forward was healing to my soul.

HEIGHTS CAFE

The entrance was signaled by an arrow to our left and we were led towards an elevator up to the twenty-third floor. From there, to our right, was an outdoor path which took us through a transparent tunnel. Birds flapped their wings in the sky around us as we walked, and beneath us cars ambled the streets.

The smell of grilled chicken was in the air, along with a citrus mix of alcohol as the double mirror doors to the restaurant parted.

"Over here," Kathy called enthusiastically, waving and standing. My eyes widened at seeing her already expecting again while juggling her three-year-old.

"Su-Lia, it's been years! You look great. I'm excited that you are back for good," Kathy said as she hugged me. I extended my fingers to greet Luna, her daughter.

Luna was shy. She had very rosy cheeks, green Irish eyes, and wore a nice violet satin dress that perfectly matched her mother's. A cute black hair bow clamped her thin red curls that piled over her little shoulders as she took a sip of her drink.

Kathy and Jinee's mouth dropped when a basket of croissants, avocado shrimp appetizers, vegetable summer rolls with peanut sauce, and salmon cucumber coils were set one-by-one on our table. Even an ice cream sundae was placed in front of Luna; she happily clasped her hands around it before digging in.

"Su-Lia, what is this?" Jinee and Kathy both exclaimed, inhaling in surprise. Their gaze followed the food until my grilled chicken sandwich, with fruit and sweet tea, was placed last in front of me.

"Please, help yourselves. This is my treat…"

The girls gulped with excitement while I hastily bit into my sandwich and gulped down half of my tea. A cough broke out of me as I swallowed into the wrong tube.

"Whoa, slow down girlfriend." Jinee got up to pat me lightly on the back. "Like, we know you're a busy woman but eat normally, would you?"

"Sorry… I'm starving. And I'm on a time crunch; my furniture is expected to be delivered to the new condo in a few hours," I told them, clearing my throat.

"The starvation has certainly exploded, and your time crunch is another story," Kathy teased. Shortly, her shrimp with spinach pasta was served.

"Never too busy for you girls," I said, and then I glanced at Luna with a grin. "How's it like to take care of a three-year-old while expecting? You're glowing." Kathy looked like she was about to go into labor any day.

"Oh, it's rough having a busy family but being a mother is amazing. Darren is usually traveling for work so it's just me and Luna most days." Kathy reached to touch her daughter on the cheek. She had a beautiful, complete family.

I blinked as happiness consumed me. "Your strength as a mother is admirable… I once thought I'd have a family too, but that was in the past."

Below is the main creek. I'll teach our children how to fish.

If we had a son, he'd look just like you, my mind spoke.

The voice that lived in my heart had resurfaced. For years, I refused to speak of him, say his name, or do things to make me remember but hearing the word 'family' for the first time in a while tugged at my emotions again.

Jinee stopped chewing but didn't comment. She would have known there was no use in bringing up a past I wanted buried away.

Kathy reached to caress my hands. "You're even more admirable for continuing to be strong for everyone. You've changed. A lot."

Nodding, I replied, "Changing was really the only option…" I shoved a piece of croissant in my mouth and chewed composedly. Food was a way to divert thoughts most times. "Mmm, these are so delicious," I said and stuffed more croissants in until my cheeks were full. After managing to swallow I then finished my drink.

"That's some elegant eating for someone who's supposed to be ladylike." Jinee laughed.

Pausing, I replied, "Hey, only with you girls I can eat without being reserved."

We spent a leisurely couple of hours catching up, and before long, my phone was ringing again. It was my realtor.

"Miss Chang, your appointment to sign the contract for the condo is confirmed at 3:00 PM."

"3:00 PM?!" Where had the time gone? I turned to the girls with a frown and told them, "Looks like I'll have to leave to put in my deposit for the condo. I'll catch you ladies later at the venue."

The girls quickly approved, and I rushed out the door, hearing the AI voice announce: "Ticket paid for Table two. Thank you, Miss Chang, for dining with us."

Auto biometric payments via mobile devices had become a new convenience. When dining or shopping, you would walk out with your items and payment for the goods would automatically deduct from your bank without a need for physical cash or card payment.

After a while of waiting outside the restaurant building, I waved, and an autonomous Uber stopped in front of me. "Miss Chang, Uber291 is delighted to service you to your destination," the system voice from the vehicle sounded as I settled in.

"Thank you, Uber291. Please take me to the Blue Moon Village."

The drive was a quiet thirty minutes. I loved that the space was on the outskirts of Asheville which oversaw Mount Mitchell—away from the noisy downtown where I'd had lunch with the girls. The structure was built with curved edges. Each alternating floor was either a white wall or mirrored, reflecting the stunning distant city lights.

My realtor waited for me by the door. We exchanged and signed contracts, I transferred my deposit, and my fingerprint was scanned for recognition as the door key.

"I've wondered, Miss Chang," my realtor asked while I observed the cityscape from the balcony and saw the silhouettes of mountains in the expansive view. "Why of all the better condos in the area have you chosen this space?"

My arms were crossed. A breeze surged the gray chiffon curtains behind me. "This scenery reminds me of a place I once lived. Only in this location can I see the stars as if they were right in front of me…"

The realtor looked impressed with my answer. "That is quite an insight you have there. After all, you are on the thirty-fourth floor which has the best view." The short man with baggy eyes pushed up his glasses and smiled.

The truck with all my house furniture and belongings pulled up beneath, having traveled from New York to Asheville. The realtor left shortly, and I began to instruct the moving crew where to set my items.

Miss Chang, I have arrived. My directing manager's text message projected while I was still getting dressed. Staring in the mirror, my hairline was parted at one side, tucked behind my ears, and tightly secured into a ponytail. Curls of hair ran down my back.

I drew a finger to my lips to touch the plumped surface, and a flashback of his familiar mouth came to mind. Twisting my red lipstick, I applied it both to top and bottom before pressing them together. Perfect. I smiled, staring at my own reflection. "If only you could see me tonight as I celebrate you."

I walked out of my condo with confidence—feeling like a new person. Soft white feather designs overlapping one another were sewn elegantly over the shoulder of my fitted pearl-white, satin dress. A golden belt was secured tightly around my waist. Star shaped diamond earrings dangled down, matching a simple golden chain necklace with a crescent moon pendant. Rhinestones sparkled from my clear pointed toe pumps as I exited the sliding doors of the forty-story apartment block.

"You look stunning tonight," Directing Manager Leah said, as she sat across from me in her black dress suit. Her neck-short brunette hair was cut in an A-line bob. She had a beauty mole beneath her bright caramel eyes.

"Thank you. How do you like Asheville?"

"Quite a difference if compared to New York," she commented.

It was already 7:00 PM. Thankfully, my newly purchased gallery was only fifteen minutes away from my condo.

The Flames Fighter exhibition was set to last three hours. We were able to greet and meet visitors of all ages, clients, and journalists. The exhibition held over 100 hand brushed paintings displayed throughout the building. Curtain drapes of gold and white spilled from the massive windows.

"Miss Chang, can we ask who the muse man in a lot of your paintings is? Many across the world ask why only his back is always shown in the events and landscape series of your pieces?" a reporter who wore a bright pink dress suit asked, reaching out her microphone to record the answer.

Proudly, I replied, "He is someone from my dreams but a real person who lived during the Vietnam War."

A confused look fell upon the few journalists and reporters around me. Manager Leah was no exception.

"So, are you saying you've dreamt of him but have never seen his face or know his name?"

It took a moment before I could find the right answer without sounding secretive. "He indeed is very attractive and charming. His name will remain undisclosed, but he is a man of minimal words, who cared genuinely about those around him. He was an advocate for the freedom of his people.

"Little did the world know that he and three other men fought with heart and soul during and after the Vietnam War. They wanted to reunite families, save lives, and destroy corruption within their own people—those who were preventing crossings to Thailand."

The reporters marveled and interest rose through a crowd that filled almost every space in the Flame Fighters exhibition.

"We love the Peace Fighters of Vietnam!" several of the Hmong crowd members called out. An enormous energy overwhelmed me but also filled my heart with happiness.

"Thank you, Flames Fighter!" another person shouted. The Unit never named themselves but, in 2084, the followers of my wanderer journey used it fittingly. The fire of corruption was settled by the peace fighters which had now made a new-found history to be remembered by many.

As my personal journey has never been forgotten, it was a joy to know the experience—especially the muse man—captured the hearts of many.

Then a different journalist with short brown hair, glasses, and blue eyes asked, "Will you ever release a front profile painting of him, Miss Chang?"

"Maybe one day…." I said, grinning.

"You've really made the world curious," Jinee said, nudging me after the interview had concluded and the crowd had moved to explore the surrounding artwork.

"If he turns around… I'll miss him more. His back is enough…" I told Jinee and her mouth parted like she was surprised by the reason.

"So, you've stared at his back for six years?" Jinee asked semi-seriously. She peered closer at the painting. "He does have a great looking back. I can see why he remains a hot topic."

Fans had even sent drawings and artwork of what their vision of the muse man was, but none truly looked like him; some made me sad, and some were so silly they made me laugh until my belly hurt.

"What are you smiling about?" Kathy said, tapping me on the shoulder, her big belly covered with a red cotton dress.

"Oh, nothing. I was thinking about my next event tomorrow," I told her.

"Are you visiting the campus?"

"Jinee told you?"

"Yes. It'll bring back a lot of memories, for sure."

A Fateful Hope

CHAPTER 28

"Right this way," Mrs. Caplin said, greeting me at the front office when I arrived the next day to visit the campus. She was the new president of the academy.

A pearl necklace ringed around the loose skin of her long neck. Her hair was wrapped into a low small bun above her nape, and she wore a light-blue knitted sweater that tucked nicely in her black dress pants with black kitty heels.

The school changed a lot in six years. Once an all-girls' school, it had recently turned coed. The east wing had a boys' dormitory while the west housed the girls. Passing each classroom window brought back so many memories.

I remembered studying and working through two summers just to catch up, so I could graduate early. It wasn't easy to want to be a *star* but after many sleepless nights working odd jobs to save money, and nosebleeds while painting feverishly for years, it had all paid off. I was given another chance to live with purpose.

Before long, we were on the third floor, walking through the hallway to the main library. The lovely portrait was still there hanging wide across the wall. Slowly, I stopped, facing directly at it. The image reminded me of my days with the person I loved.

Mrs. Caplin had gone ahead but came back to wait patiently. "That was taken by a famous German photographer, Helmut Ludwig."

H.L. were the initials in cursive at the bottom-left corner of the frame. Lifting my eyes, I then realized something I hadn't noticed before. A standing shadow of a family by the creek: a father, a child sitting on his shoulders, and a mother. It was still as breathtaking as the first time I observed the portrait.

We walked further and the library doors opened. The professors and students of different art and design classes greeted me with bouquets of flowers and snacks.

I looked around to see if Mr. Benz was still there and, sure enough, he had paused from putting books away using the five-foot metal stairs and was waving. I waved back in delight. He was still the general librarian but with a few more years of age packed beneath his eyes. The sweet gentleman was balder now at the top of his round head.

"Su-Lia!" He was panting by the time he got to me. "I wondered what happened to you until I started hearing a lot about you from the students. How have you been?"

"I've been excellent, sir."

"I can see that all over social media, and you were on T.V. last night. You've really become a successful artist." He squinted and scooted closer to whisper, "That muse man must be proud of you too."

My eyes twinkled and I slowly gazed at Mr. Benz, wanting to talk to him more but Mrs. Caplin ushered me away as the students cheered. The general librarian only beamed and sat down with the rest of the crowd.

The college president made her introductions and students were given the opportunity to meet me. The event went on for a while until Mrs. Caplin turned to ask her closing question on behalf of the crowd, "Miss Chang, your story has really inspired many of our students. Tell us, what do you have in store to further exhibit the Hmong Culture? 100 years into the past has taken history into a twist that many of our students and younger generations have yet to grasp and understand. What advice do you have for aspiring artists?"

Mother had arrived and was closing the door behind her. Warmth melted over my heart, seeing her face while attending my event. I acknowledged her and proceeded with my response, "My vision is no more than that of each artist in this room; it is to seek the best of me in all things.

"The Hmong have truly been an example of what fighting for freedom is, along with what living and hoping for a better future means. With this, I plan to extend opportunities in Asheville. Bring your talents, your work, and your insights. Together, we can transform our culture by creating virtual experiences of our history. We can establish educational museums and exhibitions across the world to bring a lost and forgotten past to this new age.

"My accomplishment is only a small part of my journey. With you all, we can take Hmong culture to the next level."

The library exploded with cheers. Mother acknowledged me from the back of the crowd and tilted her head like she was proud.

The meet and greet was over after two hours. Most of the students left but some stayed back to chit-chat for a bit. Then Mother finally reached me and wrapped her arms around my waist. "My sweet Su-Lia is finally back. Shall we go out for a late dinner?"

I agreed but told her I wanted to give Mr. Benz my farewell

before leaving.

"I'll wait here for you then. Be quick," Mother said and took a seat by one of the desks.

I waited in the back of the library where Mr. Benz usually came out with books to put away. But when he didn't appear and I was about to leave, a glint from under one of the shelves caught my eye.

A mysterious atmosphere weighed over me, followed by a sensation that drove me impulsively curious. Dark shadows clouded the room except from where the glimmering came. My heart began pounding.

Slow to move, but like a string that tugged me forward, before I knew it, the side of my cheek was already touching the carpet; palms flattened as I peered into the tight space.

The sight of a familiar stone glowed before my very eyes. My limbs went senseless, and my pupils dilated until the tremors from within surfaced, striking me into a spin of disbelief. It was impossible! I had believed for six years that nothing was left that would allow me to reach him again.

Holding my breath, I reached as far as I could and slowly pulled the mineral out. I held the stone with care against my heart as I worked to catch my breath. My mind rushed for answers. I leaned against the bookshelf while emotions ran through me; feeling lost, unreal, and confused all at once.

Was there still hope? Or was it just me daydreaming and wishing it was real?

Opening my palm slowly, as if not wanting the stone to disappear, its warmth resonated with my soul, and I was convinced it was really the piece I once thought shattered.

The incident had happened in the very spot I now sat:

The library thief swung fiercely at me. I blocked, impacting the delicate stone into two pieces. The lost piece was smaller. It broke off and must have landed on the ground. What kind of fate was this?

"Mrs. Chang, it's almost 8:00 PM. We'll be closing the library soon," a lady with short, wavy red hair called out to me from the front desk.

"Su-Lia?" Mr. Benz's head popped out from the end of the aisle and I raised my eyes to meet him. He frowned at seeing how disconnected I looked.

"Why are you sitting down there?" He came to my side and helped me to a stand.

I looked up at Mr. Benz a bit teary. "The book of Dual Destiny tells about these stones," I said, opening my hands to let him study the fragment. "It's warm… this was what connected me to the past."

Mr. Benz took the stone into his grasp and raised it for a closer look. "Where did you find this? I've walked these book aisles many times but never seen it. Someone must have kicked it away." He handed it back to me and smiled. "That man must still be waiting for you, Su-Lia."

"Did you… already know?" I asked him with sudden interest.

Mr. Benz paused before his eyes softened. "I knew from the day you went missing from the library. When I picked up your bag, a note slipped out from the book. I've been meaning to return it to you all these years…"

A piece of lined paper was folded into a square. When I opened it, it read:

March 8th, 2078—Not just a dream. Time traveling is real… YingShua Pha is real.

Hesitation fell over me when my mother called out my name. She noticed Mr. Benz and waved at him.

"Time is not forever. Love is for every lifetime you choose. You have a tough decision to make," he said, nodding at Mother.

I folded the letter over the stone carefully and settled it in my tan blazer pocket.

"Go along now. I believe you already know where your heart truly is…" he finished, before turning his attention towards my mother and greeting her.

They exchanged small talk for a moment. "Shall we get going, Su-Lia? It's getting late and they are about to close."

Before stepping out of the library, I glanced back at Mr. Benz and his eyes glistened a farewell.

Finding the stone again was breaking me down to making decisions. Time just never waits.

Mother has been such a great part of my comeback. Returning from the past burned my heart to ash but it wasn't enough to destroy my spirit because I had her. A mother's love is life's greatest gift. She would never betray me like him… but why was my heart still unsettled and empty when my career had just taken off and life was at its peak for me?

He was still missing in my life.

I squeezed Mother into my arms and told her, "Let's go home instead…"

A look of surprise hit her. "But I thought you wanted to have dinner at Green Leaf?"

"I want to cook for you… it's been so long since I've made you dinner," I insisted, hooking arms with her.

Mother breathed and patted my hands. "Well, alright. I haven't seen your new condo so let's drive out there. I'm interested in seeing what you can cook."

"It'll be your favorite."

"Su-Lia, when did you learn how to cook such exquisite dishes?" Mother's mouth had dropped.

"Lobster tail is your favorite. Here, try this balsamic salmon in spinach as well. It's delicious. When I was in New York, I learned from Leah, my manager." I placed a big spoonful on Mother's plate and poured her a glass of red wine.

Mother ate with joy. After a while, we moved onto the balcony to continue chatting.

"Don't be afraid to remarry. I wouldn't be upset with you," I began when we had both sat down.

A sigh escaped her lips before she answered, "Not until I've received closure from your father—then I can move on."

"You never spoke much of him except that he left when I was little. Where is he? And why hasn't he returned?"

"He left us when you were only three years of age. I was twenty at the time and worked two jobs to support us. Your father was a good man, but his benevolence separated us. He'd rather give up on himself than to put someone through hardship."

"Was my father ill?" I asked with a saddened look.

She nodded. "He was your age when he took his own life with

a gun. The pain of glioblastoma deteriorated your father in only a matter of months. Treatments were of no use and there was little I could do to ease his pain. One day I came home from work to a letter he had left on the kitchen table: '*By the time you receive this, my body will be freed of this pain. Please take good care of yourself and our Su-Lia. May we meet again*'. To this day, I still question why he chose such a selfish path."

I hugged my mother in shared grief, understanding why she didn't like speaking of him. It was heart-wrenching to remember things that hurt.

Mother fell asleep and I covered her with a warm blanket and whispered, "I love you, Mom. Be strong for me…"

I reached into my pocket and pulled out the note which had the stone inside. I raised it up to where the stars sat glimmering in the quiet night.

Trust that no matter what happens, we'll be the stars in each other's sky.

I promise you my next lifetime, so I can love you dearly.

Now that I've become your star… there *is* no next lifetime.

A Chosen Destiny

CHAPTER 29

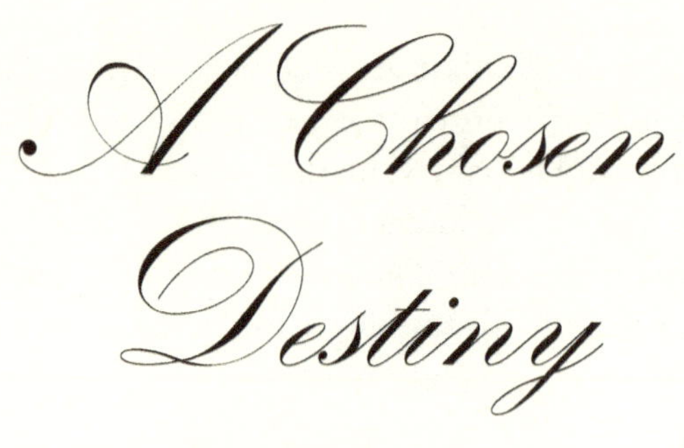

~ **S**ix weeks later

"Su-Lia… this can't be real," Jinee said, taking my hands and squeezing them tightly. "How do you even know if it will work as it did in the past?"

"I can feel the warmth of the stone… it's only this way with me. The past is calling for me… he's still waiting."

Kathy moaned as pain struck her. "I think I'm having contractions…"

"Oh no! I didn't mean to—" I got up and helped Kathy lean comfortably on my beige leather couch.

"It's okay. It's not you but this baby is giving me Braxton Hicks," Kathy said, exhaling heavily and trying to steady her breathing before turning to me. "How will you explain this to your mom?"

Gloom came over me, followed by a scowl. "I don't know where to begin… it hurts to stay, and it hurts to go."

"You must tell her—write her a letter if you can't bear to face her," Jinee insisted and kept smiling while pushing tears out of her face, pretending she was okay.

Kathy pressed her fingers gently into her belly and said, "Go where your heart is. Now that you've found this gem, let the magic work one last time."

Bursting out in tears, I hugged both girls. They were the best ever. I squeaked between cries, "Where will I ever find friends like you? I'm thankful to have known you."

"Su-Lia, we'll be friends forever..." Kathy's eyes glimmered and tears streamed down her face. "We'll take good care of your mother. That's a promise."

I stood up and grabbed Jinee's hands, opening her palms. "Please pass all these to my mother..."

Jinee raised her head. Her eyes widened, stunned at the numbers written on the documents. "That's your entire life..."

"I'd give her the whole world if I could."

Then Jinee remembered and dug in her tote bag. She pulled out an outfit wrapped nicely in a square, cream-color box. "When you came back six years ago, the hospital gave your mother the clothes you wore but she let me hold on to them. She was afraid you'd be hurt seeing them."

I opened the box, and it was the outfit YingShua gave me long ago.

"I actually repaired and added my own style to it, so it looks brand new again," Jinee said. "This is perfect timing... it feels like you are going off to get married in this dress filled with vintage and modern touches," she added with much satisfaction.

Feeling loved, I pulled the top off the box and unwrapped the plastic.

Jinee had added to the skirt with sheer fabrics made as an overlayer of red and green that trailed to the back, which complemented the finely embroidered sash belt. It had been altered into lotus designs mixed with vines and coiled hearts. Bright green triangles matching the rest of the outfit outlined the apron; sterling coins and bells jingled as I spread my fingers across it. The skirt had been kept with its original vintage look but the top was newly refined into a deep purple halter-neck. Flowy chiffon sleeves hugged both sides of my arms elegantly.

"This is such an extraordinary piece—it's stunning. I love the mix. Thank you." I had already put on the outfit and both my best friends sat, watching in awe.

Kathy waved for me to bend down slightly. "And I bought this for you as a token of our friendship. I'd been meaning to give this to you but you were away for so long." She secured a shiny three-ring authentic silver necklace around my neck and settled the coin chain over the balls of my shoulders. The jewelry chimed harmoniously.

"Su-Lia, if you're going to go… go now." Jinee stated. "Before I change my mind about letting you go." She covered her eyes with her arms, pointing to the entrance of my home.

It was such an emotional moment. I paused, my face broken into sadness before reaching to take Jinee and Kathy's fingers into mine. "Friends forever… no matter where we are in this universe."

With that, I left with an aching heart and painful tears.

Should I part from you, you better keep fighting to stay alive. As you've always waited, I'll always find my way back to you.

The day came as I had once promised him. Mother's words never ceased to amaze me:

Nothing is ever an end if you believe in fate.

What I thought was impossible became possible for the last time. A chance I couldn't turn away from.

At the highest peak of Mount Mitchell, I stood carefree above the city of Asheville. I sucked in the scent of sugar maple trees and elusive, citrusy wildflowers. Calm sequences of wind caressed my face, seeping beneath my hair and swirling down my neck. The magic was beckoning every inch of spirit inside my body, wanting to take me back to where I left off.

Then a stinging pain surfaced from within, when memories of my childhood with Mother and my loving grandparents came flashing back. I'll miss camping each year with them and watching the starry nights together. I'll miss my mother's cooking, her cheery face, and how she cries with me in moments when I need her most. Don't cry too much, Mother… I'll be in a safe place.

I'm going to miss Jinee's silly romantic jokes, upbeat personality, and most of all her presence that made heads turn just because she was so pretty. Kathy always wanted what's best for me and cared for everything that was important in my life. Our cherishable moments will always be with me no matter where I go.

It was one of the hardest decisions I'd ever made. I was really leaving the world that my body belonged to but not my heart and soul.

Curling my fingers around the stone, feeling its delicate edges, with all my might I squeezed until a bursting sound crackled in my shaking fist. Parting my eyes, anticipation, fright, and excitement overwhelmed me as I opened my hands and brought the stone into view. It had crumbled in fragments where I saw a reflection of myself. Then it flew away into the vast sky in gold and blue stardust of glimmering glass.

Within seconds the world shifted, distorting my sight with blinding forces of colors that ate through every cell of my being. I tried fighting off the darkness that caved into my focus, but the energy force was so strong, even the breath in me was taken by the speed of time.

~1984—Luang Prabang, Ban Xang Khong Village

"Mommy, Mommy!" a little girl's voice shouted.

"What is it, Kabao?" her mother responded.

"Look! Who is that?"

Darkness separated into a burning light of warmth. Two curious figures stood over me. I shook my head and slowly opened my eyes to endure the head spin I was still experiencing.

"Did she come from the sky?" the little girl asked, and her mother pulled her back behind her. She carefully leaned a little more.

"Daughter, did you see how she got here?"

"She appeared right there by my rice bowl."

Two pigtails came silkily down from each side of the girl's head, fastened with a red ball hair tie that looked like two cherries. Her white cotton shirt fell over her skirt that had a blue and purple zig-zag design. The mother, who looked to be in her early twenties, had long, black hair which was secured back with a silver barrette.

I blinked and a look of amusement spread across my face when I saw rice grains stuck to the cute girl's rosy cheeks. Then my gaze moved to the mother as I looked around. "What year is this?" I whispered.

The woman observed me and made sure I was okay before answering, "It's 1984."

Little Kabao touched the coins and lines of pearls on my outfit. Her eyes grew and she asked, "Your clothes... you're so beautiful. Just like a Hmong princess from heaven because I saw you appear out of thin air!" She threw her hands up like it was the most amazing thing.

The mother covered her daughter's mouth and tittered. "She's been listening to too much storytelling from her grandparents. Excuse her rudeness."

"Keep on believing. Dreams DO come true," I told the girl with a smile, and reached to caress her cheek. "I'm from a faraway place but not as far as heaven."

Then another spinning sensation came throbbing at my temples. With a hand against my head as I tried to maintain my balance, I questioned, "Where is this place?"

The mother grabbed her daughter, settling her onto one side of her hips and said, "This is Luang Prabang, Ban Xang Khong Village."

Contentment filled my heart. I really was back!

Emotions surged from within, the shock of foreverness lingered in my soul. There were no second thoughts, no matter where this chosen destiny would bring me—I was ready to live the past again.

Where are you, YingShua? my heart called out quietly. Anticipation flooded me and I didn't want to waste any more time.

I had no idea where to begin searching the area, but I had to start somewhere. "Can you tell me which direction I need to go to see the mountain aurora in the sky?"

A look of confusion fell upon the woman's face, but she answered, understanding that I was lost, "There is only one place for that. You'll have to head west towards Mount Phousi." She stared for a moment before asking, "Do you not have any belongings?"

I considered the question, realizing I only wore my Hmong outfit and red and black sneakers. "It's easier to travel without luggage," I said lightly.

The kind woman walked me out of the bamboo home to see me off. I stopped when noticing artwork of so many different colors along the path. Mulberry floral designed papers, encased by wood frames stood around the front yard, while pink, yellow, and blue bamboo umbrellas hung gracefully above me. Lanterns of all sizes scattered the streets.

The lady and the child made these for a living, as well as neighboring stores that had other crafts and souvenirs for sale. The village was small and crowded with people wearing happier faces than I was used to.

Cute children walked the streets, playing together—girls jumped their rubber bands as sports back in these days, and some groups sat to play pebble-catching games. The boys had their slingshots; chasing and shooting each other as they rounded corners of homes. Six years later, Laos was breathing a new life and style.

A motorcycle sped past and the driver's head turned a little at the sight of me. Villagers began to stand up and a man shouted from across the street: "Come and watch the cockfighting. It's about to begin!"

Cockfighting? Where did I remember this? My mind found the word familiar.

Curious, I decided to cross the street and onto a very narrow path between two homes; everyone had to squeeze through to get to the ring where the cheering got louder.

Multiple groups of boys, looking like they had just returned from middle-school, were gathering for an afternoon of gameplay. Sliding through the crowd, I finally got a closer look, and to my surprise, one boy stuck out to me right away when he shouted, "Red, Fighting! Fighting!"

TuPao? It was no mistake! He didn't look much different than when he was five, except much taller.

The word *red* and *fighting* was something I taught him back in the days when he wanted to learn English. He still remembered.

TuPao's voice was a little deeper and his hair had grown a lot longer. It was now stylishly swiped to one side, slightly over his left eye. The light-blue collared top he wore was buttoned crookedly. His black tie was loosely hanging around his neck and his navy shorts stretched to his knees.

Seeing the child had grown up handsomely delighted me. I was particularly pleased to find he was a student.

"Come on Red. You can do this!" *Red* was his cockerel's name. I wanted to shout out to him but held back. The uproar and general excitement around the game drew me back in with gaining interest.

Despite the brutality of it, cockfighting definitely seemed a popular sport with teens and adults alike. The two shamo roosters went on with their fighting. Their black wings whirred as they jumped at one another—sharp beaks poking and yellow clawed legs striking out.

"Yeees!" TuPao jumped the first round and quickly collected his monetary winnings, stuffing it hastily in his pocket.

Before the next match started, a hefty boy with hair cut in the shape of a mushroom, wearing a red tie, and white top from a different school, interrupted the game in a shout: "Hey TuPao! You still have to pay up for the last time you lost!"

TuPao looked up, startled. He groaned irritably. "Not now, Rog!" He rolled his eyes and grabbed his rooster from the fighting ring and stormed through the crowd. His opponent looked puzzled as he watched TuPao leave, and the crowd voiced their disappointment.

"TuPao! Wait!" I shouted with my hands in the air, but he didn't notice and zoomed right through the layers of people as if he was running for his life.

Two more students from Rog's school raced by with sweaty hair, chasing TuPao. One boy was slender, had a small tail at the ends of his hair, and the other was husky and his head was shaved bald.

Without much thought, my feet were already dashing after them. I needed to see what the issue was. Had he offended someone?

"You owe us money!" Rog said, panting hard. He took a breath and stopped to shout: "Get him!" His friends nodded and continued the pursuit.

Through the tight gap between the two homes and back on to the streets, TuPao jumped past a row of lanterns, dodged the arts and crafts stand someone was wheeling out, and swiveled around the girls jumping their rubber band game.

Sweating already from the workout, I was enjoying the show. In haste, I managed to get ahead of the other boys. I hopped slightly to snatch one of the hanging umbrellas and twisted to a stop— pretending I was walking by.

The boys gasped and tried pushing but they pulled their hands back upon seeing my long, dark hair flowing gracefully around my face. "Am I… in your way?" Raising my long, dark eyelashes, I greeted them with a pleasant smile.

The boys stood dazzled, their mouths hanging open.

"He's getting away!" Rog shouted from behind, snapping them out of their daze as their hefty friend caught up to them.

"Excuse us, miss," the kids apologized. They stood aside for a moment before speeding off.

Surveying ahead, I saw TuPao swerve around a corner and towards a grocery shop. I paced quickly to catch up and abruptly stopped when a dark silhouette stepped out from the entrance and stuck out a long black stick. With quick reactions, TuPao managed to leap over, knees and knuckles hitting the ground. He tossed his head up and danger was written all over his face.

"Tij Laug!" he called out in exasperation, with Red still tucked under his arm. He jerked his head to the side and didn't appear to dare move any further, knowing he was trapped between his brother and the other kids.

"Stop right there!" Rog shouted and all three boys skidded to a halt when they saw the man in the shadowed alley.

My eyebrows narrowed and my lips pursed as I examined the scene.

"Where have you been?"

My expression softened. That refined medium-low voice hummed in my ears. A boiling buildup of harsh memories burned in my chest as I stared ardently.

He stepped out from the shadow and my heart collapsed into my stomach. The stiffness in my body posture went numb as the umbrella slowly came down to my side.

"YingShua…" a whisper escaped from my lips.

YingShua turned his head slightly, noticing the other boys' presence before turning back to TuPao. "You were supposed to come home hours ago—why are you causing trouble here?"

TuPao stood up from the ground, brushing dirt off his pants. Red clucked and squirmed in his arms.

YingShua scowled disapprovingly. "I already told you: Red is not ready to be brought out to the fighting ring yet. Why didn't you listen?"

"But he won today, Tij Laug!"

"And he should pay us for losing last week!" Rog said as all three boys pointed.

"Why haven't you paid them?" YingShua asked calmly.

"Because I wanted to buy better food for Red so he can get stronger." A shameful look crossed TuPao's face.

YingShua reached out to TuPao's shoulders and smiled. "Give today's winnings to them."

"Then I won't have enough money to buy food for Red," TuPao argued, but his concern was washed away when YingShua pulled out a white bag containing multiple items. TuPao peeked inside before excitedly rubbing his hands over the rooster.

"So, you came down from the house to buy Red food?"

"I'm thinking about returning it now," YingShua said, pulling the bag away slightly.

"No, wait!" TuPao brought out some coins and a few bills of currency from his pockets and quickly pushed it to the boys. "Here, take this. I'm sorry, I didn't mean to not pay you last week. I was being greedy," TuPao told them. The boys gave him dirty looks as they ran off, but he remained staring at the ground.

"You did the right thing. You shouldn't allow yourself to owe anyone money. If you study harder, you may not have financial needs when you grow older," YingShua said, offering his wisdom.

The coins of my dress chimed when a gust of wind blew from nowhere. TuPao was the first to notice me. Mortified, he turned slowly towards YingShua with an expression like I was a ghost. He opened his mouth, as though about to call out my name, but I shook my head. He clamped his lips and slowly stepped back to give us space.

"TuPao, who is it?" YingShua asked, turning in my direction. A look of uneasiness consumed him. The tension in the air felt heavier than normal.

The thought of forgiving him and telling him how much I've missed him crossed my mind, but I had so many unanswered questions that needed addressing.

Closing my umbrella, I walked slowly towards him. As the coins of my dress got louder, he began to realize my familiar presence. His eyes enlarged to almost comic proportions. Then they started to quiver, and I could see his breathing shortening as I got closer.

My sneakers stopped right in front of him, leaving only a two-foot gap between us. I inhaled before muttering, "So, you managed to stay alive this long?"

Speechless, YingShua appeared unable to move or find the right words to answer.

Then after a long moment of me simply staring at him, his response was more composed than I expected, "Su-Lia? Is it... really you?" His eyes, which I so wanted to see, were partially buried behind his longer soft hair, but I wasn't brave enough to get any closer.

As I bit my bottom lip, wetness clouded my vision. I hastily wiped the tears forming away and raised my chin up. "Who did you expect? Did you hope that I'd move on and live happily?"

Anger ignited within me. All the wrong things came out—contrary to how I truly felt.

The tension eased when the ends of his lips curled, undermining the cool front he had managed to put up. "I've waited for this day to come. Staying alive was the easy part…" He slowly extended an arm with an open hand. "Letting you go was like dying every day."

My fingers formed into a fist. I wanted to remain angry in the face of his sweet talk, but when I saw his jaws clenching so hard, the emotion subsided. Even he had been in pain all these years.

Fighting was useless when it came to love. My fingers raised hesitantly, finding his as he squeezed, and finally I was able to breathe.

Just as he blinked away, tears glistened in his eyes. "Let's go home…"

I wanted to pull him back so I could see his face, but he had already left. Then I noticed a difference in the way he walked. He used a stick to guide his way. I observed carefully, gazing at his broad back, clothed with a blue and black Hmong top, complemented by satin black pants.

Following him onto the main street, the harsh realization of his poor eyesight hit me slowly—the powder substance thrown in his eyes six years ago.

After the incident I had asked many times if he was still affected but he always played it smoothly—it had all been a show. He hadn't wanted me to worry while he was struggling alone.

Tears poured down my face as I brought the back of my free

hand to wipe them away. The truth was excruciating. It hurt more than our separation because, even as prepared as I was to see YingShua, meeting again was merely one-sided—lonely and dark for him. He couldn't even witness how happy I was to see him, and all he got was my pretentious tone that wanted him to say more.

I want to see… see you as my wife and be the mother of my children…

I've never been afraid… I just hope you won't be disappointed in me.

The darkest days in my life are coming and I refuse to put you through it.

His hard-squinting when the sun reflected in his eyes, making him feel pain. I revisited every moment, word, and detail I had misunderstood long ago.

All these years the darkness in his life was his vision. Grounded in silence, I was wrong for resenting him.

TuPao waited for us at the last of the village homes, and when he noticed us walking up, he hurriedly took the bag of rooster food from YingShua's hands. "Su-Lia, it's really you. You've changed…"

YingShua stood calmly, his head angled towards TuPao as though interested in hearing what he had to say about me.

"You look like my long-lost sister-in-law," he told me and grinned. TuPao turned to YingShua and teased, "My sister-in-law is even prettier than she was years ago."

Flushed, I observed but YingShua didn't smile. Rather, he looked saddened, no doubt because he could only try to visualize what TuPao observed.

TuPao frowned as if grasping he shouldn't have said that. "Tij Laug, now that Su-Lia is back, we're together again. I hope this time it's for good."

YingShua merely blinked, which I took as him waiting for my response.

"There is no other way back to my future," I answered in a bittersweet tone, gazing at his handsome side profile.

The Sight

CHAPTER 30

Walking through the familiar grounds of Laos again, the tall weeds tickled my bare legs. The sheer fabric of my dress cascaded over green weeds and soft grasses as I passed. The jingle of the silver adornments harmonized with the sound of nature.

Crickets chirped while dragonflies buzzed in and out of the trees. A bird landed on a branch, while multiple squirrels stuck their heads to hear the coins chiming.

YingShua seemed to welcome the melodic bells of my dress; it was how he could sense the motion of my movement.

"Su-Lia, you left so suddenly. We didn't get the chance to say goodbye to you. We were all very sad." The entire way home, TuPao had glanced periodically from me to YingShua, like he was waiting for one of us to talk.

"Your brother sent me back," I said, glaring at YingShua. Guilt twitched at the ends of his eyes.

TuPao paused for a moment with a hint of confusion before

offering a response: "Tij Laug won't say it, but I know there was not a day he went without thinking about you."

I stopped and waited in case there was anything YingShua wanted to say to me, but when he remained silent, I pulled my hand away from his grasp. "I can walk on my own…"

The ground rose as we continued until we heard the flow of water to our left.

"We are finally here," TuPao said, stopping and turning around. "Su-Lia, welcome home…" He threw both his hands into the air and that was when I saw the turquoise-blue stream babbling along. The current sprung over limestone rocks while pebbles endured the twisting liquid—casting a glittering glow from the creek.

"You and brother belong together, no matter which world you are from. If today wasn't fate, then I don't know what it is." TuPao walked away with a grin, patting his rooster, and headed towards the bamboo railing that trailed up the mountain side.

"You… really live here?" I tried to move closer to YingShua to see his face, but he started walking again towards the soaring heights of the mountain where TuPao was already halfway up.

"We'll talk when we get to the house…" YingShua finally answered and grasped the railing to feel his way naturally. With his walking stick, he tapped ahead to inform him when to lift his leg. I could see his head was angled towards the silvers of my dress, making sure I was still close behind him.

My hands caressed the smooth, bound bamboo railing. Ebony wooden stairs made the elevated walkway. The sweet, spirit-raising fragrance of flowers breezed from the mountain above. Fuchsia petals of bougainvillea fluttered down, touching my skin before falling off.

On the final step before the top, I tugged at the end of his black shirt and asked "YingShua, why won't you face me? Did you know that in the future… for six years, I shared with the world paintings of my journey here, but I dared not to paint your face. Only your back… I didn't want to see you."

He tightened his grip around his walking stick, but I continued speaking, "Seeing your face was hurtful—remembering the pain of leaving you for what I thought would be forever."

YingShua's fingers fell off the bamboo railing and curled into a fist. "Why did you come back if seeing my face tortures you that much?"

My breathing deepened. I swallowed hard and slowly before responding, my voice now raspy, "Because even after an empire I built from the ground up in a world filled with wealth, fame, and thriving technology, what I couldn't have was still missing."

His shoulders eased and a moment later he whispered, "Is being with me truly what you want?"

"Yes!" Just as I attempted to get in front of him, he turned around and our gaze met only centimeters apart. I wobbled and gripped his sleeve as he caught me by the waist in one arm and grabbed the bamboo rail with the other. The walking stick fell out of his grasp and tumbled down the stairs.

Panting, he regarded me sightlessly, tears slowly filling his eyes. I allowed him to sense the closeness of my breathing as I examined his gorgeous face with care.

Those eyes that once could never look away from me no longer distinguished colors, form, or light from darkness. He gathered me closer against him, his lips trembling as he spoke, "*This* was why I wanted better for you… I'm dying to see you. But no matter how much I look, I can't find where the light is…"

Crying with him, I lifted a palm to caress his face. "I'm right here, YingShua. I am the brightest star in your life, as you are to mine. Where there is darkness, I'll light the way for you. Where there's pain, I'm going to heal you." My other hand shifted to his chest and I hit him softly. "How could you think of going through this alone, dummy? Don't you know how much... I love you?"

YingShua choked. The ocean in his eyes poured over my thumb as he shifted his lips to my palm and let out a breath. He murmured tenderly, closing his eyes, "I didn't mean to hurt you..."

"I'd already forgiven you long ago."

With a second palm to his other cheek, I pulled his face down past mine and whispered in his ears alone, "YingShua, there IS no next lifetime. This lifetime is ours." With that, I attempted to pull back, but YingShua caught my arms. In palpable hunger, his mouth seized mine in heat—sucking the breath out of me.

Beyond trapped, the world turned into hazes of fuchsia flowers racing against green nature as our kiss intensified. Years of craving throbbed my rose-pink lips, asking for more as I dug my nails into his tensed arm muscles, tasting his hot breath in my throat. His neck-length hair tickled my fingers as he tilted his head and caught my lower lips gently in his teeth and released. Our noses brushed and neither of us wanted to pull back; it wasn't enough just yet, especially now finally being in each other's arms again.

"Su-Lia, I should stop..." YingShua whispered. His swollen, cherry lips hung over a racing heart. Stray strands of his hair plastered his cheeks.

"Don't stop..." I answered, gripping onto his shirt, concentrating on him alone.

Hesitation fell over YingShua's expression but I approved as my arms draped on his shoulders submissively. With fierce strength, he bent and lifted me onto him, bringing my legs to settle around his strong body, abs hard against my inner thighs. He held me close with chin resting over my breastbone. Then I couldn't wait and brought my mouth back to his with lust.

YingShua carried me without missing the last step of the stairs as we walked over to the flatter terraces of the vast land.

"But, your eyes…" I tightened my arms around his shoulders and broke our kiss.

YingShua answered confidently, "I've walked these steps for the last six years."

My head turned and happiness filled my heart at seeing how stunning the golden home was. It was nothing like the rest I'd seen in this country. Built with sturdy bamboo walls all around the home, even the stairs were nicely laced with palm fiber.

I had asked for a garden of flowers and here were trees of bougainvillea that decked the front yard and grew around the home—giving me more than I'd ever imagined coming back to.

"How did you do all this?" I wondered out loud.

YingShua replied with a satisfied sigh, "During the first year, I finished building the home before the stairs. It was a struggle because of the height of this mountain. Meng, Nujai, and Yue—along with TuPao—had to help me. They even questioned why I chose such a place. I told them it was what I promised you."

"So, you both made up," TuPao stated, smirking from the front porch.

I hurriedly hopped out of YingShua's embrace, pushing hair strands behind my ears. YingShua didn't appear embarrassed and only grinned.

"Come inside. It's been years since we've had a meal together." TuPao waved his wooden cooking spoon in the air.

It smelled like frying cabbage, pork broth in greens, and a hint of tomatoes. TuPao was still the brightest child I'd ever met.

"Let me help you," I called out, grabbing YingShua's wrist. We walked up the narrow, wooden steps to the home which sat four feet above the ground. YingShua had not spared any materials. Inside was more spacious than what I was used to in this time. An open concept as we walked through the entrance, the kitchen was to my right, and the left was separated into two rooms. It felt cozy and warm.

"I hope you will be comfortable living here," YingShua said from behind. He leaned against the front door with his arms crossed, head slightly tilted.

"Comfortable? It's more than just that!" I twirled around tearily. His eyes gleamed at the sound of my happiness.

I couldn't help but adore TuPao who, to me, was still the little five-year-old boy weaving bamboo baskets and just about anything.

He was cooking at only eleven years of age. Walking next to him, I requested the wooden stirring spoon and told him, "You go study or play with Red. I'll finish making dinner."

"You can cook?" TuPao questioned in surprise, letting go of the utensil.

"Of course, I'm no longer the college girl from six years ago. I've grown into quite a woman." YingShua's mouth parted. He blushed but I could tell he was also intrigued by the statement.

TuPao went off to feed his rooster and, later on, two of his friends from school called for him to go play with them. I watched as the boys ran off happily, like there was not a care in the world.

I tossed the dish water in the backyard and noticed some writing in the dirt. At a closer look, it read:

Hello. My name is TuPao.

Amused, I realized that he had written more than just his introduction in the yard. He practiced writing different sentences, scratching them out when he didn't get it right. TuPao had always been a bright child who enjoyed learning and exploring.

A while later, after the dishes were put away, and I was tossing another bucket of water outside, I was caught off guard by YingShua snaking his hands around my waist. He pressed my body into him and his large chest breathed against my back.

"You scared me…" I stretched my neck and tilted as he hunched to rest his chin on my shoulder.

He squeezed a little tighter. "Your stomach… is soft," he whispered, lips behind my ears. "Is this what you mean by becoming more womanly?"

"Did I make a mistake by saying that?" I squeezed my eyes shut when my red embroidery sash belt and dress apron fell to the floor, coins hitting the ground with a cling. He removed my silver necklace and set it aside.

"This time… I'm not holding back," he mumbled, his breath warm on my neck.

The round pail fell from my grasp as I turned to face him, hands landing on his shoulders. My fingers played with his hair. "And you made me wait too long…" I said, pulling him down to my yearning lips and kissing him softly.

Without further thought, I was on top of him on our bed. We both paused to catch our breath, during which a sudden curiosity grew on him.

I watched with pleasure as his fingers touched my eyelids. When I closed them, he moved on to trace the contours of my cheek bones, and parts of my jaw. His thumbs pressed gently over the corner of my lips, against my teeth which exposed them slightly. A warm sensation started nibbling in the back of my throat when his fingers outlined the curves of my body.

"Everything about you… is perfect," he told me, and a handsome grin flashed across his face as his hands slid down to grasp my legs beneath my skirt, "Why did you have to dress so thin?"

Feeling senseless, I still managed to answer, "What's wrong with dressing comfortably?"

"Because this body drives me insane." With that, he moved his lips up to mine and wrapped me in his arms. We rolled off to the side and we made up for the many years we had lost—close and intimately. He became mine and I became his in the foreverness of a destined past.

"Su-Lia?" I heard YingShua's voice call out to me. The evening came before we knew it. I sat on the staircase, staring at the faint aurora that appeared like a moving ocean of neon colors.

He slowly moved to sit next to me, feeling the flatness of the wooden front porch. "Do you… miss your mother?"

"I will always miss her but she knows by now that I've come back and I'm safe here with you." I stretched my arms in front of me and placed them back on the floor.

YingShua laid his hands over mine, protecting them. "Mother… don't worry," he said, speaking to the sky. "I've loved Su-Lia all my life and will never stop loving her. From this day forward, I will take her as my wife and the mother of my children. Please give us your blessings."

I stared at him, awed by his genuine vow. "Mother *will* be happy for us," I assured.

"What fate is it that led you back to me?" YingShua asked, the keenness of his tone implying that he had been waiting to know.

"The last piece of Destinite was found in my world, buried in my college library. The last time I came back, there was a library theft incident. The thief knocked me down and broke a piece I once thought was shattered. It was found beneath one of the bookshelves when I visited the campus for an event. Who would've known I'd stumble across it and be prompted back to you."

Happiness glowed from YingShua's face. "The heavens have really blessed us." He paused for a long moment, like he adored me, before continuing, "You're going to live a simple life here in Laos, up on this mountain as we raise our children and grow old together—will you truly be happy?"

I rested my head against his shoulder. "The six years I was away, I learned to grow from our separation. Every day became better, which then turned to years of burying your face only in my thoughts—refusing to speak your name so I could move on. I thought striving for success as an influential artist, having wealth, and multiple businesses across the country would make me forget you but that was far from the truth. Although I had many who loved me as fans—along with my girlfriends and Mother—you were still missing. I realized before leaving my entire future how much I needed you in my life."

YingShua then flipped my palm up and firmly intertwined his fingers with mine. "Thank you for coming back to me. After letting you go, I wanted to throw myself off this mountain and—maybe, just maybe—I'd hope to follow you to your future. But it was unrealistic and too easy. I deserved to live each day worse than the other. I raced against my deteriorating vision to fulfill every single thing I promised you on this mountain, even if it meant I'd never see you again.

"I'd watch the sky and pray daily for stars to fall. I thought perhaps they would bring you back to me, as they once had. I waited and waited, but that silk orchid scent that always flowed from your hair never came. Until today, and yet even then I thought I was only dreaming, but hearing your voice was like a cure to my pain. All these years of torment had not been in vain."

YingShua pulled the heart charm I made for him from his inner shirt pocket. "The only thing I had to keep me going was this."

"You still have it!" I said, regarding it in wonder.

"Every moment, I kept it with me."

Love is truly a journey—a place and time. Our sacrifices were worth every drop of tears, bloodshed, and pain while fighting for a love we once thought could never exist. Dual Destiny intertwined our fates. It gave me another chance to choose my path, my love, and my destiny.

~1987: Three and a half years later

"YingShua, are you ready for this?" asked Dr. Henny, an Ophthalmologist from America who had been treating YingShua's eyes for the last four months. We had returned home for three days from Bumrungrad Cornea Transplant Center, in Thailand.

"It's been so long since the incident—there was no way to identify what substance was in his eyes but it did cause a bacterial fungus to grow in the outer layers of the cornea. We are grateful to the donor." Dr. Henny, who spoke Hmong very well, unwrapped the white bandage around YingShua's eyes. The flat, square cotton sheets were peeled off.

"Thank you for making miracles happen," I told Dr. Henny.

My heart raced as I watched YingShua slowly open his eyes. He squinted hard at the bright light before he gave up and closed them. Beneath his lids, his eyeballs moved side to side, and then he tried again.

Our second child had been born almost a year. YingShua heard Sunshine's voice and smiled warmly as anticipation flowed from his expression. After many rounds of testing, he had waited impatiently for the day he'd receive the surgical treatment to repair his vision.

The extreme glare from natural light was initially harsh on his eyes but his vision soon sharpened into images of Sunshine, me, and Dr. Henny. He saw his daughter for the very first time—she was blinking at him with large, adorable hazel-green eyes and a head full of short black hair.

"My Sunshine has her mother's eyes," YingShua said with an awestruck look as tears welled up.

He held the happiness at his chest and received his baby who reached her tiny chubby fingers to her father's face. "Gaaa…"

Sunshine made happy baby noises with a big toothless grin.

YingShua glanced up at me, studying in a daze, and pulled me down for a hug. "Thank you for being strong all these years, my love. You're even more beautiful than the last time I saw you." He stroked my hair and brought his nose to touch mine.

"I'm so happy you agreed to be treated."

Dr. Henny stood with us in the house with a look of delight. Some tears sparkled along his eyes, and he removed his thick heavy glasses to wipe them away. "What a lovely family," he said beneath his breath.

TuPao's head popped through the entrance. He had raced home from school to see YingShua and play with our first born, named Supeng.

"Daddy!" Supeng, who was turning three in a few months, shouted. He hopped out of TuPao's arms and climbed up onto his father's lap as YingShua held his daughter and son, one on each leg. Supeng touched his father's chin and giggled when YingShua leaned to kiss him on the forehead.

"Here." TuPao handed me a yellow envelope with a letter which I opened quickly, knowing it was from America. It was from Ia and Nujai. They had made it safely and reunited with Meng, Yue, and Mainong who had left a few years earlier.

I was happy to know they were living and adapting well to the new lifestyle and culture.

TuPao took the letter and tried reading it, sounding the words in Hmong before staring up to YingShua who was still enjoying his children's company. Then he looked at me and said, "Five years ago, before Meng, Mainong, and Yue were leaving for America, they asked YingShua if he was sure he did not want to go. Tig Laug said 'not until Su-Lia returns. This is our home'. Even though he was hopeless, he still waited."

TuPao held his breath, as if hoping the bit of information would be news to my ears and it was—I was speechless. Then he grinned like he had done a good deed, shrugged off his backpack, and walked over to the rest of the family.

I love you... I mouthed towards YingShua. As always, he noticed right away and acknowledged me with a soft blink between talking to TuPao and Dr. Henny.

Warmth spread across my face and softened as I then turned to admire our little family, feeling overly joyed suddenly. Time had gone by so fast and I now had the family I once wished for. Despite the fact that time only moves forward, time also gives if you chase it.

"I'd recommend taking a walk outside to explore. It'll help strengthen and re-train your center vision," Dr. Henny told us, bringing my attention back to the moment.

Supeng wanted to see the creek, so YingShua lifted him to sit on one side of his shoulders as they walked down the steps to the stream.

"Dr. Henny, please spend a day with us before you go home." I handed him a cup of water and a plate of juicy yellow mango and melon slices.

"Oh, that looks refreshing. Now that my work is done, I'd love to rest here before heading back to the city," Dr. Henny said, taking the treats and sitting on the front porch to observe the scene. I paced down the bamboo stairs with Sunshine in my arms.

Along the other side of the mountain, layers of golden rice wheat swished back and forth. Red poppy flowers sprouted, scattering the lively field. It was nearing the time to harvest the rice again.

The stream during summer was filled with fish. Supeng jumped every time he thought he caught one and frowned when realizing he hadn't—pouting and making his father continue to reattach the fish string.

TuPao even went down to the stream with a sharp hunting tool and caught a few that were flowing by.

Then multiple camera flashes caught my attention in the distance.

"Who is it?" YingShua asked, taking baby Sunshine.

Curious, I answered, "They look like travelers visiting the area."

We watched for a long moment as the couple continued to hike the trail that led them directly to us.

They first spoke in a language I didn't understand, but when I asked if they knew English the man's eyes lit up. "Yes. Yes. The scenery here is magnificent! I was speaking Deutsch," he said, holding a camera with a lengthy lens.

His wife, a redhead with freckles, smiled and complimented, "You have a lovely family. We are traveling photographers and love capturing wonderful landscapes. May we take a look around the area?"

"Yes, of course you may," I answered kindly and nodded.

"May we please know your name?" the man asked.

"My name is Su-Lia Pha and yours, sir?"

The man with a clean brown mustache and curly hair threw his hands for a handshake. "We are pleased to meet you and your family. My name is Helmut Ludwig."

THE END

Epilogue

To my dearest Mom,

As you are reading this letter, I've already left 2084. I've come to realize that, even with all things I have in this wonderful future, I still long to have a life with YingShua. This decision has weighed heavily in my heart, as I never thought that I'd be living the rest of my life without you.

I wish you were here to wipe these tears away as I think back to our days while growing up. I know you did your best in raising me through all your struggles and sacrifices. When it came to me you spared no expense. You never allowed me to feel less than others nor did you let anyone look down on me. By working multiple jobs, you barely had enough to wear or eat, but still prioritized my happiness above all.

You worked so much, we rarely had meals together but, when given the chance, eating with you were the moments I cherish most; seeing you with a mouthful of food and lecturing me to eat more always brought me warmth and comfort—knowing you loved me dearly.

I still remember my very first pair of Start Light kickers you bought for me, that I still treasure to this day. The sneakers were so expensive that I dared *not dream about owning a pair, but you surprised me with them. On the day you presented them, I shed tears of disbelief knowing how much they would have set you back. You hugged me tightly and stated, "Sweetheart, Mom knows what it's like to want what you can't afford."*

Mom… in this lifetime, I know that I will never be able to return the unconditional love you've showered me with, but I still want to thank you for loving me and for believing in me when I didn't believe in myself. In my darkest moments, you filled my heart with light. And on my worst days, you made the best memories a mother could give.

Because you raised me earnestly, I studied hard for years and worked through sleepless nights wanting to ensure your efforts would not go in vain, hoping you would be proud of me. If only I could give you the world, Mom, I would.

In the black box are the codes and keys for my two condos in New York and Asheville. You are the sole owner of all five of my event venues and the historical museum centers I've established. The yellow envelope holds documents of all rights and ownership of my assets, legally signed over to your name.

As you age, I should be here to spend it with you and take care of you, and I'm sorry for being such a selfish daughter.

When you miss me, Mother, look out into the night sky and watch the stars. As they shine, know that I will always be under the same sky, thinking about you in the past I call home.

I love you, Mom. Don't cry and please take good care of yourself.

Yours dearly,

Su-Lia.

ABOUT THE AUTHOR

Reena Lee is a Hmong American romance writer who lives in Oklahoma, United States. Her parents migrated from Laos to America when she was only three years of age. Growing up, she had always dreamed about being a fantasy romance author and writing about her visions, experiences, and inspirations.

Dual Destiny is Reena's debut novel, which was brought to life from being a heavy dreamer, wondering what if *dreams* were not only *just a dream* but another life one was actually living?

The new-age novel was also inspired by young Hmong generations who are continuing to re-grasp the Hmong identity of the past, hidden secrets of corruption, and divided cultural experiences that come with the modern days in comparison to the past.

In Reena's free time, she spends 'staycation' days with her husband and three children. When she is not writing, she likes to read educational books, web articles, watch romance and food entertainment. Cooking is another hobby she enjoys as she believes that is the fruit to having a loving family when being able to have a meal together.

www.ingramcontent.com/pod-product-compliance
Lightning Source LLC
Chambersburg PA
CBHW031958150726
47990CB00005B/1761